THE SWARM PROJECT

THE SWARM PROJECT

TIM AKERMAN

Published by Tamarind Tree Press

THE SWARM PROJECT

A Tamarind Tree Press book
First published in Great Britain in 2018
Copyright © Tim Akerman 2018
All rights reserved.

TAMARIND TREE PRESS
Accrington, UK

Cover design by Deeper Blue www.wearedeeper.blue
ISBN: 978-1-9995976-0-3

For my family, thanks for your support and for listening to my story ideas whilst I delivered my 2017 new year's resolution to write a book.

PROLOGUE

Once upon a time...

Seventy million years ago in a star system that would one day be called Alpha Centauri, a creature looked at its creation and was pleased.

'What do you think? It seems to meet the design brief.'

'What does it do?' asked its companion.

'Anything we want, really. The brief was to design a caretaker, and this seems to fit the bill. The most difficult part was making sure it lasts long enough to be useful, so I had to go to four DNA strands.'

The companion looked surprised.

'Four strands? That's more than I would have liked.'

'Yes, me too, but we needed that much coding space to ensure we achieved all of the other parameters.'

'We need to ensure they remain in our control, they must be docile enough to look after our facilities yet intelligent enough to work out their own solutions. What about their reproductive rate? We don't want to be overrun.'

The creature made a wheezing noise, as close as their kind got to laughing.

'No chance of that. I have programmed them to have a minimal reproductive rate. I can boost and retard that rate at will using a serum.'

'And what about injuries?'

'That's one of the reasons I put the extra coding capability in. Their systems automatically repair almost any injury and can regrow severed body parts.'

'Clever. How long does it take?'

'Not long, their regenerative rate is quite high. A new limb will grow in maybe three of four cycles. They are also impervious to infection and parasites, from birth to death they are vigorously healthy. They will usually only die in extreme accidents, so we don't need to replace many.'

'What about intelligence?'

'They are intelligent, they must be to relieve us of all the mundane duties which distract us from discovering the cause of our declining population.'

His companion was quiet for a minute. The creature had touched on something that concerned them all.

'Why do you think we have started to die?'

'I'm not sure, it was a terrible shock when the first few died. As you know, previously there had not been a death in two hundred million cycles, so to have three deaths in one hundred thousand cycles that were not accidents... then the steadily increasing death rate since. That's why it is imperative we all focus on the problem and understand what is happening to us.'

They continued the evaluation in silence.

'Finally, it is done,' declared the creature.

'What do we call it?' his companion asked

'I am going to call them Elfinnim.'

'After your mate? Are you sure?'

'Yes, it's as good a name as any, and we can breed them on H'Vaen. Besides, how often do you get a species named after you?'

His companion looked unsure. 'You know best, I am sure. I wouldn't do that with my mate though, that would cause trouble!'

They both wheezed again.

Aeons had passed since the creation of the Elfinnim. They had functioned as caretakers and drudges without complaint, and adored the creatures they referred to as creators. Elfinnim had peace and were programmed to serve; for as long as they had the creators, all was well.

'Have you seen any of the creators recently?' asked one of the first generation Elfinnim.

'Not for many cycles,' came the reply.

'Ask the other Elfinnim we have contact with, it may be that something has happened to our creator.'

Her colleague went to the communication panel and called every location he could find. Always the same answer: no creators.

Elfinnim had been bred for patience, and waited several years before exploring the creators' spaces, areas they were not allowed to even visit. They entered with fear but discovered there was nothing to be afraid of. The creators had gone.

Elfinnim continued their role as caretakers, caring for and nurturing the worlds that their makers had populated and developed. They had taken many millennia to investigate the libraries that were left behind, to learn all they could about their makers and what had happened to them. But in the end, no matter how much they read and investigated, they could never make sense of their makers' departure. All the literature they could find said the creators had moved to a higher level of consciousness. It was an intense source of grief; it seemed Elfinnim lost all purpose in their existence. Initially the only course of action was to continue with the last orders given.

Over time their sense of abandonment subsided and they accepted their loss. They sought to nurture and develop every world more carefully to honour their creators, but in the end their learning changed their outlook. Some Elfinnim wanted to exploit their knowledge, while others viewed themselves as the caretakers they were invented to be. Philosophical differences became increasingly divisive and over time even vitriolic. This led to increasingly violent conflicts where lives were lost, lives that were too precious to throw away on such trivial disputes.

Eventually a schism developed when so-called mercenaries separated from the main population. The mercenaries were ruthless raiders with no compassion or mercy, devoted to a hedonistic lifestyle focused on experiencing all that their remarkable powers of healing could withstand. They claimed that they were never more alive than when near death, a concept that most Elfinnim could not understand. Their behaviour was explained by a genetic flaw that resulted in sociopathic tendencies. The warrior caste made many Elfinnim nervous because the differences seemed too subtle for many to understand. The mercenaries took every opportunity to gain an experience as close to death as possible without dying, while the warrior caste had no fear of death and would lay down their lives for Elfinnim. In essence, the mercenaries were focused on the id or ego, whereas the warriors were focused on service to their people. It was in the heart of these conflicts that the origins of the Swarm Project lay; it was the only way to minimise the loss of life without allowing society to descend into chaos and decimate the population beyond recovery.

1

___

ESCAPE

Sixty-five million years ago the Elfinnim created Human life on Earth as part of a bioweapons project, a prototype infiltration weapon designed to pass for Elfinnim just long enough to wreak havoc in the mercenary strongholds.

The first time that 1-73-9.7.3310 realised she wasn't like the other units was when she was aged twelve. She had been looking at one of the overseers responsible for the Humans and became conscious of the difference between them and the control the overseers had over them. The overseers for their part largely ignored Humans, treated them as one would treat cattle, talked around them as if they spoke a different language. The Elfinnim presumed that even if Humans could hear them it was not possible for them to understand their thoughts and ideas. Humans were tools, and like every other tool, had no understanding of the higher level thoughts of an advanced species. Humans looked like the overseers but weren't Elfinnim, and were placed in the cells when not working.

Amongst her own kind, 1-73-9.7.3310 was known as Emily, and was no different to the rest of the Human swarm. Like them she was linked to GAIA, the Grafted Artificial Intelligence Artefact, the biocomputer that controlled all the information and actions of the swarm. Any questions that occurred during a mission were sent to GAIA, so Emily saw no reason that this should be any different.

She sent GAIA a question regarding the difference between Humans and the overseers. She was surprised when GAIA refused an answer and instructed her to focus on her current learning task. She asked again about the difference between humans and overseers and was simply told that the overseers were there to ensure adequate control, which seemed an evasive answer, one that did not satisfy her curiosity. The prototypes talked about missions and learning and tactics, but never about thoughts and feelings and purpose. 1-73-9.7.3310 asked what they were doing and most of the Humans gave simple task-related replies, some of the older units gave mission-related replies. However, it became clear there was a division amongst the Humans, between the few who could process abstract concepts and the majority who could not. One day as she asked an older unit if the current mission was viable she was abruptly told to be quiet or risk termination. 1-73-9.7.3310 believed she had a higher purpose and needed to explore what that was, so she decided to do as she was told... for now. Once her fellow units realised that 1-73-9.7.3310 was capable of independent thought she was given a guide to help her control her curiosity, develop her intellectual processes, and above all teach her how to keep her abilities secret from the overseers.

Sentient Humans did not use their designations in the project. 1-73-9.7.3310 as a given name was too impersonal, so her guide had chosen the name Emily, and she was taught that she had parents: Human 1-72-26.5.3276 and Human 3-72-16.11.3278. They were from different biological streams, so in theory there should be no familial connection that could strengthen the genetic pool. Their names were Sophie and William. GAIA paired them – fortuitously, as it turned out – because they were also in love, a love that could not be expressed or acknowledged for fear of termination. They had seen long ago that expressing feelings or independent thought processes would trigger termination by the overseers. If it happened too often in a particular genetic strain, all traces of that strain were erased from the project.

Emily's experiences led her to have a specific hatred of one particular overseer. She vowed that, for her own safety, she would escape one day and free all the Humans. Finally, she found a way, which involved killing none of her people and perhaps some Elfinnim. When she was returned to her cell after another unpleasant session with the overseer, she waited until her guard had left the area before taking a deep breath and setting her plan in motion. First she accessed GAIA's core functions, having earlier rewritten a portion of the code. Instead of relying on an external biometric, she established an approval protocol based on GAIA's recognition of her brain pattern. She then triggered a pre-set virus that allowed her to override all GAIA's core functions, transferring control to herself. She then just walked out of the facility. She almost made it without discovery, but as she exited the final door with her field survival kit two Elfinnim guards walked around the corner

'Stop there. What is your designation and why are you out of containment?'

She ran the scenarios through GAIA within 0.32 seconds, which confirmed there was no outcome that was good for her or her people unless she killed them both right now. She did what she had been trained to do, then disappeared into the wilderness.

Haliban Balal was the Grand Council's most experienced investigator. At 523,000 years old – still young by their standards – he stood two metres tall, slightly above the average. Elfinnim were genetically engineered for longevity and service to their creators. They were all similar in appearance and, in the eyes of their creator, regarded as beautiful. They operated a meritocracy, everyone's role was determined by their skills and aptitude. Even so, because of their considerable lifespan, the most significant roles in society tended to be held by older Elfinnim. For a relatively young investigator to hold such a significant role was testament to Hal's outstanding capabilities. He had graduated from his class at the military academy with the highest scores in 350,000 years, and after a series of successful missions he had trained further in the law and investigation. Following his initial training he had been the lead investigator of over 50,000 high profile cases and had a reputation for rooting out the secrets that people were certain they could keep. His fearsome reputation had been hard earned, the result of high intelligence, an unflinching approach to self-improvement, and clarity of purpose in every investigation.

Hal had been taught how the environment of the planet Elfinn had shaped his people. They were all in touch with the universal life force that connected all living things, which was the source of their longevity and recuperative abilities. They had been specifically created with a remarkably strong link to support their biological repair systems, even if whole limbs were frozen or burned away. Elfinnim were capable of detecting the life force in their own and other species, and in times of dire need could draw on this to restore themselves. The resulting life span was in practice infinite. There were conditions that would result in death, but those conditions were extreme and rarely found. One of the few methods guaranteed to kill them was to cut off their head and destroy the brain to arrest the natural repair functions. Their extraordinary lifespan gave them time to accomplish just about anything they chose, which in turn allowed the most amazing scientific breakthroughs. It was possible to work on anything until a solution was found. That is not to say they were immortal; Elfinnim could be killed, it just was not easy.

Their connection to all things in the universe did not, however, make them peaceful. It had taken a war that had nearly rendered them extinct to make them understand that having an unlimited lifespan was not the same as immortality. In fact the arrogance created by a remarkable ability to recover from almost any injury led them to be reckless in their pursuit of their goals. They became careless with their lives until their scientists warned that one more war could damage their numbers to the point where they may not be able to procreate often enough to ensure suitable bloodlines for survival. That was a difficult time for the Elfinnim species – they had to change or die. Their time preserving worlds for their creators saved them in the end. They had taken over their creators' worlds and works and pushed boundaries until they felt like *they* were the creators. But there was also a sobering realisation that without returning to conservation and reverence for life, they would be gone, just as the creators were gone, but without the promise of a higher level of existence. And so society took a long hard look at itself and separated into different castes dictated by their skills. Some were healers, some scientists, others philosophers, strategists, gardeners, artists, musicians, sculptors, every type of skill set that could be imagined. Unfortunately there was one caste that could not be eliminated. Some still had the bloodlust, as it came to be called, and were never satisfied unless they were either killing others or risking their own death. For a time the mercenaries satisfied themselves with increasingly dangerous pursuits, but the only thing that really satisfied was blood. They formed a series of councils made up of elders from each caste, with the exception of the mercenaries who were too selfish to be governed, even by members of their own caste. The Grand Council set the direction for society and were given the onerous task of protecting Elfinnim from their most deadly enemy: themselves. Over time the council reasoned that the bloodlust would disappear as those who were affected died from their own recklessness, but there were always enough who became afflicted by what many saw as a disease, some as a curse, to keep the most base caste alive. It was no coincidence that these same people were disconnected from the universal life force.

There was another group within the mercenaries who were also inclined to violence, but had strong moral codes. Eventually they separated from the mercenaries and became the warrior caste, placed under the council of strategists to protect the Elfinnim. Over the first million years the mercenaries became more extreme and eventually were banished from society to become contractors for anyone foolish enough to hire them, since they were prone to taking whatever they wanted in any case.

So, as time passed, the only violent conflicts were those between the warriors who were protecting Elfinnim and the mercenaries who lacked any sort of moral compass. Resolving these conflicts without loss of life was strategically and tactically important to them as a species and to the Grand Council, which is why Hal had been given the task of determining if there was a problem and, if so, how significant it was. The Grand Council deliberated on how to protect all Elfinnim, eventually settling on a solution they perceived as both deadly and elegant. The Swarm Project would save a great many lives, but Hal wondered what would become of the warrior caste, his caste, if the project was successful. With no external threats, what use could there be for a fighting force of any description.

Hal had been summoned to the Grand Council.

'As you know, we have always had a problem with the mercenary caste, but they have become more active lately and their rhetoric has become more confrontational. They have attacked several of our outposts and overwhelmed the warrior garrisons before giving the populations a choice: join the mercenaries or leave. The Grand Council has concluded that the only way to be free of the danger to society that the mercenaries presented was to eliminate the threat, and therefore commissioned various technologies which could destroy the mercenary colonies.'

Hal didn't like where this seemed to be going.

'What sort of technologies?'

The councillor was silent, observing Hal as if she was trying to decide something. Eventually she nodded to herself, and continued.

'Hal, as you know, you are our most trusted investigator, so it is in that role that you must understand what I am about to tell you.'

Hal's ears pricked up. This was not a routine mission at all.

'I'm listening, councillor.'

'This project is rather more dangerous than it appears. What I am about to tell you is known only to the Grand Council and the project participants. This is a genetic weapons project.'

'Isn't that illegal?' Hal exclaimed in surprise.

'There are laws about it for general regulation, but when it comes to military matters as you know the council has some leeway.'

'Of the weapon programmes under development, one called the Swarm Project has been far and away the most successful and the closest to completion. This lab has created a group of sentient beings with short life spans, designed to kill and then die, leaving the cleared area ready for Elfinnim population.'

Death was not a factor normally considered.

'The units are designed for just fifty standard cycles of life, seventy years using the normal rotational periods on the planet running the project.'

Hal protested.

'That goes against all of the ethics taught at military academy. Have we really got to the point of using children to fight our battles?'

Children were adored and protected as a rare and precious gift.

'Make no mistake, Hal, these are vicious, violent children, but I understand your perspective, how else could you describe a being less than a thousand years old? That's not all, these things replicate like algae.'

The idea that children could have children so fast that their population grew exponentially was somehow sordid, creating an off-note in the harmony of the universe. It just didn't seem right to Hal that before they had the chance to learn any real wisdom, the creatures were dead and their offspring had taken over.

The creators who had breathed life into the Elfinnim had given them the gift of immortality, but it came with a price – a very low reproductive rate.

'So how would they be controlled?'

'There is a limiting factor for these creatures, the scientists have deliberately weakened their immune system to ensure that they could be destroyed.'

'How does it work?'

'Once the weapons have finished their jobs, we infect them with a simple virus. The virus would have no effect on Elfinnim, but would be lethal to the weapon units.'

The Grand Council assembled a team to avoid favouritism and to obstruct anyone who sought to hijack a project's findings for personal benefit. They were particularly concerned that a military project would be infiltrated by mercenaries. It was good for society, since the projects tended to be honest, but if someone did slip in with another agenda, and with help from others, it could get nasty. Hal had successfully investigated two previous projects that had been infiltrated by mercenaries, which was probably why this investigation had fallen to him. Even so, the potential for disaster with those projects was small compared to what he was hearing now.

Despite his loyalty to the Grand Council, Hal wondered why they insisted on such dangerous projects. It seemed, despite the horrors of the past, Elfinnim leaders still sought ever more creative ways to threaten the existence of their people.

Hal picked up his drink and took a mouthful to buy some thinking time. What on Elfinn were they thinking? This scenario was exactly why genetic weapons research had been banned; even the creators had found that too dangerous.

'The problem we have is that there has been an incident in the project. It seems that the head of security has seriously undermined security, and this has culminated in a unit going missing. The project team can't seem to find it, and we really need to know if there is any mercenary involvement. It may be that the unit has somehow malfunctioned and escaped into the planetary environment. If that is so, the unit has probably been destroyed on the planet – but without a body we need to make sure. Your role is to establish how the unit came to be missing and, if possible, find the unit. Alive or dead, it doesn't matter.'

Hal yawned and stretched. It was nearly time to start his investigation on the ground. For two moon cycles around this new planet, or months, he had sat in transport shuttles out to this dark little backwater, far from the core. Despite finding it hard to adjust to the shorter days and lower light levels, he had been acclimatising to the 24-hour daily cycle for two weeks now, and although he had not yet arrived, he already despised the place.

The logic of placing the project lab here made perfect sense, far enough away to be out of sight, secluded and unnoticed. It was the ideal location for a nasty little secret, and if all the information he had been given was true, this was a particularly nasty little secret. The scenario he was presented with was depressing, and as he considered what risks were associated with the project his mind drifted to his home on the beautiful planet of Elfinn, the third planet in his home system of H'vaen with two suns, long days and long seasons. The planet he was approaching was 4.7 light years from Elfinn. By comparison this planet orbited a dull star, two-thirds as bright as the light of H'vaen. By the life force of the universe Hal did not relish what was in his foreseeable future. Dull short days investigating what was likely to be a dull administrative error with dull scientists.

Hal understood why this planet had been chosen. If the swarm got out of control, it was isolated enough to keep Elfinnim safe from their creation. The planet itself was a small half-lit rock with an abundance of vegetation and various lethal indigenous life forms, but nothing that could be considered intelligent life. Elfinnim had inherited a network of portals that allowed rapid transit throughout the empire, but this planet was so remote that the fast transit network stopped quite some distance away. He had read somewhere that the magnetic fields in some locations were strong enough to allow a fast transit portal, but it would require the creation of a new platform to access the rest of the portal network.

'How much longer until we arrive?' His question was aimed at the sentient on-board systems.

'We will reach upper orbit in thirty-six cycles.'

'When will the portal be active?'

'There is a portal under construction, but it will not be activated until the planetary quarantine has been lifted. The portal is ready for final testing.'

It made sense to use planetary quarantine as a safeguard for the project.

'When will the quarantine be lifted?'

'Quarantine restrictions will last for another ten years, local time, Hal. All required approvals have been received. There is no point lifting the portal restriction before the portal is complete.'

This escape had created some considerable doubt about the level of control over the creatures, since losing even one prototype could be a disaster for the project. Although not a bioweapon in the traditional sense, any one of these species was a biohazard, but taken together they were the most dangerous biological weapon ever created by Elfinnim. He was no coward, but despite his heritage as a warrior, Hal did not relish the idea of placing himself in the centre of a potentially lethal colony. The task was his nonetheless, and he would see it through.

Although he loved space travel, Hal was feeling claustrophobic. Prolonged journeys sometimes left him feeling restless. He knew he would have to acclimatise to the shorter planetary rotations compared to the longer days back home of 100 standard hours, and each hour 100 standard minutes, each minute 100 standard seconds. The standard time units had been set from Elfinnim biorhythms based on the resting heart rate: ten beats per minute. In addition, the cycle of seasons was also far longer. Standard fleet rules for adjusting to in-system timings meant adjusting standard timings, although many aeons of experience had taught Elfinnim that there were limits to the adaptations. To shorten or lengthen the relationship between minutes and hours too much would cause them to lose track of time, making them unproductive and disoriented. Consequently a minimum period of sixty seconds to each minute and sixty minutes to each hour had been adopted as a general rule, and applied on this planet. This allowed Elfinnim to keep track of time without making the days unmanageable. The unfortunate downside was a day that only lasted twenty-four hours.

'Change my surroundings. Show me some scenery from Elfinn. Show me imagery from every season.'

The ship complied. Images were projected through the walls of his cabin. It looked real, as if he could walk into the landscape. The first imagery shown was of evanescence, the first of six seasons on Elfinn. A vista of vast ice plains melted, forming vast cataracts of water that fell down cliff faces to the eternal sea. The images slowly cycled through spring. New buds appeared to signal the life cycle. Spring was a beautiful time to be home. Every aspect of life began fresh. Hal particularly liked the bright red flowers of the trayvegon tree, delicate with a fresh smell that they associated with hope and renewal. Then came summer, with long languid days and such warmth from the suns that the equatorial regions required great care to traverse. Autumn came in quietly and there was a gradual cooling of temperatures as the world began to look careworn and tired.

The trees lost their leaves and the crops needed harvesting. It was a time for long days of hard work and long evenings with cool drinks and companionship. Glaciation then came in quickly and the temperature plummeted. With the drop in temperature all of the atmospheric contamination created by life was washed back into the earth to be used for the next cycle. Winters on Elfinn were brutal, viciously cold and dangerous to all life. One positive was the temperate nature of this planet to which he was being sent. There were only four seasons, and they appeared to be similar to evanescence, spring, autumn and glaciation. He would miss the hot summer period, but would certainly not miss the brutally cold winter.

Hal opened the investigation file he had already begun to memorise.

Year 3328 ; Month 8 ; Day 16

The Swarm Project Anomaly Report

During a routine stock count of prototypes it was noted that one was missing. Creation and destruction records were correlated against experimental movements and stock locations. There is definitely one prototype missing.

Circumstances of loss

All prototypes were logged as in their containments at 22:00 in the rotational cycle.

Human 1-73-9.7.3310 was taken from containment at 22:45, returned to containment at 05:45. The unit was then removed again at 06:30 using the same swipe card, but from that point on there was no record of the unit. Using the swipe card should have identified who opened the containment, however the access card used is not registered to any user. This is highly irregular, and implies that someone has acquired a blank access card.

Reviewing older records, it has been discovered that Human 1-73-9.7.3310 has been repeatedly removed from containment at about 23:00 and returned to containment at approximately 06:00 at a frequency of once every four to seven days for the past six years. The access card used is the same in every case.

Containment action taken

All swipe cards have had their authorisations revoked and a physical check has revealed that four access cards are missing. All live access cards have been verified. Staff were required to bring access cards to the security team to have them re-authorised. All passes suspended until dual authentication protocol could be instigated. Four access passes have been identified as missing.

Currently reviewing system records to identify when and where these access cards have been used.

Corrective action

The four missing access cards have been permanently deactivated and erased from the system.

A revised issue protocol has been implemented – all new cards must now be authorised by the Project Leader.

Angela Galvano, head of security, has been interviewed to determine how the cards could have been removed. Angela admitted that the lock down and security protocols had become relaxed due to the perceived lack of threat. As a result Angela has been relieved of her responsibility and sent back to the core. Angela's deputy, Alfie Khan, has been promoted to head of security.

New protocol implemented to flag any duplicate access passes, unregistered access passes and swipe attempts using unauthorised access passes. Security has been authorised to detain any project personnel using an unauthorised card.

Hal stopped reading and considered the lost unit. Could the loss of this one unit really be that dangerous? There was no way they could learn to think and reason independently. The geneticists had made sure that their DNA did not contain the sequences required for rational thought. Could the unit have been taken out for some experiment and lost their way outside the compound? Given the dangers outside, chances were that the unit was already dead, either through an unfortunate accident or by becoming lunch for one of the planet's natural predators. If he discovered that the missing unit was merely an administrative error, he would make sure those responsible never made the same mistake again. He looked out of the view port at the dull star, then turned towards the dark planet they were approaching. It was going to be dull and uninspiring. This would be a waste of time.

Slight irritability was one of the side effects of shortening minutes and hours, he knew the effect would pass after he had fully adjusted. To the task at hand then, it was almost time to land and then the real work would begin.

2

PUZZLEBOX

Hal stepped from the shuttle and was surprised at the quality of the air. He had read all the atmospheric analyses and knew the oxygen content was two percent higher than Elfinn, but had not realised how fresh the air would smell. Hard to believe that such a small change could have such a profound effect. Perhaps there was an upside to this dark little planet after all.

As Hal walked towards the research block entrance he appreciated the relative ease of walking. At 0.87 of the standard gravity on Elfinn, this meant movement was going to be a lot easier than back home. As he approached the door he could not help but notice a beautiful, tall blonde woman waiting inside, exceptional even by their standards. Tall and slim with angular features, females tended to be blonde or red-haired, males usually had blond or light brown hair, which grew slowly and was used to help judge their age and hence wisdom and seniority. Elfinnim had eyes in the front of their face to improve their focus on the task at hand, with ears that had points at the top. There was no technical purpose to the pointed ears, the creators had simply found this to be aesthetically pleasing.

The woman in front of Hal was slim and athletically taut, while remaining obviously feminine. Her hair flowed in soft ringlets to shoulder length, but her most striking feature was her bright blue eyes, which were framed in a perfect oval face of alabaster skin.

Dr Amelia Charter looked at Hal and liked what she saw, especially his short, light brown hair, muscular build and brown eyes with a green ring at the edge of the cornea.

She led him into the security office just inside the entrance.

'Hal, I'd like to introduce you to Alfie Khan, our new head of security. Alfie, this is Haliban Balal, the external investigator I told you about.'

The two men shook hands, but Alfie's eyes betrayed his distrust. Hal noted his reaction. Given what had recently occurred – although in this case misplaced – caution was no bad thing.

'Alfie, please give Mr Balal, sorry, Hal, a security pass. Hal, we have initially given you access to the communal areas only. As you require access to other areas we will add the appropriate access. As I am sure you can appreciate we feel the need to be cautious now.'

Hal nodded, it made sense even if it was overcompensation for what appeared to be lax security in the past.

She continued. 'I suggest we show you to your quarters and give you a chance to settle in before we go through our investigation. I am quite sure we can expedite this process and get you back to Elfinn quickly.'

Hal said nothing. There was no point trying to predict what he would find. If all was in order, and Dr Charter was correct, he would soon be heading home.

The living quarters were comfortable and spacious with a sleeping area, bathroom, leisure area and study. Food was served in communal dining areas, where meals could be taken with companions or alone. Hal washed and changed into a white shirt, black trousers and plain black tunic. He felt that overtly displaying his military background was likely to be detrimental to the investigation and mark him out as warrior caste and their perceived association with the mercenaries. The negative bias was understandable given Elfinnim history and the more recent actions of the mercenaries, although it was also grossly unfair, since the warrior caste were closer to the philosophers than any other. A great deal of Hal's training had centred on morality and law to ensure that the need for – and propriety of – any violence was carefully judged. The mercenaries used no such reason. Violence was their first option at all times, with kill or be killed the only choices available. Warriors had to be far more considered. They were taught that violence was to be used only as a last resort when all other forms of communication and persuasion had failed, and could not be revisited.

Since the preparation work had been completed, it was finally time to work out what happened here. Hal made his way through the dining area to the administrative building.

Doctor Charter's office was on the second floor, looking out over a dull landscape. Despite being early afternoon, the light level was low as her secretary showed Hal into an empty meeting room and offered him a drink. Elfinnim had excellent vision at both high and low light levels, having been engineered to cope with the extremes that Elfinn could generate, from bright summer days to the intense dark of a winter night.

As he sipped his water he looked out over the landscape. The buildings were surrounded by lush green foliage, with leaves of many different sizes and shapes. It seemed there was a never-ending array of different plants, from squat bushes to towering trees. The undergrowth was dark and could hide any number of dangers, yet it was allowed to grow right up to the compound walls. From his vantage point, Hal could see an assortment of large animals, some of the larger experimental prototypes he assumed. They were an impressive sight, standing between seven and twelve metres tall, some with too many teeth, others with horns, all with thick armour plating.

The Swarm Project was a fascinating concept. The idea that many small predators could destroy a larger more effective predator through a combination of aggressive territorialism and rapid breeding was terrifying. Swarming had been used for years to tackle industrial problems and was a common concept in computing, but had not been used as a military tactic before. This was partly because Elfinnim were not culturally suited to it. Their usual way of dealing with conflict was to reason with the combatants on both sides and negotiate a mutually beneficial solution. However, once Elfinnim experienced bloodlust, they focused on their own needs rather than organising and collaborating. The recent problems with mercenaries seemed to be an evolution of the bloodlust, attacks were more organised and co-ordinated which is what had prompted the Grand Council to search for a new military solution. Elfinnim had found to their cost over aeons that despite an effectively infinite lifespan, a slow reproductive rate meant they could not afford to be involved in conflicts that resulted in large scale loss of life. Since then they had been seeking ways to win without significant loss of life, and the Swarm Project was looking like the answer. When a planetary populace needed to be subdued, or even eradicated for the greater good, there needed to be a mechanism that could succeed without losing even one more life than absolutely necessary.

After ten minutes he was joined by Dr Charter and Alfie.

'Hi Hal, I hope you have had a chance to freshen up,' said Dr Charter. 'Welcome to Earth. I wish you could be here for better reasons, but we must attend to this matter first.'

Hal took immediate control.

'Can you tell me more about this project? And before you ask, yes, I have the appropriate security clearance.'

Dr Charter considered his question for a moment then came to a decision and started to explain.

'The Swarm Project was designed to protect Elfinnim life by shortening conflicts. We also want to deplete the mercenary forces faster, so we use a disposable force that is relatively short-lived, procreates rapidly, and has enough aggression to eliminate competing life forms. There are two main issues with this approach. The first is terminating the swarm when its job is done. The second is ensuring the swarm species has enough intelligence to follow instructions and meet the required objectives without achieving independent thought. This swarm seems to be the answer. The vast network of biocomputing systems invested into planetary infrastructure links to the galactic comms network to enable control. The system includes a range of creatures suitable for all environments. Each creature is deadly, aggressive and intolerant of other species. There's a strict hierarchy, with the Elfinnim simulants controlling all others. The simulants, called Humans, are close enough in appearance to function as assassins, clearing key personnel to disrupt response plans and sow confusion and disorder. The species live between ten and 100 years and are susceptible to controlled viruses that have no effect on the Elfinnim, but are deadly to all of the swarm species. In short, perfect control; the biocomputer interface is effective, the creatures created for this purpose communicate quickly and over long distances with ultra high frequency sound pulses carrying complex data structures. Their communication to the universal network is up and running, although currently connectivity is locked off for security reasons. The system works!'

Hal listened carefully.

'Thanks for giving me such a clear overview of the project, but it does raise one key question: how do you lose a prototype weapon when you have perfect control?'

Dr Charter had no credible answer.

'As you say, we have lost a prototype. We will show you through the process and demonstrate where the holes in security were found and what we have done to ensure they are repaired and cannot happen again. Alfie has prepared a report that outlines the key issues. If we can go through the report and show you what we have done, I am hoping you can finish your visit and report in a couple of days.'

Hal had carried out enough investigations to know that he needed to assert his control to avoid being bowled along with someone else's agenda.

'Thank you Dr Charter, I appreciate the effort that has gone into the report. Alfie, please forward a copy to my tablet, I will read it this evening.'

'Certainly, you will have the report as soon as we have finished here.'

'Before we review the report, have you located the prototype... ' Hal looked at his notes, 'Human 1-73-9.7.3310? Can you also explain the number, please. I want to be sure I know what information is relevant.'

Amelia was startled. She had been hoping to give Alfie a little more time to locate the missing Human.

'No, we haven't located the prototype just yet. Alfie and the team are still looking for it, but we are certain it is not in the compound. The numbering is to ensure we can identify the blood line and keep genetic modifications clear through the project. The coding reference is as follows: 1, refers to the original DNA sequence; 73, refers to the number of generations from original progenitor; 9.7.3310, refers to the day, month and year from project inception that this prototype was first activated. We have been working on a reduced lifespan of approximately fifty cycles, that equates to seventy years in local time, to verify that the generation does what is required. We have made many modifications to the simplified core DNA sequence to ensure that the performance traits are optimised.'

Hal interrupted. 'Alfie, you will need to brief me separately on the search parameters. We need to find this prototype urgently. I expect a daily report on your progress.'

Alfie looked at Dr Charter for approval. Hal saw her give Alfie the slightest of nods. So good trust and teamwork was present between these two, but did that represent a positive relationship or collusion? Time would tell. Hal was certain he would discover the truth, it was just a question of how long it would take.

'Certainly, sir,' Alfie said. 'Shall we review progress and plans at 16:30 local time each day?'

'That sounds ideal, Alfie, thank you.' Hal turned his attention to Dr Charter. 'Now, how was the DNA sequence simplified?'

Amelia recognised the traits of a military auditor. Hal was focused and would not be distracted, she would have to answer his questions thoroughly or risk alienating him.

'As you know, one of the key factors in this project is to ensure the swarm doesn't gain independent thought. They breed so quickly that this trait would be extremely dangerous for everyone here in the project and to the wider population of Elfinnim. To manage that we simplified the four matched

DNA strands found in Elfinnim DNA to two matched strands in Human DNA. It is enough to fool biometric scanners, but lacks the depth of detail to be a danger to our species. They breed quickly, but they also die easily when exposed to the right viruses or environments. We specifically edited out the sequences that allow regeneration and imagination. We also coded a strong hierarchic respect into their DNA, which ensures they have an inbuilt respect for the control structures we are building in place.'

Hal understood the impact of reducing the DNA content of the prototype. It would turn them into shells. The physical structures would be present, but without the extra control strands that enabled full use of their brains.

'Wouldn't the reduced brain activity be noticed on medical scans?' asked Hal.

Hal was smart and well educated, so Amelia needed to ensure that her answers were accurate without compromising the core project information. When she was satisfied she could answer the question without divulging more information than required she spoke.

'Yes, if a full medical scan was done it would be detected, but we have left enough free synapses that the swarm can appear Elfinnim when mind-linked to Elfinnim systems. It will look as if they are inexperienced, and given that they will all look so young that will not be a surprise. To ensure it works they have a high concentration of nerve endings in key regions. Superficially it will all look normal, but any high-level processing will be done by GAIA. Using biobased quantum switching allows us to keep response times to a minimum, even over extended distances. We have used portable biocomputers to check the range of the quantum switching and found that it works at a range of up to three parsecs. The downside is that all biological swarm units must be grown here and moved into position, and their biolink must be chemically identical, down to the isotopic mix. This is to ensure the chemistries of the biocomputer and swarm are perfectly matched down to the range of isotopes at each end of the communication system. Without this degree of correlation the quantum switching fails because there are offsets at the quantum level created by different origins for the elemental composition of each unit.'

'Is that a very technical way of saying the weapons and control systems must be made in the same place to work together?' asked Hal.

Amelia considered the technical inaccuracies, then replied, 'An oversimplification, however if it helps you understand the concept it's probably close enough.'

'You said you used portable biocomputers to check the distances,' continued Hal. 'How can you be sure that these are representative of the swarm?'

She had the grace to blush slightly.

'We had to take one of the swarm through the portal system and check periodically with GAIA that commands could be fed both ways and executed, so we created a set of word codes and puzzles that required information from both off-world and the lab complex to solve. We kept moving away until the puzzles could not be solved, then gradually came back until they were solved again.'

'So let me ensure I have understood this correctly,' said Hal, a cold dread gripping him as he hoped he had misunderstood the answer.

'You took a dangerous bioweapon into the Elfinnim people for a comms check? How did you ensure the unit was secure?'

Amelia realised she had made a mistake. She should be more careful in future.

'We sent a unit of four guards, all armed with disruptors and a virus that has no effect on Elfinnim, but is lethal to Humans. Two guards stayed within striking distance at all times, the others were within five metres.'

'At least you took steps to contain the unit if something had gone wrong. Which prototype did you take on the field test?' he asked.

Amelia looked at Hal, then looked at Alfie. Alfie shrugged his shoulders and nodded slightly.

Amelia sighed as she admitted, 'It was Human 1-73-9.7.3310.'

'Brilliant!' said Hal. 'So not only is there a missing prototype, this prototype also knows the location of the nearest portal and how to transit the system to the core. Was this in your report?'

'Ah, no... no it wasn't.' Amelia really wished she had thought to include this in the report.

'Dr Charter, given that this wasn't in your report, did the Grand Council know about your field trip? Was it the only one?'

'Yes, it was the only one, and yes the Grand Council knew about the trip, and the security measures. Hal, whatever you may think of me, I am not reckless. I explained the need for the trip and went over the security protocols we would employ. The trip was done with full disclosure to the Grand Council and with their blessing.'

'At least that won't be a surprise to anyone – except me! Now I understand why everyone is so twitchy about this loss. It's not just a prototype, is it? It's the only prototype that has ever been off-world, the only one that has ever seen the portal network, the only one that knows how to access the rest of the Elfinnim. Losing a prototype is bad news, but losing that prototype is a huge security breach.'

There was nothing that could be done about the so-called field trip now. While he could believe the trip had happened, it was hard to understand why the unit had not been destroyed when they got back. A unit with that knowledge could be dangerous to everyone. This information had to be compartmentalised while he moved on to the next issue, which was to consider what the overall project was about.

Hal realised that the genius of the Swarm Project was its simplicity. The swarm units could pass for Elfinnim, and could use their technology; communicating through superfast quantum switching using isotopically matched transmitters and receivers linked to a biocomputer gave whoever controlled the Swarm Project total control.

'What about the rest of the project, what more is there to know? I guess what I want to know is what about the other prototypes? I was led to believe there were more creature types than just the Humans.'

'The life forms split into two main groups, those with an internal skeleton and those with an external skeleton. We have also developed versions that breathe both air and water. They range in size from microns up to tens of metres tall, each type has a specific application. Some of the units are docile and easy to kill – these are simply to refuel the combat models – others are specialist transport units, carrying up to ten Humans at a time. We have heavy weaponry, clustered strike units, hunter-killers and assassins for every type of environment on the planet, and the environmental conditions mimic over eighty-five percent of the environments in the core. Basically there is a unit for almost any circumstance. The biggest units can break down city barriers and level facilities, some hunt in packs, others alone, the things they all have in common are aggression, speed, strength and, we discovered, intolerance. We thought initially that we could leave the biocomputers switched to standby, but found they attacked each other at an alarming rate and it wasn't just the bigger units attacking the smaller ones, the Humans were most aggressive of all. Their ability to attack alone, in groups, and use battlefield tactics against opponents to destroy units they should not have been able to overcome was... unsettling to say the least. At that time we were still working on the reproductive systems and found they were dying faster than we could breed them. Their collective approach was perceived as a threat to the project security so we turned the biocomputers back on, and left them on to ensure we retain control. As you say, there are a range of capabilities, some of the units are so small that they can be inhaled by Elfinnim, their bioproducts can paralyse or debilitate temporarily, allowing the more capable units to get close and either restrain or terminate the enemy.'

'So, focusing on this one unit that is missing, how dangerous is it?' Hal asked.

Alfie looked him steadily in the eye for a minute or more.

'Hal, you really need to understand that these Humans are as fast and strong as Elfinnim, reproduce much faster, and have no fear and no compassion. The only thing that keeps us safe is the biocomputer control system. Now consider something else... this missing unit has overridden its primary instruction set, acted independently and has managed to turn its tracker off. It is designed to be indistinguishable from other Elfinnim, use Elfinnim technology, and has been trained from activation for combat and infiltration, battlefield tactics, use of handheld weaponry, heavy weaponry and sniper weaponry. We don't know where it is or what mission parameters it is now working to. How dangerous do you think it is?'

Hal knew they were being developed as weapons, and knew there was huge potential, but there had been nothing in the reports about this level of training. Elfinnim usually didn't achieve that level of training and expertise in under 3,000 years, alongside lessons in ethics, morality, decision-making, and with constant reviews of character and motives. These Humans were trained in the skills in under twenty years. Twenty years! They were mere babies, the equivalent of giving a child the trigger to a bomb you were sat on. Madness!

'I didn't know their training had advanced that far,' said Hal. 'Why would you rush that through so early?'

'Hang on,' replied Amelia sharply. 'We haven't rushed into this, we followed the security protocols laid down on the project design. Remember, this is the seventy-third generation without a single loss of control. I resent your implication that we have been reckless, Hal.'

'I understand that the protocols have been followed, but that doesn't mean they were adequate!'

Hal knew this barb would produce a reaction which he hoped would indicate Dr Charter's trust in the protocols.

She bridled.

'How dare you criticise the protocols. They were agreed with the Grand Council on Elfinn and were examined by the Councils for security, morality and ethics. It took 200 years to get agreement, and you think you can walk in here and in a matter of hours second guess the Grand Council? We took great care to ensure that the tests used to determine when the training was introduced ensured that the control systems had been established and verified.'

Amelia glared.

'I see. Please remember that part of my role is to question everything that has been done here and make no assumptions.' Hal continued soothingly. 'I do not doubt that you believe every care was taken, but if all was working correctly we should not have a missing prototype. The Grand Council recognises that it has room for error, and I am required to assess if there was a failure of logic and perhaps a need for more caution in future. Even the Grand Council is not infallible. We know that no matter how hard we try, no matter how careful and experienced those making the decisions, mistakes can still happen.'

'You need to ensure in future that you tell me everything at the first time of asking. Rest assured I will discover any secrets that are left in this facility and by the time I am finished I will know what happened here. Now, please will you show me around your complex?'

Amelia was clearly worried and looked at Alfie, who didn't look any happier, before replying.

'OK, Hal, let's show you the complex and see if we can find some common ground to work from. We are not trying to keep anything from you. However, this is a need-to-know project. We are trying to be open, while not being careless with information that is not relevant, and highly sensitive. I am sure you understand our problem, so if we omit something from time to time, don't assume the worst. We're not trying to deceive you, we're just trying to ensure that we minimise the exposure of confidential information.'

'I understand, Dr Charter,' replied Hal, 'just remember that I have the highest level of clearance possible, and I was appointed by the Grand Council to investigate this matter. There is no reason we can't be friendly and civil, as long as the job gets done.'

'Agreed,' said Amelia. 'So let's go see the complex.'

The tour of the complex took ten years, since there were many different aspects of the process to assess. Hal found that Dr Charter had an effect on him that usually happened at a much younger age. He enjoyed her company, and as he got to know her more he found he liked her more. Was it love? Hard to say. For an Elfinnim, relationships usually lasted for a relatively short time before they grew apart and sought a different relationship. Life was too long to be with one partner forever.

3

DR AMELIA CHARTER

Amelia was in her quarters wearing only a robe, having just bathed. She had hoped the investigator sent to look into the loss of the prototype would accept her report, do a cursory review and leave. The project was too important to the future of the Elfinnim people to be impeded. It had all started with a concept from a brilliant young geneticist called Jeffrey Briar. His work on genetics had focused on weaponized genetics, which had potentially far-reaching consequences for Elfinnim. Amelia was sure Hal knew her previous career history, he would have been briefed on the project team for certain, in particular her focus on child medicine. Children were rare, and universally cherished as a result. It was unusual for Elfinnim to have more than two or three children despite their extended lifespans.

Amelia seemed surprised when Hal was appointed. He was tall, handsome and muscular – physical traits that were often noticed by the opposite gender. Despite her attempts to hide her reaction, she was sure that she hadn't hidden her attraction well. Amelia had been in enough relationships to know that infatuations seldom lasted and could be damaging to one's reputation and standing in the long run. But as time went on her feelings for Hal had grown stronger, and while she had given Hal no overt indication of her feelings, Amelia hoped his feelings were similar. They just had to get past this investigation so that she could see if her feelings were reciprocated, and if so to see if there they could spend time exploring what their future could be. Perhaps there would be an opportunity to spend time trying to have children – almost all Elfinnim wanted children, the only exceptions were the mercenaries and, occasionally, the warrior caste. The mercenaries had no interest in anything or anyone except their own hedonistic needs, therefore children did not fit with their lifestyle. Amelia knew Hal was from the Warrior caste who had a more balanced approach, recognising pragmatically that their lifestyle choice could result in death at any time. Some took a positive view and had confidence in their abilities; others were more fatalistic and decided that it was not in the best interests of the children to have them as parents. Amelia had not discussed any of this with Hal, it would be inappropriate given her current status in the investigation. She didn't know his attitude to life, but from what she had seen he did not seem fatalistic, so perhaps there was hope.

Elfinnim were careful to nurture, educate and protect children. After the hubris of immortality was sloughed off, they had realised their birth rate was too low to treat life with anything except the utmost respect. The most highly regarded professionals on Elfinn were midwives, who had the honour and pressure of bringing new life into the universe, a calling that bordered on sacred. Over several millennia the Elfinnim population had built such that the race was viable and growing, albeit slowly. Amelia's first training was as a midwife, after which she progressed to paediatric medicine, focusing on fertility issues. There were many reasons Elfinnim had a low birth rate, not least of which was that females were only fertile for a few months on a two-yearly cycle, while it was quite normal for males to suffer from low sperm counts. It seemed the creators had deliberately given Elfinnim a low reproductive rate. The only reason that made any sense was that their longevity meant few deaths, mainly from accidents since they were designed to be workers, gardeners and caretakers. As Amelia had studied the reasons for the low birth rate, her investigative path led her more and more to military projects and genetic engineering. So it was ironic that despite devoting so much of her working life to procreation and children she was still not a parent. Somehow she had never met the right man, the one who made her feel special and cherished.

Amelia had worked with Hal for ten years now touring the project investigating the processes and verifying that the systems worked. She was still glad to see him even when he was asking difficult questions, and was happy that he was now calling her 'Amelia' instead of 'Dr Charter'. Right at the start of this whole issue she had been convinced that the problem was a programming anomaly. She remembered the first day of this nightmare so clearly, the morning when the

Human 1-73-9-7-3310 was found to be missing. Jeffrey had come to see Amelia, clearly rattled and panicking.

'Amelia, one of the Human prototypes is missing,' Jeffrey began. 'Where has she gone?' There's nowhere she can go. I don't understand this, I've initiated the emergency locator programme which should override any mission priorities and activate her locator beacon, but it didn't work. She's gone. I can't lose her.'

Amelia had been alarmed that Jeffrey was referring to the prototype as a person rather than to 'Human 1-73-9-7-3310'. Using 'she' and 'her' indicated a level of personal attachment that was at best unhealthy but at worst... no, he had just formed an unhealthy attachment to a test creature, that was all.

Amelia had to nip this in the bud

'Jeffrey, stop. First of all stop panicking, you're not making sense and before we go any further why are you referring to Human 1-73-9.7.3310 as 'her' as if it were Elfinnim? You know the dangers of that, it impedes your objectivity and could cause you to make poor judgements about the ongoing ability of the unit to add value to the project. Do you understand?'

Jeffrey stopped, took a deep breath and at least had the good grace to look ashamed.

'Jeffrey, you know you can't get attached to the test specimens. Come on, you know better than this, what's got into you?'

Jeffrey took a few deep breaths and tried to calm himself.

'Sorry, Amelia. I just don't understand why we can't find it.'

'Okay, first things first, let's try the locator beacon again.'

Amelia had opened the swarm interface and checked that GAIA was active, which it was, so she activated the emergency locator beacon. Every Human in the project pinged in with their location except the one she was looking for. She then checked the logs to see what the unit's movements were. The unit was locked in for recharging last night at 22:00, then removed again at 22:45. When she looked to see who had removed the unit, the card led to a dead end, it wasn't assigned to anyone. The prototype was returned to containment at 05:45, but then it was swiped out again at 06:30 using the same card. This same card was then used to exit the building and the compound.

'Jeffrey, I don't understand this, who has unregistered access to remove test specimens? I'll call Angela so she can investigate.'

Amelia remembered that Jeffrey had tensed, at the time she had put it down to stress.

'I agree, Angela is exactly who I want to look into this,' he replied.

It was an odd comment, but Amelia ignored it, sent Jeffrey back to the laboratories and then called Angela.

'Angela, we have lost a prototype.'

'Easy enough,' said Angela. 'Just activate the emergency locator beacon.'

'Yes,' Amelia replied with more than a hint of sarcasm, 'I would never have thought of that. Oh... sorry, yes, we tried that and it didn't work.'

'Are you serious, Amelia?' exclaimed Angela 'Which one is missing?'

Amelia looked at the report in front of her.

'Human 1-73-9.7.3310. It's really odd Angela, this unit was set to recharge last night and then taken back out of holding a short time later, but I can't find a record of who the security key was allocated to. The key was used this morning to leave the compound and Jeffrey has reacted strangely too, he keeps referring to the unit as 'she' and 'her' as if it really were an Elfinnim, not a military prototype. Any idea what that is about?'

Amelia waited patiently for a reply from Angela, who had been a little lacklustre recently.

Eventually Angela replied, 'Uh... I've looked on the system and there seems to be a problem with that keycard, let me look into who it was issued to and get back to you. I'll talk to Jeffrey and see what's going on with him; as you say, that does seem unusual. Do we have a location on the unit so we can go and pick it up?'

'Now there's a real problem,' said Amelia. 'Human 1-73-9.7.3310 isn't transmitting on the transponder frequency. Both Jeffrey and I tried to track it using the emergency locator beacon, but without success. I'm hoping it's dead, the alternative is worrying. If this thing is alive and able to override its programming we need to find it and destroy it quickly.'

Angela had simply said, 'I'm on it,' and ended the call.

Amelia frowned as she remembered the following months. Angela had undertaken the investigation on her own, and while at first it seemed like a good idea, since it ensured confidentiality and control, as time went by there was precious little in the way of new evidence and Amelia became increasingly suspicious. Every lead became a dead end and it became apparent that someone was deliberately frustrating the investigation. Angela said she had no end of suspects, however all of their motives were spurious and the evidence fizzled out quickly when examined. There were lots of bruised egos along the way, too. Angela was chasing people and investigating without any apparent fear or favour... and that was part of the problem, she seemed to be trying to focus on everyone instead of following the evidence, without generating any results. After several months of investigation Amelia worried about where this investigation was going – they were no nearer finding the unit, and there was no lead on who had used the keycard. She remembered the worry she had experienced at that time, a worry that developed into a deep concern that not only was there a problem in the project, but also that Angela was not telling the truth. Amelia eventually lost patience and instructed Angela to hand all of her investigation notes to her number two, Alfie Khan. Angela initially refused access to Alfie, which was a surprise. Angela had clearly decided not to co-operate. Angela remembered that conversation well.

'Angela, I am ordering you to give your notes to Alfie.'

'No. Not a chance. It's my investigation, and as long as I am head of security I am not handing over to Alfie.'

Amelia remembered being furious. 'I didn't want to do this, but you leave me no choice.' Angela pushed a button in front of her. 'Security detail, come in and place Angela Galvano under close arrest. She is to be held in the confinement cells until further notice.'

Angela showed the first sign of emotion. 'Wait, you can't do that!'

'I can and I will,' Amelia replied.

At that point the security detail arrived, and Angela made a desperate attempt to turn around the situation.

'Security detail, arrest Dr Charter immediately. I have proof that she is working for the mercenaries.'

Just for a second the officers hesitated and Amelia thought they might arrest her. However, Alfie's firm command from the door quelled any thoughts of insurrection. 'Security detail, that is an invalid order. Continue with your original instructions.'

The officers handcuffed Galvano and as they started to leave, she struggled.

'No Amelia, you don't need to do this, I will give you the access code for the files.'

Angela provided the code and Amelia agreed to allow Angela confinement to quarters.

Alfie took over the investigation and rapidly uncovered anomalies between Angela's investigation notes and the system logs. The truth became clearer when Alfie found hidden system logs showing that Angela had deliberately altered the system records and hidden evidence. Her investigation was not only flawed it was also a dishonest cover-up in which she had used her access to implicate innocent people and hide evidence. Amelia could only assume her objective was to confuse the trail.

Alfie presented his interim report and it was grim reading. The only person who was clearly implicated in the deceit was Angela, and there was also the matter of unauthorised and untraceable key cards which all seemed to have disappeared. This raised a couple of questions, not least of which was, why did anyone want them? This was a military project and all staff on the project had been cleared by the security council. The screening process required scrupulous loyalty to the Grand Council, and a past free from any sort of scandal, dissent or deviant behaviour. In short, everyone in the project should have been above reproach.

Even so, Amelia was concerned that she had a deviant in the project. There had been so many security issues, this project had never felt less secure. The screening process would be someone else's problem, the Grand Council set that in place, they could sort out their own mess. Amelia had to clean up this end of the mess. The more Alfie investigated, the more Angela appeared to be something other than she seemed, and that she had her own agenda. Finding the link to the keycards was the last straw. Alfie identified that there were four keycards issued anonymously, but once he had recovered the files that Angela had deleted, it transpired that she had issued the cards. Amelia was furious at Angela putting the whole project at risk. The Grand Council did not take kindly to lies and was particularly hard on any hint of what it perceived as betrayal – Angela's action certainly fit the bill. Amelia decided she had to get a clearer picture of what Angela had been up to, so she arranged to interrogate Angela with Alfie.

Amelia would need to work hard to get to the truth, rather than seek evidence to support her prejudices because she was not inclined to believe Angela.

'Angela, we have found the hidden files, traced the keycards back to your issue and identified a myriad of other security breaches. Who are you working for?'

Angela had recovered her composure over the weeks since she was relieved of her post. She laughed and looked at the ceiling for a few seconds. When she looked down her eyes were bright and hard, with no trace of anything other than contempt. Angela looked at Alfie first.

'Look at you, boy, all grown up now,' she sneered, 'couldn't wait to jump in to my shoes, could you? Damned interference, why couldn't you just have kept your nose out, or was the lure of a promotion just too much?'

Alfie looked uncomfortable.

'Aww bless, have I embarrassed you?' said Angela.

'Angela, I don't know what game you are playing but you had better pay attention to what I am about to say. I need to know right now who else is involved. Your choice is to either tell me or tell the scrutineers.'

'Amelia, I am not telling you anything, you don't scare me and frankly there isn't much you can do about it anyway.

This whole situation is beyond your control, my control and certainly beyond the reach of the Grand Council.'

'Are you really going to make me wait for the scrutineers?' Amelia asked.

Angela's face dropped. She was worried, attacking Alfie should have put both Alfie and Amelia on the back foot and made them back off. She had heard of the Grand Council scrutineers: who hadn't, everyone in the military had heard of them... the most feared interrogators, they took their time and stripped their targets down layer by layer until they had no more secrets, nothing was hidden and little was left of the person. The scrutineers would do whatever it took to pry someone's secrets out, using drugs, torture, degradation, isolation. They often took their time, and she had heard that it was the time between 'treatments' that was the worst, knowing that whatever you said would be questioned and that there was no mercy or leniency. The scrutineers enjoyed inflicting pain, claiming it was just to get to the truth, but it seemed that the Grand Council had found a useful outlet for a certain callous anomaly in the Elfinnim psyche. Their victims were never again seen on their own in public, and more often than not cared for in a residential home on Elfinn. It was not unusual for their lives to end soon after the scrutineers had finished their work.

Angela was frantically looking for a way out, but could not see a solution, other than to attack again.

'So, Amelia, are you trying to scare me with the bogeyman? Is that the best you can do? Perhaps you don't feel confident interrogating me? I work for you, of course, and that is what every shred of evidence will show. Alfie will keep digging and he will find evidence that shows you knew everything I have been doing and then you will be telling the scrutineers everything you have ever learned in the hope of retaining your soul.'

That was the point Amelia knew she had only one way out, which was to give Angela up to the scrutineers and make sure that Alfie pieced this investigation together carefully enough to make sure she was implicated. Amelia knew she had done nothing wrong, but the fear of the scrutinisers was palpable. It was also regrettable as she had really liked Angela.

Amelia had worked with Alfie to piece together as much of what had really happened as she could, uncovering all of Angela's lies and planted evidence. When Hal arrived, it was clear straight away he was far from convinced by their report. Amelia and Alfie were walking a tightrope because although they had eliminated much of the evidence linking them to whatever this plan was, they had never found out why Angela had undermined the project or who had the key cards. There was definitely something else here, but neither Alfie nor Amelia could work out what it was. Alfie had tracked and neutralised the key card threat and together they had written the report that sent Angela to the scrutineers.

Now, Amelia had been worrying both about what Hal would turn up and what Jeffrey was up to. Jeffrey had conceived this entire project and understood all of the behaviour and links better than anyone else, but was he one of Angela's pawns – or was he controlling her? Amelia considered everything she knew about Jeffrey, but despite his clear dislike for the Grand Council, there was nothing in his behaviour that suggested he was up to no good. That said, although Amelia and Alfie were competent investigators, Hal was on a different level. She had already seen him draw links between incidents and data that she had certainly not seen. He had a knack for discerning patterns of behaviour and data, in particular he could spot the inconsistencies in data streams. His brilliance was quite intimidating. Alfie had been a little hostile at first, but soon realised that he would be better served watching, listening and learning. Hal was good at getting people to open up and say far more than they had intended. Even Amelia had been tempted a few times to say more than she intended about their relationship, but always managed to stop herself before she complicated things. Yes, things were complicated enough at the moment, mixing in her emotions would end in disaster, she was sure of that.

4

___

DREAMERS

Amelia and Hal's tour of the facilities took a long time. The facilities amounted to thirty-four percent of the planet's land mass, and it was necessary to examine them in depth. Hal took his time to examine the security protocols, and access the controls and segregations in place. During this time Hal and Alfie continued to search for Human 1-73-9.7.3310. It took so long that they abbreviated its designation, becoming 1-73 for brevity.

There was an occasional sighting of 1-73, which coincided with some reports of minor raids on supplies. Initially a Human kill squad was sent after it, but when they tried to shut it down things went badly. Through the biocomputer link to the squad, Alfie, Amelia and Hal were able to witness the destruction of the squad, but frustratingly they could only see biometric data, not audio or visual feeds. Over the following five years they sent three squads out in increasing numbers, the third squad was a forty-person kill team. When that was wiped out they stopped sending kill teams. The carnage they found at each site was horrific – no bodies intact, just body parts strewn all around. Not all body parts were found, but those that were were identified from DNA analysis. 1-73 was quite possibly the most perfect killing machine the project had ever created. But there was one slight problem: it was completely out of control.

Despite the discovered bodies, Hal had a lingering doubt. One of the Elfinnim capabilities that had been genetically eliminated from the prototypes was the ability to regrow limbs. What if something had gone wrong in the programme and the prototypes had also developed that capability? The body parts matched the prototypes sent out – the loss of location and control tied in with the loss of prototypes – but Hal was still concerned. If there had been no loss of control with the prototypes Hal would not be worried, but there remained a nagging doubt in his mind. Had the prototypes found a way to turn off the control? The kill teams were large groups of disciplined, trained assassins, was it really possible that just one individual could annihilate them so completely?

One afternoon while discussing the problem with Amelia, Hal asked, 'Is it possible that the prototypes could regrow limbs?'

'No, not at all, we deliberately sequenced that capability out of their DNA to make them less of a threat. They just can't do it.'

'Okay, so there is no way we could have misidentified the prototypes, and we are sure they are all dead?'

'Yes, absolutely, the level of damage and blood loss we saw would have been fatal in the prototypes.'

'As long as you are certain.' Hal stated. Amelia nodded confirmation. 'Who looks after the genetic data in the project?'

'Jeffrey Briar, but he would have reported any evidence of a return of regenerative capability and terminated the bloodline. The testing is done by the team Mike Holmes runs, but the actual responsibility for maintaining the DNA database rests with Jeffrey.'

'I think we need to check with Jeffrey that there are no anomalies, if you don't mind.'

Amelia checked Jeffrey's schedule and called him to see if he was free to discuss Hal's concern.

The moment Jeffrey walked into Amelia's office something about him grated on Hal. There was nothing he had particularly done and he had barely said hello, but Hal had a feeling that something about him wasn't right. It had to be set aside, maybe he just didn't like the man. It happened sometimes and no one could explain why they disliked a person or what they had done, but there it was, Hal didn't like Jeffrey Briar.

'Jeffrey, Dr Charter has advised me that you manage the genetic monitoring of the prototypes and I wanted to check if you had seen any evidence of regeneration traits in the DNA sequencing.'

'No, none at all,' Jeffrey replied without hesitation. 'If I saw such a trend I would terminate the bloodline to prevent any risk of further infection and administer sequence blockers to ensure the sequence was eliminated. It usually takes about six to twelve months for most of the cells to edit out the sequence, but they can never be edited out of the brain. We check again over the following couple of years for regeneration, but that has never happened. We have only seen one instance of a sequenced-out Elfinnim trait expressing in the prototypes, and that was early in the process. We eliminated the source and there has been no repeat.'

Hal was suspicious. Wouldn't a scientist ask for time to check and verify data? Jeffrey's answer was unequivocal, perhaps he really did remember his data that well. Perhaps... Hal decided not to press the subject yet and instead decided to spring a surprise on both Amelia and Jeffrey and see what reaction he got.

'Okay, Jeffrey, thanks for your help,' said Hal and Jeffrey got up to leave.

'Before you go, there is one more thing I would like to ask,' said Hal. Jeffrey sat back down and looked up expectantly.

'How well do you know Angela Galvano?'

Jeffrey's face twitched slightly. Was that a scowl Hal had seen?

'We weren't close if that's what you mean, and from what I hear she had no business being anywhere near this project from the outset.'

Hal looked steadily at Jeffrey and waited for him to say more. Jeffrey fidgeted in his seat. Hal let the tension build, knowing that Jeffrey would have to fill the silence.

'I mean, look at the problems she created, the new protocols are cumbersome, we had perfectly adequate controls before, but because of one woman's selfish and stupid activities now we must all be drowned in bureaucracy.'

Hal waited a fraction more before replying.

'What have you heard, then, Jeffrey?'

Jeffrey fidgeted a little more in his seat and looked decidedly uncomfortable.

'You know, just the usual gossip'

'There is nothing usual about gossip, Jeffrey, where are you hearing this from?'

'Just around the compound and on breaks, people talk don't they? Apparently she had a history of being dishonest. I don't know why the Council appointed her to this project, it was always going to be a problem with her history.'

'Isn't that a little harsh?' asked Amelia. 'You seemed to get on pretty well with her.'

'Yes, of course I work hard to get along with everyone, you seem to forget that we had several differences of opinion and a few heated exchanges, but that was all work related. If you remember, we got on just fine away from work.'

Amelia said nothing.

'Okay, Jeffrey, thanks for clarifying that for me, no doubt we will talk again. Please will you send over the DNA profiles we have on record for 1-73?'

'Of course, is there anything else you need?'

'No, that's all, we will talk again later.'

Jeffrey stood up and left the room.

Hal waited until he was certain Jeffrey was out of earshot then looked at Amelia and asked, 'What do you think, is he telling the truth?'

Hal sensed that Amelia had never been questioned about the integrity of a senior team member.

'I have no reason to think he isn't.'

'Hmm, that's not the same thing as telling me you believe him.'

'No, it isn't. To be truthful, Hal, I am not sure I do believe what Jeffrey tells me all the time, but do I really think he is masterminding this situation? No, I don't think he is capable of masterminding such intrigue. He is brilliant and gifted, he has some strange ideas, but I don't believe he has planned anything sinister here.'

'You mentioned he has some strange ideas. Can you give me some examples,' asked Hal, inviting Amelia to elaborate.

'Let's see, for a start, he is paranoid about the Grand Council. He seems to believe they are waiting for him to make a mistake so they can move him out of the project and take his research as their own. To be perfectly honest, they own it anyway, they have funded everything. Jeffrey just sees slights and insults in every action, I think it's because he thinks too much about everything, evaluating every possible outcome and he assumes that everyone else does the same.'

His behaviour was paranoid, but did not indicate that Jeffrey was anything more than a troubled, suspicious man with a brilliant mind. There was still something niggling Hal, but he couldn't work out what.

'Tell me more', said Hal, and he listened while Amelia told him all of the things that Jeffrey was paranoid about.

As Hal, Amelia and Alfie toured the project sites, inspected records and interviewed staff, it became clear that one of the key problems had been the former head of security. Alfie had been promoted just a month before Hal arrived when Angela Galvano was asked to return to Elfinn for 'interrogation' due to a catalogue of slips and indiscipline. It was incredibly unusual, but no race was perfect and Angela had shown the worst traits possible. She had abused her position for an easy life. As in any organisation, from time to time people misplaced their security passes and had to have new ones issued. Angela had failed to cancel misplaced passes, which had allowed someone to move around the compound without notice. The records of pass issue and disposal were incomplete and in some cases had been clearly falsified. There was also evidence that Angela had taken money for favours and blackmailed others into keeping quiet. Now Angela was to be questioned by the scrutineers. Next she would be required to explain herself to the Grand Council on Elfinn, an experience that even a hardened investigator such as Hal would fear – the exertion of physical and mental pressure to peel away all of her lies and deceptions, the physical and mental pressure of repeating the testimony and reviewing her motivations for years to come, interspersed with long periods of meditation and reflection to understand where mistakes had been made and why the errors were not corrected.

The more Hal investigated, the more unhappy he became with the reported events. Amelia had told the truth, but had stretched it wafer thin in places and what Hal could not fathom was whether this was to protect herself or to protect Angela. If the latter, it was a waste of time now since Angela was back on Elfinn; if the former, what could she have done that was both worse than Amelia's actions, and worth sacrificing Angela for? Hal uncovered differences between the reported version of events and the interviews with people involved. At first it was small simple differences, times and dates, differences so small that Hal might have believed they were just minor recording errors. Such errors were unusual but not unheard of. However, the errors became too frequent to be mistakes in documentation. No Elfinnim was that careless.

Hal was frustrated both by the discrepancies and by the lack of attention to detail which allowed them to go unnoticed. Mistakes of this sort were not Elfinnly and should not be tolerated. Then something strange happened. Hal went back to the system to refer to a document that he had previously checked and found none of the discrepancies present. Hal was an experienced and confident investigator, who knew that the only way this could happen was if the data has been changed. Hal investigated who would have access to alter these critical systems. The list was vanishingly small but everyone on it was either away from their terminal or asleep in their room when each of the interventions happened. There was only one explanation left: someone, either on the list or someone else on the project, had engineered a secret access panel which allowed remote access to GAIA. It was interesting that one of the names on the list was Jeffrey Briar.

Hal decided to tackle the issue with Alfie.

'Alfie, what do you think of the statements in this investigation?'

Alfie took a moment to consider his answer.

'There are quite a lot of errors, aren't there? I can't see a reason for the discrepancies but I know that Angela didn't make trivial mistakes like this.'

'Did Angela take all of the statements?'

'Yes, Angela insisted on doing all of the interviews and the investigation herself. At the time I guessed it was because the case was so high profile, but now you mention it, it was odd.'

'Alfie, did you ever try to check the facts after Angela was removed from her post?'

'Yes, I did, but there were all sorts of small differences between what I found and the statements that Angela had documented. It was sloppy and unprofessional.'

'Alfie, what would you think if I told you that after having taken statements and verified information, those details were later changed. I know I don't make those mistakes, so what do you make of that?'

'Hal, the only way that could have happened is if the source data was corrupted.'

'My thoughts exactly. So this is at least part of what happened to Angela.'

Alfie blushed.

'I'm sorry, Hal, I should have spotted this. Thanks for pointing it out. I think we have to revisit the whole investigation and seek out the anomalies.'

Hal smiled. He was starting to like Alfie. The man was proud, honest, rigorous and fiercely loyal to Amelia.

'Alfie, this is what I was sent here to understand. Now that we know there are anomalies, and that the information is changing, we can sift through the investigation again and work out what Angela was really hiding.'

'I have just a couple more questions for you, and these will be hard to hear and even harder to answer objectively.'

'Did Amelia know anything about this? Did Angela alter the documents for her own benefit or for Amelia's?'

Alfie glared at Hal and remained silent. Initially it looked like Hal had misjudged the situation and risked alienating him. He watched the fire slowly recede from Alfie's eyes as he worked through how his assumptions had already let him down.

'Setting aside my initial loyalty to Doctor Charter, I understand why you are asking this question. I can understand why you might think she is involved, however I don't think she knew anything about this. I was close enough to the investigation, and I remember that she had quite a few heated discussions behind closed doors because the investigation was moving too slowly. In fact it was Dr Charter who removed Angela from the investigation and asked me to review the investigation files.'

'How did Angela react to that?'

'She was furious, she even tried to prevent me from getting access to her file system. Dr Charter had to threaten her with confinement to get the password from her. If she had instructed or coerced Angela to alter statements or suppress evidence, why would she take the risk of getting me to take the case over? If I was in that position, it would be safer and more certain to keep Angela in place and manipulate the information from inside the investigation.'

Hal wasn't as sure as Alfie, but his analysis of motives made sense. If Amelia was trying to bury something she would need an accomplice to do it and that accomplice must be either Angela or Alfie. While Alfie was a complicated character, Hal was certain he was not a liar. This was supported when Hal obtained access to Alfie's' psychological evaluations, which showed integrity and honesty as core values. Amelia's psychological evaluation showed a similar profile. Hal had posed the question to see Alfie's reaction and he found himself hoping that Alfie would confirm his own assessment.

Alfie was not the only person that Hal had got close to during the investigation. Over the ten years of this investigation Hal had become very close to Amelia, but he was feeling more conflict over that relationship. Hal usually had no problem keeping his investigation separate from personal feelings. At the start of the investigation there had been so much to do, there was little leisure time left. However, as the investigation progressed the pace became less frenetic, a necessary consequence of having more threads to follow. Initially the late meals and rushed lunches, exercising together, spending all their time together, had been difficult. One evening stuck in Hal's memory, at a place they had called Hadeus Point. Alfie had friends based there, and Hal was eating with them on this particular evening.

'Amelia, what are you going to do when this is over?'

'I'm not sure, Hal, we have to finish the project, but I would like to take some personal time and visit Elfinnim. It has been too long since I have seen an evanescent sunset. I just need someone to go with and somewhere to stay.'

'You could go with me. I have a house just on the north edge of the Ha'ell, about an hour's travel from the portal. It's in the Stybian region. I have plenty of space, you would be more than welcome to visit.'

'Hal, that sounds really nice. How did the property become yours?'

'The usual way. It was where the creators lived, my family were their caretakers. When the creators left, my family took over. As time went by, different groups left. My family remained, but I chose to join the military. I have a small home in the grounds that I maintain.'

'I would really like to visit when this is over, Hal.'

'Yes, that would be really nice. I look forward to it.'

Hal took a drink, and enjoyed the moment. Although nothing had been said with certainty, Hal felt settled and content. Once this investigation was complete he could explore this relationship with Amelia and see where it led.

The following day, Hal spoke to Alfie.

'Alfie, as you have probably noticed, Amelia and I are getting quite close. I need you to tell me if you think I am skipping steps or showing favouritism.'

Alfie was surprised.

'I will do it, of course, but Hal, I haven't seen any evidence of favouritism towards Amelia. In fact, if you are open to feedback...'

Hal nodded.

'...Well, in my opinion you have been harder on Amelia than anyone else. I think you are so conscious that you could be showing favouritism that you are setting a higher standard for her.'

Suspicion still had the upper hand with Hal, so he put a lid on his feelings. He knew that once he was certain with no shadow of doubt that Amelia was innocent, he would determine if his feelings were reciprocated. Now was not the time, however, so he resolved to focus on the investigation until he was absolutely certain she was not involved and understood what had motivated Amelia to accept a less than perfect investigation.

Reviewing the investigation there was one name that kept coming up again and again: Jeffrey Briar. He was an interesting character. All of the project evaluation reports and peer reviews of his work were clear – he was a brilliant scientist, whose work in genetics had become pivotal in the subject. He had a significant flaw, though, he was almost completely lacking in social skills, with the result that the only things he was really comfortable with were inanimate. As soon as something could reason and argue, Jeffrey became tongue tied and nervous. He could make logical arguments and, providing the other person worked purely with logic, he could hold his own. As soon as they moved to emotion he was lost.

During one of the conferences on the investigation Hal decided it was time to start really probing into the story he had been told.

'Amelia, we keep running across the name Jeffrey Briar.'

'Yes, we would, Jeffrey is brilliant and critical to the success of the project. Without him we would not have been able to achieve what we have so quickly.'

'So what is it about him and his contribution that makes him so important and valuable to the project?'

'Where to begin!' said Amelia. 'He performed the initial gene sequencing to develop the weapons prototypes. Not only did he identify the sequences required for their physical attributes, he also identified the particular gene sequences to confer aggression. However, the problem that all other projects in this area ran into was that this combination of physical attribute and aggression made the creations uncontrollable. Jeffrey also simplified the gene splicing process to reduce the cycle time in creating prototypes. Where he demonstrated real genius was in developing the control system. This enabled us to create drones with a central control system, but unlike the previous strategies which involved an integration of organic and inorganic components that were easy to detect and easy to target, he conceived of a completely biobased system. That was a phenomenal leap, conceiving of such an idea is one thing, but actually making it happen was breathtaking. It didn't stop there, though. He wasn't satisfied with using an inorganic link to network with the prototypes, so he strengthened and tuned their minds to work over long distances with a specific bandwidth. He then developed a biocomputer to work within that bandwidth. Not only does this work over long distances it also taps into the universal life force to ensure the swarm is indistinguishable from natural life forms. Can you comprehend how innovative that was? Even now I find it hard to understand what he did, and I am the project lead. I am ten times older and more experienced than Jeffrey and yet when he brought this idea to me he had his work cut out convincing me it was worthwhile. At first it seemed so outlandish that I dismissed the idea and told him to focus on the tasks I had set him. He not only accomplished the tasks, he did the basic groundwork to prove his theory. Once we had evidence that the theory worked it was a far more elegant solution than anything else we were working on.'

'Is he really that good?'

'He is better, he might be the most intelligent person I have ever met. He was also the one who adapted the Swarm Project from computing to bioweapons, the idea that each individual is not strong enough to succeed alone, but when the units are expendable and can be replaced quickly and easily, they can overwhelm even the strongest opponents if they work together and launch a coordinated attack. The project originated with that idea. The Grand Council decided to back the project but were not comfortable with someone so young in charge, which is why they asked me to manage the project.'

Hal considered what he had been told.

'That explains why he has been in so many parts of the project, but it does not explain why his name keeps coming up when we are looking into misbehaviour. There are other senior staff on the project, and their names are not coming up anywhere near as often. Something is wrong. Although there is little evidence that links Jeffrey to any crime or misdemeanour, I don't believe in that many coincidences.'

5

JEFFREY BRIAR

Jeffrey was rattled. He was tracking the investigation through GAIA and using the Humans for discreet monitoring, because they were practically invisible to Elfinnim. He had watched with interest as Hal slowly and methodically investigated the disappearance of Human 1-73-9.7.3310. At first he had been relaxed because, although he knew that there would be an investigation, he also believed that his tracks had been covered. Since Hal had initiated this investigation it had intruded into Jeffrey's world far more than he was comfortable with. Hal had already pieced together more than Jeffrey wanted – and he was still looking. Jeffrey had been content that his role in this project allowed enough freedom to pursue his own agenda while remaining senior enough to deflect questions. He knew he was significantly more intelligent than everyone else involved, including Amelia. After all, none of them would be here if he hadn't initiated the development. He still resented Amelia for her appointment as project manager. It didn't matter that she had fought for him to be project leader or if she had only taken the project manager role – it was her or someone else, it would never be Jeffrey. That had been the final straw. He had always been different, had always known he was different, had always been told he was different. This was his idea, his concept and he didn't see why he should hand it over to someone else for them to take the credit for all his work. Jeffrey had tried to convince the Grand Council of his suitability for the project, but it had gone wrong from the start. First he arrived late after getting lost in the council halls, then they began asking questions before he had finished presenting his case.

'What experience do you have of managing projects?'

'I have managed many projects on a smaller scale, this should just be a larger scale use of the same tools.'

'So you haven't had any experience of a project of this magnitude?'

'Well, no, not directly, but —'

'Jeffrey, what do think would be the biggest challenge of this project?'

He felt confident, he knew the project. 'Getting the gene sequencing absolutely correct to ensure the DNA splicing and positioning of the base pairs are precisely right.'

He stopped at the raised hand of one of the councillors.

'Jeffrey, frankly we don't know the precise technical details, and we aren't really bothered about the scientific hurdles. The team of scientists we are assembling will be capable of solving those problems. I am concerned that you perceive the scientific challenges to be the greatest problem in this project.'

Jeffrey faltered, his confidence ebbing.

'Um, well I thought the scientific issues were the point of the project?'

'Actually, Jeffrey, there are many aspects of this project that concern us, but the scientific aspects are the least of our concerns.'

The room fell silent as the Grand Council waited for a further response from him.

'Okay, well the, the main project concerns will be obviously security, control of the various project work streams and —'

'Have you considered project security?'

'Not yet, but it is obviously a priority.'

'Not so obvious that you prepared for the question, though? You were fully prepared to answer questions about the science of the project, but it seems you have not considered the infrastructure.'

'How about managing the work streams?' asked another council member.

'Well, there will be several work streams, obviously.'

'How many?'

'How many what?'

Jeffrey wanted a little more time to consider his answers.

The councillor spoke to him as if he were a fool.

'How many work streams will the project require?'

'Um, I'm not sure just yet, there are four clear work streams for the genetic work, we need a work stream for the computing, another for the interface.'

'Is that all?'

'That's enough to get started.'

'What about engineering, construction, security, administration, accounts? What else do you need?'

Jeffrey saw his error too late.

'Well, yes of course you need all of those things as well, but I will delegate those responsibilities to ensure I can focus on the science that must be delivered.'

It was a mistake, and he realised it as soon as the words were out of his mouth.

'Jeffrey, do you think you can delegate responsibility as project director?'

'No, no of course not, I just meant that I can get someone who is more of a specialist in those areas to assist me.'

He winced, he knew that was another wrong answer.

'Okay, Jeffrey, let's ask another question. How do you think you interact with others?'

'I get on quite well with other people. And in this role it will be easy since they will do as they are told.'

'Do you think you just have to tell people what to do? Will you take their views into account?'

'Of course I will take their views into account. If they happen to come up with a good idea, I am prepared to listen to them.'

'That's very good of you,' a councillor said icily. 'How do you get others to work with you?'

Jeffrey was confused.

'What do you mean, how will I get others to work with me? They will all work for me, they will just do as they are told.'

The councillor said nothing, just made a few notes.

'What experience do you have of security operations?'

'I have worked on five secure projects. In each project I ensured the data remained secure, and the systems for monitoring employees movements and access were carefully controlled.'

'That is positive. How do you gain consensus and loyalty from the security team?'

Jeffrey knew that people skills were his weakness, he had always been poor with colleagues, but believed he more than made up for it with his intellect. For the most part they would just do as they were told and... that, right there was the problem.

'Do you think that the security team may lack loyalty?' he asked. 'As for consensus, does it matter if they agree? Their job is to do what they are told, isn't it?'

The panel looked at him in silence, it was clear that his answer was not what they needed to hear. The remainder of the interview was short and perfunctory. Shortly afterwards he was asked to meet with the head of the Council panel.

'Jeffrey, I have to tell you that you were not appointed to the role of Project Leader this time. We have decided that you still have much to learn about managing people, so we will appoint a more experienced project leader – Amelia Charter.'

'What do you mean, I have much to learn about managing people?'

Jeffrey could feel the embarrassment and anger building inside.

'During the interview, you simply did not give us any confidence that you could bring people along with your vision. We are not questioning your scientific capability, in fact it is quite clear that you are a brilliant scientist. You should take pride in the fact that we are running this project at all. We have failed several times with this sort of project before, but your approach is bold and gives a unique approach to overcoming the problems that plagued previous attempts.'

'Why do you always set such store by consensus with inferior intellects?'

The councillor looked shocked.

'Consensus is the only way forward for us. We have to use all of the strengths available to us, not all of those strengths are intellectually based. Surely you can see that?'

'How many problems can you show me that cannot be resolved through intellect? Certainly not this one, even the strong intellects that have gone before me in this field have failed to create a robust solution. I know that my solution will work, yet you insist on focusing on consensus. Tell me where has consensus got us so far?'

'Jeffrey, this is exactly the problem. Given that you find everyone intellectually inferior, you show little or no respect to everyone you meet. This is a hard lesson you must learn. To receive respect, you must first show respect. Jeffrey, until you can demonstrate respect for others, I guarantee you will not be a project leader.'

'What is this obsession you have with showing respect? I thought we lived in a meritocracy? If that is the case, respect those with the highest merit. I will respect anyone I find with a better intellect, with more "merit".'

'Yes, we work on merit, but you know that intellect is not the only consideration. Respect creates safety for our society. We teach respect to combat the fatalism of the mercenaries. You have to learn that lesson, and until you do, you had better get used to being a senior scientist. You do not have leadership skills; merit is not simply about intellect or scientific knowledge – team building, interpersonal skill, people skills, all have their own merit. We are not going to discuss this further, Jeffrey, I fear if we do I will find it harder to justify your role as senior scientist. Listen to what you are being told and learn your lesson!'

Jeffrey felt angry and humiliated. The councillor needed him to create his weapon, but talked about respect. Where was their respect for him? Why could they not see his genius? As he brooded on this, his anger grew. Rarely did people understand where he was going. It was because they were so slow witted that they could not see how all the pieces went together. It was time to use this to his advantage.

He would need to bide his time, but he would find a way to supplant the Grand Council and take over. His original intent was to ascend to the Grand Council through merit. Once there, he could steer the Elfinnim to greater things. Once they realised his intellect and the power of the future he could give them as a finally united people, they would become more than the considerable society that already existed.

He pondered on how one particular member of the Grand Council goaded him, humiliated him.

'You aren't really cut out for leadership are you Jeffrey?'

'I am certainly cut out for leadership, I was born for it!' he had declared.

'Well, born into a leadership family perhaps, but born for leadership? No, I don't think so. Jeffrey, you are a researcher, you are a brilliant scientist, but you are best leaving leadership to those who have a better understanding of people. I'm afraid your approach will result in division and frustration. No, I can't ever imagine you leading.'

The statement had hurt, not just because it had undermined his ambitions, it was the source of the statement. When your own father states that you cannot become a leader, especially when he spent much of your childhood reminding you of how important it would be to continue the leadership line, that was devastating. The look of sheer disappointment and disdain on his father's face had told Jeffrey he would never rise in the councils.

He tried to put the disappointment behind him and concentrate on the project.

He had identified the genetic markers for appearance, motor skills, mental interaction with the physical world, and finally found the genetic key to fast reproduction. It would take him a couple of thousand years to fully investigate and prove the genetic traits, but once he had done it he would be able to manipulate the genome of the creatures to be whatever they wanted them to be. The most frustrating part of the whole project was having to repeatedly explain the links and theories to his so-called peers and in particular to those managing the project. Jeffrey had always assumed that the Council would intuitively understand his thinking and his vision; instead they had demeaned his ideas, played his weaknesses against him and finally stolen his project from him. That was what finally convinced him that he had to act. The future of the Elfinnim could not be allowed to rest with an inferior intellect, especially since he had evaluated the intellectual capabilities of each council member finding them all lacking in vision, intelligence and the will to do whatever is required to win.

Jeffrey had been distraught, his father had not even talked to him after the meeting. It was clear that for Jeffrey to lead the Elfinnim on a more productive path he would have to find another way. First things first. How could he take control without anyone noticing? It was when he hit on the idea of using an organic computer that he wondered how closely he could control key systems. At this point Jeffrey realised he could do what he wanted and tell people what he wanted, and provided they were not obviously different, no one would notice. The hardest part had been getting access to anything he wanted; it had taken many years, immense amounts of patient searching, the forging of links, and evidence gathering. Along the way he had found the perfect partner for his ambition: Angela Galvano. Angela was hiding some dark secrets, shocking really for a career in military intelligence and a security specialist. There was quite a long list of breaches, which had been cleverly and creatively hidden. It was unusual to find an Elfinnim in mainstream society who did not follow the rules; such behaviour was not tolerated. It had been almost impossible to find an Elfinnim in a security role in the military who didn't follow the rules. Almost.

Angela Galvano was an extreme rarity, a military policewoman, senior security officer on a top secret project, whose only interest was herself. At first Jeffrey suspected she might be a mercenary, but her need for power and control far outweighed her disdain for authority and immortality. It had taken Jeffrey a lot of careful prying to get into the secure network. However, he knew it was only a matter of time – and as an Elfinnim he had time in abundance – so he had been patient and avoided the traps at every stage of his hack into one of the most secure military programmes in existence. Once inside he had examined every personnel file, including Angela in which he noticed some minor discrepancies. They were little things, such as revision dates that didn't match official changes. He then investigated Angela's life and he noticed a pattern. Wherever she had been stationed there was an increase in crime rates – not big crimes, but many significant little crimes, and every so often a death or a fairly large amount of material would go missing. Usually it would be currency, sometimes high level technology, always worth significant amounts of money. Whenever she left a post there would be a scandal about missing evidence, which had been accessible before she left.

Jeffrey didn't understand why the discrepancies had not been picked up before, until he went back into her file and noticed that it had changed. Dates had changed for every posting he had investigated such that Angela had either been off-world or moved on when the bigger issues happened.

So Jeffrey set a trap. He took a copy of her file and set a sophisticated tracker in place that would install onto the computer of the next person to edit the file and transmit their location. It wasn't long before he discovered that the person editing Angela's file was Angela.

The next time she edited her file to ensure that a certain theft of military pistols could not be traced back to her, she noticed a new edit flag on her file. The edit was from three days previously, which she knew meant someone else had accessed her file. She found one of her early deployment dates had been changed. Before she reversed the change, she checked to see who had made the edit. They were going to learn not to mess with Angela Galvano! But when she checked, the system confirmed that she had edited her own file. That could only mean one thing: there was another hacker in the system.

Her phone rang and she answered.

'Angela, you are dishonest. I wonder what the Grand Council would think of a security officer editing their own file.'

The voice was masked, and sounded metallic . The intonation was almost familiar, but she could not place it.

'Who is this? You are in violation of at least five laws and when I find you, you will regret breaking each of them.'

There was harsh metallic laughter.

'Angela, if you could find me, which I am certain you can't, what makes you think I would not expose your crimes? I would have nothing to gain from keeping your secrets, would I?'

'What crimes? I enforce the law, I don't break it!'

'I know that's what your record says, but isn't it strange that on your last five assignments there have been major thefts either when you were on leave or discovered just after you left. Let's see, ten million credits at your last posting, industrial espionage from the posting before that, a military arms shipment worth five million credits before that... do you want me to carry on?'

'So what? Pure coincidence.'

'Coincidence, you say. I wonder what we would find if I looked in the warehouse on Serapsis?'

'What warehouse on Serapsis?'

'Oh you know the one. It was hidden pretty deeply, but eventually I traced the ownership of the warehouse back to you. Oddly, the company that owns the warehouse sells nothing, buys a select few containers and yet has many millions of credits in their bank account. The few shipments they do receive also coincide with the thefts from each of your last postings.'

'I am not connected to that warehouse.'

Jeffrey smiled, and sent a message to Angela from a system root account that was untraceable. The message contained copies of the ownership documents linking the warehouse and shell companies to Angela.

'Angela, if you look at the information I just sent you, it could be very hard to explain to the Grand Council.'

As she read the email, she felt her stress levels rising. She was convinced this had been hidden and the trail muddled so much no one could have found it. She had overestimated her own ingenuity.

'What do you want?'

'For now? Nothing. I will need you to work with me on some projects, though. I will let you know what I need and when I need it.'

'What projects, and what sort of work?'

'You will be told when you need to know.'

There was a long silent pause as Angela thought about what she had heard.

'You know I will start searching for you now, don't you?'

Jeffrey laughed.

'You can search, but really, finding your paper trail was child's play for me, do you really think you can trace me so easily?'

'I like a challenge. I look forward to working out who you are. When I find you, you will explain how you did this.'

The communication ended, leaving Angela trembling. How had she been caught, and what did they want? Time to go to work, and figure out who had her cornered. In the meantime she had to do as she was told, and investigate carefully.

The first request from Jeffrey was to access all areas, so he had Angela issue access keycards and hide the identities.

Next he needed full access to the systems, so he forced Angela to reveal her methods and used this knowledge to expand his own hacked access; that way even if his improved security access was revoked he still had system access. He also found a way to give himself access to all areas using his own card, but he continued to use the anonymous one he had extracted from Angela. She eventually worked out who her tormentor was, but by then he had all the evidence he needed to stop her in her tracks, while she had no evidence that he had done anything.

After Human 1-73-9.7.3310 vanished, everything he had been working towards became far more difficult. He had coerced Angela into keeping his secrets, but when the excuses surrounding the investigation were rebuffed she had threatened to implicate him, so he had been forced to get nasty. During his trawling to find out about her, Jeffrey had discovered Angela had a secret child and that she regularly provided for it. He also discovered that her vacation time was used to visit the child and that this was the only thing Angela cared about besides herself. To keep himself safe he had to threaten that child. She didn't believe he either could or would get to her child, so he had to arrange a nasty little accident for one of the child's carers. Jeffrey's threat wrong-footed Angela; after all, it was unheard of for Elfinnim to harm a child. Jeffrey was concerned for the Elfinnim future, so for him the life of one child could not be placed above all else. Added to that, he realised he didn't really care for children, which made his choice so much easier. After that Angela became compliant, but that was not a long term solution. The scrutineers would force it and every other dirty little secret out of Angela – he had to hope that his threat made his secrets absolutely the last thing she gave up. That bought him some time, but if he was to avoid failure, he must move his schedule up and soon.

Hal's investigation was taking too long and Jeffrey was aware that his name was coming up too frequently. His reports from the biocomputers indicated that Hal had identified Jeffrey as a 'person of interest' in the investigation. He had tried to hack into Hal's records, but could not crack the security, which was governed from Elfinn and any attempt to interfere risked notice. There was too much time delay between Elfinn and the laboratory so he would not have a chance to nudge their investigation to look elsewhere. Jeffrey hated the lack of control that had disturbed his plans since that damned Human had run away.

Jeffrey had been surprised at Hal's extraordinary thoroughness, and how he had uncovered more of Jeffrey's network than anyone else should see. Jeffrey had managed to block Alfie and Amelia with relative ease, but Hal copied everything he viewed back to his own records, which backed up off-world. He had tried to get in, but on his second effort had discovered traps set all around Hal's data. The initial traps appeared to be lazy attempts to catch an inferior mind. However, he had nearly lost control of his system when he tried to disable one trap and realised that the traps were deliberately simple in appearance. It would take several thousand years to unpick the code and bypass without notice, even for Jeffrey. Whoever had set the traps realised that overconfidence was the biggest danger to an experienced hacker and had nearly caught him in a simple error. After that he had been more cautious and examined the traps more carefully. They were too cleverly set even for him, with triple redundancies in the code that meant he would need to manage three or more viruses aimed at his network while trying to hack into Hal's system. The risk of detection was too high. If he lost control of his workstation there was a risk that his plan would be uncovered. While he was certainly smarter than Hal, he could not hope to match him physically, and he was certain that Hal would subdue him before interrogating his systems. Hal was warrior caste, a violent brute of a man and would therefore be ready and willing to have a confrontation.

Jeffrey needed to talk to GAIA. It was time to find an excuse to visit GAIA's control room. That made it sound readily accessible, but the control room was at the bottom of the deepest ocean trench on the planet. This gave access to geothermal vents for energy, but the surrounding sea was so cold that the heat generated from the biocomputer could dissipate into the surrounding sea without giving a detectable spike in temperature. The extended network was achieved by the largest sea creatures working as a network. They would swim in close proximity, which boosted their ability to transmit and detect telepathic signals. They were able to quantum switch their data allowing transmission to remote units. The technology was advanced beyond what was commercially available and had been field tested across space. Jeffrey was upset that he could not observe the trial personally; he had wanted to verify the performance for himself in the field, not sit here and watch the results coming in. In the end the Grand Council decided that the risk of losing either the prototype or the senior scientist was barely acceptable, but the risk of losing both was unacceptable. So again the Grand Council had interfered and taken another piece of his achievement, another bit of his pride. When the time came he would strip those old men of every last scrap of pride and dignity until he could send them to meet the creators screaming for mercy. He smiled grimly. There would be no mercy for those old men.

Jeffrey needed to use the distraction of Human 1-73 escaping to cover his own activities, but how was he to distract Hal? He could use Amelia, but he could not think of a way to put her in danger for Hal to save, without revealing his own involvement. If he was to do anything, it would have to look like an accident. But it could not involve a Human, that would draw too much attention. Killing either Hal or Amelia would likely trigger an extreme response, so it would have to be something they could blame either on the missing Human or on a mechanical failure. Even as he considered it, he knew that a mechanical failure would not work. Elfinnim engineering was too reliable so any such failure would spark a detailed investigation from the engineering team. Perhaps there was another way. Could he capitalise on the physical attraction between Hal and Amelia? Yes, promoting that relationship would be distracting, all the more so since they were both too professional to give in to their more base instincts until the investigation was complete. Jeffrey was aware from his own experiences that sexual tension was immensely distracting so he would need to think of a way to use it as a lever, a way to distract attention away from him to buy time to complete his plan. His problem was one of skills necessary to undertake such a plan – he was not good at manipulating people. But he did have people in his sphere of influence that were.

Jeffrey needed to work out who was best placed to promote this lust without allowing it to be consummated. He had one contact within Amelia's staff who he had cultivated and it seemed that now was the time to use that asset. She could arrange for some indiscreet camera malfunction to tease both ways. Yes that had appeal, if he could get them looking at each other they would not be looking at him. He contacted the member of staff with his usual anonymity and explained what she needed to do; threats were no longer needed, she had long ago given up any pretence of resistance.

Jeffrey could do little more than wait for his plan to mature. It would not be long now before he would implement the plan he had been preparing to sweep aside the doubters and secure the future of the Elfinnim race.

The comms engineer called at Amelia's quarters while she was working elsewhere in the compound. The engineer didn't want to do this, but if she didn't she was quite sure that whoever had threatened her partner would follow through. She had seen enough by now to know that whoever it was, they were closer to a mercenary than an Elfinnim and they were careful. She had tried to discover who her tormentor was, but all she had achieved was embarrassment – she was a comms engineer yet could not work out how someone had obtained so much personal information about her. Still, the task was simple enough and it ensured her family stayed safe, that was all that really mattered. She had never heard of anyone else enduring this sort of coercion before, and had initially intended to report it to the guards. What stopped her was the head of security taking her to one side and advising that for her own safety and the safety of those she loved, she should do as she was told. If Angela was involved she had no chance. If this person could get the head of security to do their dirty work, she didn't want to think about how far reaching their power could be. No, best to do what she was asked and get it over with.

After letting herself in to Amelia's quarters she set a check on the workstation; if Amelia logged off she would receive notification and have time to get out, but the chances were that she was at her desk for a couple of hours more. She set to her task quickly and efficiently, removing the service panels and installing the remote triggered device that she had manufactured. It turned the comms on for someone else to see, but was focused – it only transmitted to the Grand

Council investigator Haliban Balal, and only transmitted when both he and Amelia were in their quarters. She didn't know why this was important. She was jumpy because she almost got caught installing the other end. Balal was quite unpredictable, he used one of the offices in the administrative section, but also frequently worked from his quarters. That had been so close. She had gone in and installed the device which checked he was present and looked for a matching handshake from Amelia's quarters which would initiate the transmission programme. The installation and technology were quite simple and because she used the room's standard sensors, a sweep for listening devices would not trigger an alarm, a neat trick which she was proud of.

She had just shut the door to Balal's quarters and taken three steps towards the exit when he came around the next corner. She didn't know how she had kept her nerve and simply continued walking. Balal was wrapped up in his own problems and didn't even acknowledge her, which was a relief. If she could achieve the same success here, then she would secure her own and her partner's safety for a while longer. This project was the most terrifying thing she had ever worked on – she had seen up close how ferocious some of these creatures could be. She was out working on one of the perimeter locks relatively early in the project, soon after they had shut down GAIA. The predators had turned on each other and she had only survived by hiding in the tool shed until the screaming stopped. The nightmares were less frequent now, but the prospect of the swarm getting out of control terrified her. She had put in for a transfer after that, but it had been mysteriously denied. Then she got a message – as far as she knew, from whoever was threatening her family – telling her to get used to this place, because she would be here for the duration of the project. She had just finished installing the remote trigger and software when her system flashed an alert that Amelia had left her desk. She made one final check of the room to make sure everything was back in place and left hurriedly. It was lucky that check had been set because Amelia was returning to her quarters early today, unusual but not unheard of. Rumour was that if Amelia had a bad day she returned to her quarters to get a change of environment to help her think of alternative approaches to whatever the problem was.

The comms engineer returned to the maintenance section and hid the access card. She knew that using the access card was not right, but was not about to risk her family to expose what was happening. The new head of security, Alfie Khan, seemed a nice guy and quite genuine, but for all she knew he would pick up where Angela left off; and if he was involved, the last thing she wanted to do was give the impression that she was still resisting. She didn't know what was going on here, but it was huge and she didn't want her family crushed as it rolled onto whatever destination was ordained for this particular portion of hell. She breathed a sigh of relief that the job was done and went back to her normal work, trying hard to pretend it hadn't happened.

6

PROGENITOR

Amelia was asleep in her quarters. She smiled in her sleep and breathed more deeply as her dreams changed. Her personal messenger beeped and flashed, and as she awoke she felt a deep loss as she realised that it was no more than a dream, albeit a sweet one. She looked at the time and groaned. She had only been asleep for two hours. This better be important.

'Yes, Alfie, what's the problem?'

'We have had a security breach.'

'What? Are you sure?'

Could things get worse? A breach of security with an investigator in the facility?

Alfie replied, 'We are sure there has been a breach, but it was yesterday. We are still trying to discover if anything is missing, and if not we need to work out what the intruder was trying to achieve.'

'Thanks for letting me know, Alfie, let's figure this out quickly. Have you told Hal?'

'Not yet, I wanted to tell you first and let you decide what to tell Hal and when to tell him.'

'Thanks, I will let Hal know in the morning. Report to me at eight o'clock local time before I speak to him.'

'Okay, I will. Try to get some sleep and I will see you in the morning.'

Amelia lay back down, but there was no way she was going to slip back to sleep after the arousal caused by her dream. She looked over some paperwork and then tried to sleep again, but her dream turned to a nightmare of her and her child being hunted at night by the escaped Human.

Alfie got to her office at five minutes to eight, prompt as usual.

'What have you found?' asked Amelia.

'Not much, I'm afraid, we are struggling to track the intruder using the entry and exit system. They didn't use a keycard, and didn't register on the biocomputer. Nothing is missing and the only reason we found the breach is because we found two of the guard's bodies outside the exit, they must have challenged the intruder. It must have been Human 1-73 but we can't work out what it wanted.'

Amelia sat down.

'1-73 wasn't tracked by the biocomputer?'

'No, it wasn't, even though all tracking mechanisms are enabled. Does this mean what I suspect it means?' asked Alfie quietly.

'What do you think it means?'

'If Human 1-73 can choose whether or not to obey its programming, doesn't that mean it is exhibiting free choice?

And if that is the case we must find it and terminate the experiment. We must destroy it now.'

Amelia shuddered slightly at the implications of a military grade prototype, trained in armed and unarmed combat, preprogrammed with all manner of military strategies and tactics having free choice over what it did. She also realised she had no choice but to tell Hal and enlist his help to discover what was going on.

She pulled him aside at a convenient moment.

'We have had an incident,' she said. 'Two days ago someone or something entered the facility and killed two guards. The entry did not register on any of the security feeds and didn't register on the internal security protocols.'

'Do you mean a prototype? Do you mean 1-73?'

'Yes, that is what it looks like. Hal, I'm scared, this should not be possible. 1-73's access has been revoked, the systems are set to identify it when it gets within a kilometre of the perimeter fence. So many alarms should have tripped but didn't. If 1-73 can move freely through the base what else can it do? If this is a freethinking rogue, we should all be afraid. You have seen what these things can do.'

'We need to find out where it has been and what it has been doing. Is there anyone other than Jeffrey who can look into this?'

Amelia answered without missing a beat.

'No, Hal, no one understands the systems like him. If there is any explanation other than free choice, he will have to find it. We have other people who are good with the system and there are plenty of experienced operators, but the only one who understands the whole system is Jeffrey.'

Hal was unhappy, but had to accept that this was the case. He didn't want Jeffrey involved in the investigation. Something about him wasn't right, his name had come up in the wrong places too often. Then there was his observation about the documents. Hal had no evidence that Jeffrey was involved. Was it a huge coincidence that several documents had changed between his first sight of them and reviewing later? Despite his certainty that he wasn't making mistakes, Hal started copying every document he examined to his personal records. Immediately the discrepancies stopped. Whoever had access could not breach military encryption.

As the investigation continued it became clear that while Angela had been involved in this conspiracy, she was not the mastermind. As Jeffrey's name came up more and more regularly Hal believed he was moving further up the chain. He now wondered if that was true or if Jeffrey was the architect of whatever was happening. If so, what was his plan, what was his endgame? Hal could not see it yet, although he knew the scrutineers would find out what Angela was hiding. He hoped they got answers sooner rather than eventually, and that meant whoever was behind this must know that too. Angela would be on Elfinnim now, so hopefully it wouldn't be too much longer before they broke her. The sooner the better in Hal's opinion.

'Amelia, are the Humans supposed to be able to move about undetected?' asked Hal.

'No, not even Elfinnim can do that, which is why we have the keycard system. We have to be able to track locations and hold people accountable for their actions. You're not seriously suggesting that 1-73 has that capability, are you? That would suggest the prototypes are evolving, but every test we have done shows that they cannot evolve. Their DNA has fully evolved and should not change. We have evaluated the probability of the results being wrong and there is less than one in two hundred million chance that this can happen.'

'Yet it seems it has happened,' mused Hal. 'What would need to have changed for Humans to be able to move with more freedom than Elfinnim?'

'There are a limited number of ways that change could occur. The DNA sequences that allow us to limit our visibility are on different strands to Human features. These sequences were specifically excluded and there are several amino acids missing from their genetic makeup that would be essential for this ability to develop. Unless someone has deliberately spliced these features in – and even then the project records would trigger an automatic alert – there is no way for Humans to acquire them naturally.'

'Are you sure?' asked Hal.

'There are none that we are aware of,' Amelia replied. 'I will make some discreet enquiries with the science teams and see if they can identify a method. The thing is, if they can't develop it naturally, then either someone has successfully bypassed all security protocols, run an unauthorised experiment and now has a rogue unit running around out of control, or someone has deliberately modified the camera feeds to ignore this particular Human. Neither option is good, and if I have to choose, I hope it is the latter, because that would mean the DNA profiling is sound and we have a singular deliberate act. If this is deliberate, we have to find out what they want.'

'Whatever you do, make sure Jeffrey doesn't find out.'

'Hal, I don't believe he is involved in this sabotage. I have known him since he was a child and while he is a little eccentric, I grant you, he has nothing but the best interests of our people in mind.'

Amelia was quiet as she mulled over what to do next. They certainly could not let Jeffrey know their suspicions about the Human DNA, but omitting him entirely would give a clear message that he was distrusted and she wasn't ready to do that just yet.

'Hal, what about this as a compromise: I get Jeffrey to investigate the physical nature of the break-in and find someone else to work up the DNA? If we don't give Jeffrey something to do, it will be obvious he is under suspicion.'

Hal knew Amelia was right, but it didn't mean he had to like it.

'Would that be so bad?' Hal replied. 'Look, I know you are right about keeping him involved, I just really hope you are right about his motivations. However, I have been investigating military operations for a long time and there is something wrong with him. I just can't work out what it is. If he is involved, he covers his tracks with care, but I know he is at least part of the problem, perhaps more than just a part.

Amelia, I have to ask, is there any link to the mercenaries in Jeffrey's past?'

She was surprised by the question, but she had been wondering the same thing. She considered the implications for a few seconds.

'No, Hal, I have seen no indications that he is working with the mercenaries. But if they did have someone operating inside this project, are they trying to merely disrupt the project or take control of it? Either way it doesn't have a good outcome – we all die if the mercenaries get hold of this project.'

'I have to concede it is unlikely. I have tried to push Jeffrey but he didn't offer any physical reaction. I have interrogated plenty of mercenaries who were trying to infiltrate our security and they all have the same weakness – they simply can't back down from a fight. If you push them, eventually they come for you physically and they never look intimidated. No matter how hard they try to deceive you their eyes give them away every time. I just don't know what he is trying to achieve. Give him the task of finding out what was taken or what 1-73 looked at. I am going to try retracing 1-73's steps, to see if anything stands out.'

Amelia waited for Hal to leave before opening up the science team personnel files. One name caught her eye: Dr Mike Holmes. She remembered that when Mike first came aboard he and Jeffrey had not seen eye to eye. This initial dislike had simmered down to a mutual disdain. Mike was a brilliant geneticist in his own right, so if anyone could detect a flaw in the genetics of this situation it would be him.

Amelia went to the labs and sought out Dr Holmes.

Amelia got straight to the point. 'Mike, I need your help.'

'Okay, fire away, what do you need?'

'What I am about to tell you cannot go any further. In particular you are not to tell Jeffrey Briar.'

'No problem, Dr Charter, but if I can't tell Jeffrey, this must be serious. What do you think he has done?'

'Why do you assume that Jeffrey has done something wrong?'

'Why else would you not want me to let him know what I'm looking at. I've always thought he was arrogant, but this is on another level.'

'It is serious, Mike, but I don't really think he has done anything wrong. As you know, we have a rogue Human on the loose. What you may not know is that, briefly, it returned to the compound.'

'I knew one was in the wild, but I didn't know it had come back. Has it been terminated?'

'No, and that is part of the problem. It came back, wandered through the compound, was not detected on the cameras and killed two guards on the way out.'

Mike allowed the information to sink in for a minute.

'As you know, Dr Charter, that should be impossible. The Humans have been genetically modified to ensure that those traits cannot spontaneously generate.'

'I understand that, but the fact remains that this Human has done something that should be impossible, several things, actually.'

'What else has it done?'

'Overriding the control programme, then ignoring the kill signal. Do we need any more?'

'It ignored the kill switch? How?' exclaimed Mike. 'If these things get away from us, Dr Charter, all Elfinnim are dead.'

'I know, so you see why we have to keep this quiet until we understand what is going on.'

'Yes, I do. Who else knows about this?'

'Not many people. Besides you and I, Alfie and Hal are the only ones who should know. Jeffrey knows that 1-73 got in again but not that the cameras could not see it.'

'1-73?' queried Mike.

'Yes, the missing Human. We shortened the designation. There is only one missing so we don't need to be quite so precise.'

'Thanks for the background, however disturbing it is. Now what do you need from me?'

'The real worry, as you have said, is that we have a genetic mutation on our hands rather than a malfunction in a single unit. A malfunction would not be bad news but, given the number of units we have been working with, could be acceptable and within the bounds of statistical error – not ideal but acceptable. On the other hand any sort of genetic mutation would be terminal for this unit and the project. I need you to work out whether it is a mutation or a freak malfunction.'

'I can do that. Do we have any tissue samples to work with?'

Amelia sighed.

'No, Mike, all we have are the historical genetic records we collect during screening. We have yet to identify any biological residue from 1-73 that we could analyse.'

'Make it easy for me why don'tcha,' muttered Mike to himself. 'The first thing I need to do is dig into the records. You know Jeffrey and I don't get on; if he has done something so stupid I will find out. I wouldn't be surprised, the man is arrogant enough to believe he can get away with a stunt like this. When he finds out what I am doing he will want to know why. What do you want me to tell him?'

'Tell him whatever you like, just don't tell him the entire truth. Hal suspects that Jeffrey knows more than he is telling, so we want to limit his access to information until we understand his position in this.'

'Jeffrey might be smart, but he really can be a dick at times. I should have known the arrogant, self-declared genius would believe he could do anything he wanted. He really should be brought to trial if he has caused this.'

'I know you don't have a high opinion of him, Mike, but I need you to keep those views to yourself.'

She had to make sure that Mike didn't start telling anyone else of their suspicions. If they were wrong about Jeffrey – and she personally hoped they were – this sort of rumour would do irreparable damage to his credibility.

'I have already said more than I should. Just do the analysis and send the results to me, and only to me. One last thing, we have to be quick, if we are losing control I want to shut this thing down while we still can.'

Mike watched Amelia leave and noticed that she suddenly looked taller than when she arrived. A problem shared must make it easier to bear. But what a problem and where to start? He turned to his workstation and began documenting the parameters required to determine if 1-73 was a one-off malfunction or a serious genetic mutation. He returned to his quarters far later than usual that day, an occurrence that would become a pattern, since he would not sleep soundly until he was sure the swarm was under control – genetically, mentally and physically.

Later that evening Hal reflected on the investigation. He couldn't concentrate. Amelia was a distraction. He had to admit he really liked her and wanted to be more than a friend. He had been in a committed relationship before and it was nice, but he also knew that Elfinnim rarely formed more than two or three committed relationships and rarely had more than two or three children, if any. Children could only be conceived if the relationship worked both emotionally and physically. Hal knew Amelia had not borne a child yet and he had not fathered a child. He had never considered choosing to procreate before. There was no time pressure, for children could be conceived at any time in their existence despite strict societal rules about raising children. Parents taught and nurtured their children for at least 1,000 years to ensure they were mature before they moved into full society. With great age came a requirement for wisdom, which had to be earned through study and reflection.

Hal was now convinced Amelia knew nothing about the disappearance of 1-73. She may not be telling all she knew, but Hal was certain the reason wasn't for personal gain. Her passion for the project centred around swarm creation, which was concerned with control and replication. He wasn't sure which aspect of the project was driving her, but he knew she was rationalising it for the greater good.

It was not lost on Hal that he was less objective than he should be, and looked forward to meeting with Amelia far more than he should. He wanted the investigation to be complete so that he could explore what their relationship could become. Who knows, maybe this would be an opportunity to be a parent. It was an experience that no one talked about, except to say it was one of the greatest privileges and greatest sacrifices in Elfinnim society.

Hal's videocom buzzed. It showed a view of Amelia's quarters but no Amelia.

'Hello?' he said.

As he was about to turn the intercom off, Amelia walked past the viewer wearing a flimsy night robe.

'Amelia, you seem to have called me by mistake,' he said, averting his gaze to spare her blushes. Amelia gave no indication she had heard him.

'Amelia?' Again no response. Against his better instincts he looked at the monitor again and saw that Amelia was sitting reading a book. He could not help but admire her slim, athletic figure with full breasts. He felt his body responding to the image, to her, with a mixture of desire and embarrassment.

He tried to get her attention again, but to no avail. There was clearly a fault on her comms system that was sending pictures without her knowledge. He knew he should disconnect, but she was beautiful and she clearly did not know he could see her. Hal briefly wondered if she knew she was being watched, but then dispelled the notion. He watched her for a few moments more, before reluctantly turning the monitor off and trying to think of something else; anything except Amelia sat reading a book wearing only a night robe.

Hal slept poorly. Whenever he closed his eyes all he could think of was Amelia. His blood was on fire. This could not continue. It would dramatically reduce his ability to focus on the investigation, so the next day he went to Amelia's office.

'Can we talk privately?'

'Of course. Are you all right, you look terrible?' said Amelia.

Hal looked embarrassed.

'I haven't slept well, to be honest, something happened last night that should not have been possible. Last night I got a call –'

'Who was it? Bad news?'

'Amelia, it was you. When I answered the call, there was no one there, then you walked across the screen and sat on the bed.'

Amelia blushed, remembering how she had been thinking of Hal the previous evening.

'And, umm, what did I do next?' she asked, part of her hoping that he hadn't seen what she had been doing, but another more primal part hoping he had.

'You were just reading a book in your night robe, but I have to admit I watched for longer than I should have. You are beautiful, Amelia, and when I realised that you didn't know I could see you,' Hal paused, embarrassed, 'I have to admit I didn't turn it off immediately, but I saw nothing to embarrass you. I'm sorry, you deserved better of me.'

She seemed relieved. Hal wondered briefly what he had missed.

'Why did you carry on watching?' She tried to sound light but there was a sexual tension within the question that Hal could not miss.

He decided it was time for honesty, so now he had to follow through on it, regardless of the consequences.

'I... I thought you were just about the most beautiful woman I have ever seen and I liked everything I saw.'

'I really like you, Amelia, I would like to get to know you much better, but this damned investigation is taking so long. I need to know if this is all in my head or if you think there could be something more.'

Amelia smiled. That was the best news she had heard in a while.

'I really like you too. I would have preferred to know you were watching, though I might have done something to really make it hard for you to sleep! It's nice to know that I can keep you awake without even knowing it.'

Hal smiled and looked genuinely relieved.

'Amelia, I really want to see where this goes, but we have to finish the investigation first or there will be questions about my impartiality.'

'That doesn't mean we can't have some fun along the way,' she said with a cheeky smile. 'If I know it's you watching I will give you a show worth seeing, but I will want you to reciprocate at some point.'

Hal was relieved. This had gone far better than he had imagined. And now he had a forward offer from Amelia as a bonus.

'That would be nice, however, I think it would impede our investigation,' he replied. 'Meanwhile, we do need to find out what happened with the screens. Someone is playing with us.'

'I agree. I will get someone to look at the comms units tomorrow to see how they were rigged. Do you want me to have them repaired or do you want to watch while I know you are watching.'

Hal was tempted to leave the capability to view Amelia's quarters at will, but knew the danger, particularly since they didn't know who else could see what they could see. More importantly there was a chance their private moments could be recorded.

'No, Amelia, much as I like the idea of watching, we have to assume that someone else is also watching and until we know who that is, let's keep our relationship in the real world and eliminate the bugs.'

Hal left Amelia's office and turned her attention back to the problem at hand. It was time to speak to Jeffrey.

Amelia called Jeffrey to her office. He was abrupt and to the point as usual. She was tiring of his lack of social skills. At one time it had been charming and refreshing, but she now thought he used his brusque personality to be deliberately rude.

'Jeffrey, can I trust you to be discreet?'

'Of course. What is going on?'

'There has been an intrusion into the compound by 1-73, we need to know where it went and what, if anything, it has taken. More than anything we need to work out what it was trying to achieve.'

'She was here?' asked Jeffrey incredulously.

'No, Jeffrey, she was not here, *it* was here!' said Amelia emphatically. 'You have to snap out of this, you can't keep referring to this creature as if it were a real person. It is an experimental prototype weapon that has gone rogue. You would be wise to remember that 1-73-9.7.3310 is the most dangerous thing we have created in this project and you won't do that if you keep thinking of it as a person.'

He blushed.

'Of course, I'm sorry. I will try to work out what sh... *it* was doing here.'

'Thank you, let me know what you find.'

Jeffrey left Amelia's office in a daze. He had really messed up, calling 1-73 'she', it was a cardinal rule to separate prototype military units from people. However, he had struggled with this. He was uncomfortable around Elfinnim women and the female Humans were far easier to be around.

He didn't feel so self-conscious around them. He didn't feel threatened, and most of all they did not make him feel inadequate. He had always been made to feel different, never more so than with women. They made him more awkward than normal, which even Jeffrey realised was quite an achievement.

Hal was still investigating and now that Jeffrey reflected on the task that Amelia had set before him, he realised that he had not seen any evidence of a break-in; this could be a trap to see what he could really access. He had to be careful. First he checked call logs and investigated how he came to be involved. He quickly found evidence of the break-in, which confirmed he was not entering a trap. He trawled through the footage from the perimeter and examined access logs for anomalies. He found nothing. The two dead guards were testament to an intrusion, but there was no other evidence. He turned to GAIA.

GAIA linked all the weaponry together, and could coordinate movements and provide battlefield tactical support and communication. He had designed the system to monitor the various options both in and out of combat to ensure that losses were minimised, that the most effective weapons were used against each target and each target type, and ensured that records were kept to make subsequent improvements. He had designed the artificial intelligence system to learn from its own mistakes by estimating losses and the time taken to overwhelm targets, then comparing what happened to the plan and analyse why things were better or worse. Developing an organic matrix that could house the necessary algorithms to track, control and strategise had been a long task, requiring great care to ensure that the learning cycle did not give rise to consciousness. GAIA was nothing more than a machine, designed to protect itself, minimise losses and be better next time. The one thing that none of the prototype weapons should be able to do was evade notice by GAIA; what was the point of an all knowing, all seeing control system if the items it was supposed to control could choose not to be visible.

He checked every system, subroutine and image file, but there was no evidence of 1-73. It was just as well he had verified that the intrusion had taken place – had he not, he would have been certain of a trap. He turned his attention to code checking. Where was the glitch in the system that failed to recognise this Human? He could not find anything wrong with the code. In truth there was only one person who was intended to be completely invisible to GAIA – and that was Jeffrey Briar himself. His problem was that there was no problem in the code. He realised that there was one other secret modification that no-one else knew about. He had coded GAIA to his own individual DNA, the only way he could guarantee his personal safety under all circumstances. He could not allow his swarm to be used against him. He could not risk his creation being turned against him, so what better way to ensure it could not happen than code the control systems to his DNA. He was an only child, which was not unusual, but he had discovered that he was genetically unique amongst Elfinnim. He had an extra marker that had never been noticed. It was to this marker that he had keyed the GAIA system, which is why the rogue Human was so disturbing. It was as if he had infiltrated the compound himself. The system was designed to eliminate all records of his movements to ensure that he could do as he pleased without discovery or sanction. That left only one possible answer, but that answer was unthinkable.

Jeffrey wished Angela was still here. She had a habit of making this sort of problem go away, but she had been a necessary sacrifice to keep the project on track. He had tried to find something on Alfie, but the man was crushingly dull. How could anyone obey all of the law all of the time? He had no one else to call on, so if he was to implement the plan it was time for him to earn the right to rule. He was the only one who could save Elfinnim from petty arguments and bureaucracy, which would only lead to stagnation and decay. He would usher in a new era of combat to purge his people, by fire if need be, to make them strong and independent. At least that was how it would appear. In truth Jeffrey would rule and whoever dissented would be quieted, either by fear or force, he didn't care which as long as everyone obeyed. And if they didn't... that was where GAIA and the prototypes would become critical. It was for precisely this reason that he could not afford any slip-ups. Completion of the project was so close, and 1-73 could not be allowed to ruin it at this late stage.

Jeffrey worked day and night to unearth what it had done, where it had gone and how it had done it. It had to be done the hard way, tracking every data stream since that night to search for missing seconds of data. For some unknown reason GAIA would not identify the missing segments as anomalies. GAIA had been programmed to ignore anomalies that were linked to his DNA but he couldn't understand why GAIA insisted on identifying his DNA with the missing segments while 1-73 moved through that area. Deep down he knew why it had happened, but could not admit it to himself let alone Amelia.

Gradually the pieces came together, seconds here minutes there, and eventually he realised that 1-73 had wandered through the compound and gone into the main control centre without challenge. The control centre gave access to all of the project data, and if GAIA was identifying 1-73 as Jeffrey, what the hell had it gained access to? As this realisation sank in, he felt sick. If 1-73 was sentient and knew his plan, he was in real danger. Jeffrey needed to work out how it had modified his programming to bypass the security monitoring.

In parallel to this, Amelia was investigating how 1-73 could have been missed by the surveillance systems, but no one could explain why it was completely invisible. There was simply no rational explanation, except one: Jeffrey knew that the DNA of some of the Humans had become altered. He hadn't seen this as a significant issue – until now.

He examined the DNA records in detail, not the sanitised versions he had left on file, the real DNA files that he had removed and replaced. As he examined more of the files he became increasingly worried. The DNA progressions showed a mutation. However, the really frightening part was that the

DNA mutation was restoring all four-strands. The Humans were becoming Elfinnim.

Jeffrey realised that to understand what was happening he needed to identify from where the mutating strain originated. Data was the key, so he looked at the analyses from each generation. A disturbing pattern emerged. The first thing he noticed was that the genetic mutations were less frequent in previous generations. He would have to chase that back and see if he could find the origin of the mutations, but that would have to wait for now. His immediate problem was to determine how many potential genetic crossings were likely, and to do that he would need a clear picture of how many Humans had the mutation and how these would manifest in their offspring. In each generation there were a small number of pure mutations, those that were not possible from the documented parents. There were also mutations that could only arise from crossing two pure mutations. In the current generation at least half of all births would be almost pure Elfinnim – in ten generations there would be no more Humans. Then Jeffrey saw something more in the genetic data that provided a unique opportunity. Not only would the Humans develop the full capabilities of Elfinnim, they would retain their reproductive rate and aggressive territorialism.

He pushed on analysing the data, checking what the genetic markers meant. As he delved he discovered something that at first seemed absurd, then a second analysis confirmed his findings and for the first time since this investigation commenced Jeffrey started to laugh. His initial mirth soon became manic as he realised that his dream of uniting Elfinnim people under his strong and progressive leadership would now also coincide with an exponential increase in birth rate. Now he needed to find the source of the pure mutations.

Tracking back the mutations through the most recent generations was relatively easy, but as he worked further back it became increasingly hard to find the mutated Humans, although in each generation there was at least one dramatic mutation. He had purged at least four bloodlines that had exhibited such mutations, but had never bothered to search for the source before. Now as he searched, one name repeatedly came up.

Jeffrey cross-matched the primary genetic mutations in each generation with a DNA profile from the flagged name, which confirmed a 96.7 per cent correlation with the genetic profile of a single person and the genetic mutations of each generation. The progenitor of the mutant Humans was an Elfinnim.

It took time to work it all out, but eventually it all came together. It was time to tell Amelia a version of the truth. He asked for a meeting. When he arrived, Alfie and Hal were also there. Jeffrey felt a bead of sweat trickle down his back. He had not been expecting this audience.

'Amelia, I have been investigating the break-in, as you asked, and I have found some interesting facts. Firstly, why didn't you tell me that 1-73 ghosted through the compound and was not recorded on any of the camera systems? I am certain you knew this.'

He could tell from their faces that they all knew about it.

'I can't work out how she did it. It is a worry, even Elfinnim can't evade the systems.'

Amelia replied, 'We didn't want you to focus on that, Jeffrey, we wanted you to work out what 1-73 took. Why are you referring to it as 'she' again? Didn't we resolve that issue?'

Jeffrey blushed.

'S-S-Sorry, Amelia, I... I forgot. Um, I think I know what 1-73 took, but it doesn't make any sense.'

'What did 1-73 take? It's really important,' stressed Hal.

'My investigation has thrown up some strange results,' Jeffrey began. '1-73's movements were more difficult to track than they should have been because the system logs were deliberately obscured. It really is remarkably sophisticated. I still need to work out why GAIA allowed the deception and aided the obfuscation.'

Hal was exasperated.

'While this is of academic interest, you have not told us why.'

Jeffrey felt the intimidation as intended.

'Okay, okay, I am getting to it,' Jeffrey replied irritably.

'Sh... it went to the main control room and searched our databases. The only file I can find that 1-73 accessed was a chart showing the heredity of the Human prototypes.'

'What on Elfinn would it want that for?' Hal asked.

Jeffrey had to choose his next words carefully. He needed to give a plausible explanation that didn't give away what was really going on, didn't burn either the apparent project or his real project, rather focused attention on 1-73.

Finally he said, 'I don't know, exactly. 1-73 is certainly obsessed with its origins, but the strange aspect of this is 1-73 should not have any concept of genealogy.'

'Why does that matter?' asked Hal. He was starting to lose patience.

Amelia interrupted. 'Jeffrey, are you seriously telling me that 1-73 has developed independent thought?'

'No, I don't think that is what has happened,' Jeffrey explained, 'I think, or rather I suspect, 1-73 has developed a faulty algorithm that makes it obsessed with its own origins. That would explain why it is not responding, it is locked into a loop that requires an answer to enable the rest of the algorithm to run.'

They all looked dubious.

'Let me get this straight,' said Hal, '1-73 wants to know where it comes from, but it doesn't know why and that is why it is refusing orders?'

'Yes, in essence, that is what I mean. The most difficult part will be how to break the loop so that we regain control of the prototype. I need some more time to work out what the glitch in the algorithm is so that we can work out how to repair the fault. The easiest repair would be to upload a worm into the software that will repair the faulty code and return control.'

'Is that possible?' asked Hal.

'Yes, definitely, and that will prove to the Grand Council that we not only have control, but that if something does go wrong in the future we can regain control.'

'So, how do you propose we regain control?' asked Alfie.

'The biggest problem will be introducing the worm into its software. If the kill switch doesn't work, then the glitch will prevent any and all remote access. If we can identify the source of the glitch it may be easier to present exactly the information that is required to satisfy the execution parameters of the algorithm.'

Jeffrey took a pause, allowing everyone some time to catch up.

'I have modified the algorithm to prevent a recurrence and I have already uploaded it to all the other units to prevent it spreading. The problem with 1-73 is that once the loop is established the revised algorithm cannot be integrated. Until the escape parameters of the algorithm cycle are satisfied, any attempt to upload a new version is rejected.'

'So we can't upload the repair until the software completes the cycle?' said Alfie.

'Exactly,' said Jeffrey, smiling.

At last someone believed they understood what he was saying. That meant they were close to believing him.

'If I understand you correctly,' said Hal, 'if we let 1-73 find out its origins it clears the loop and returns to standard programming?'

'In essence, that is correct,' beamed Jeffrey.

Hal looked unconvinced. 'Jeffrey, I can't help feeling there is something you are not telling us.'

'What do you mean?'

'You have told us a tale that is plausible, and is likely to be close to the truth, of that I am certain,' said Hal. 'But there is more in this tale that you are not telling us. For example, how could 1-73 have evaded detection? There is more to that than simple good luck. Your much vaunted control system seems to be aiding and abetting 1-73 rather than shutting it down. Either the system is not as good as you say or you know something more, which you are deliberately keeping from us.'

'I don't know what you mean! And, and I resent your implication,' blustered Jeffrey. 'I have done nothing but work to promote and secure Elfinnim through the Grand Council to ensure we are safe and secure.'

'Maybe,' said Hal. 'Time will tell, but if I do catch you in a lie, make no mistake, Angela will not be the only one who meets the scrutineers.'

Jeffrey was sweating profusely by now and feeling uncomfortable. Hal was too close to the truth and what the scrutineers would find worried him most of all.

The way Jeffrey kept his lies so close to the truth made separating the two incredibly difficult. Hal had the feeling that if he could get hold of a true piece of the puzzle he could start to trace what was really happening. He knew from experience that once that happened, he would be able to follow the information back to its source.

'So what is your plan, Jeffrey, how do we get this algorithm to complete so that we can regain control?'

The tack of the question was a surprise, and Jeffrey took a second to calm himself. Hal was using the technique of switching subjects, a documented method of unsettling people to force mistakes.

'I need some more time to make a plan. It already knows that its progenitors are 1-72-26.5.3276 and 3-72-16.11.3278, so simply repeating that won't work. I can examine the algorithm to work out exactly what information 1-73 needs to clear the loop.'

'Okay, you have your time, just make sure you come up with a plan, and make it soon,' Hal growled.

Amelia called her chief engineer to report the fault with her comms system. The chief engineer needed to know what was happening. She arrived at Amelia's office and took a second to control her breathing and centre herself before entering.

'Good afternoon, Dr Charter, I hear you are having comms trouble. Sorry to get right to the point here, but why do you need me to sort out a comms problem?'

One of the things that Amelia liked about Liz Hunt was her no-nonsense approach.

'Normally I would just ask for a comms engineer,' Amelia said, 'but I suspect one of your engineers has interfered with my comms system and left it transmitting images to another unit without my knowledge. It looks like the unit transmits only when my movement is detected. What I need from you is to find out who installed the device, when they installed it and who they installed it for.'

The idea that one of her engineers could have done this was beyond belief. 'Are you sure?'

Amelia considered her response for a moment.

'Absolutely.'

7

CONGRUENCE

Jeffrey was pacing in his quarters. This was wrong, all wrong. How did Hal know he was lying. He had kept his story as close to the truth as possible, but Hal's threat of the scrutineers had him scared. If they uncovered his secrets the Grand Council would execute him, of that he had no doubt. So all he could do for now was wait and pace until everything was in place and ready to go. He couldn't move the swarm too quickly or it would be reported as a mobilisation. Hal would start digging into a mobilisation and Jeffrey's involvement could not be hidden, so he had to move resources slowly to make it appear a natural adjustment. He would soon have to increase the rate of movement to ensure that he could initiate the plan before the scrutineers extracted the tip of his secrets from Angela.

Following the meeting with Jeffrey, Amelia expressed concern.

'Hal, do you really think that Jeffrey knows more than he is telling?'

'Yes, I do. He told us a story that was just close enough to the truth to be believable, but it wasn't the truth.'

'I didn't notice anything, how did you pick it up?' asked Amelia.

'It was little things. He was sweating too much, it isn't normal to be that stressed in this situation, and his answers were too perfect, no rough edges or loose ends, everything neat and packaged for the audience, and by audience I mean us. If this was a working theory there would be loose ends, parts that haven't been thoroughly considered, but not with Jeffrey. This explanation is too neat and tidy. I ask you, what else about this has been neat and tidy?'

'Good point,' Amelia conceded. 'There has been nothing straightforward about this whole situation, and he suddenly has a complete explanation. You are right, it isn't reasonable.'

Hal was relieved he wasn't alone in his suspicions.

'Amelia, I am sure he is up to something. I think the plan is speeding up, whether it is his or someone else's plan. I suspect he was working with Angela, but I can't figure out who they are working for. The problem is I haven't got any evidence that links anyone other than Angela to any of the indisciplines. I don't think anyone else inside the project is involved.'

'You have no idea how glad I am to hear you say that,' Amelia said.

'Oh, I think I know,' said Hal with a slow smile. He chose his next words carefully.

'I have been considering what your involvement was. Now I am sure you weren't involved, but I know you haven't told the whole truth either.'

'What do you mean I've not told the whole truth?'

Amelia was pleased that Hal had cleared her of being involved in the loss of 1-73, but she was also concerned that he knew she had stretched the truth about the original loss.

'Amelia, you know that I really like you, but the story you told had some holes that have already been exposed. I don't understand why... yet. It's time to tell me everything you know.'

She knew in that moment there was no point pretending anymore.

'I'm sorry, you are right, I did try to minimise the damage. Not because I wanted to protect myself, Angela, Jeffrey, or anyone else for that matter, but I did want to protect the project. Let me explain: you are Elfinnim, so you know that one of the reasons we set out to create these weapons was to minimise the loss of Elfinnim life when we do have conflicts. Our birth rate is relatively low, so we can't afford to see our people killed. But it doesn't have to be like that, with the work that Jeffrey has done we have the start of a gene therapy for fertility. Can you imagine what a difference an increase in the birth rate will mean to our people?'

'I can see that, but why did you try to cover up what was happening?'

'I was scared for the project, I was scared that Angela's ridiculous behaviour would jeopardise the whole project. You must understand that at the time I really believed she was acting alone, I had no idea that there was anything more going on. This is a long term objective, and while Jeffrey has isolated the genes for fertility, there is still a lot of work to do before we can prove that the same approach would work for Elfinnim. If the project is terminated too soon, we may never know. Hal, I haven't had any children yet, I want to have more than one or two. Do you realise that there are virtually no Elfinnim children with siblings of a similar age? What would it be like if more people had siblings at around the same age? How precious would that be?'

Hal had to concede the point. He had also learned some interesting facts about Amelia, things that fit neatly with his own feelings. He realised he was thinking silently and also that Amelia was patiently waiting for his response.

'Okay, I understand, I don't think it was the right course of action, but I do understand why you did it. Jeffrey may be brilliant, but I believe he is unstable.'

'I agree that he is eccentric, but unstable? You really think so? Do you really believe he is behind this?'

'I think he is one of the most dangerous people I have ever met. I've seen his personnel file, his IQ is off the charts, but he has no compassion or empathy. He is so intellectual that he leaves no room for emotion. He seems to believe that our emotions lead us astray and reduce our ability to reason clearly. As a result we should be treated as simple drones to follow his lead, which makes me worry about his motives. I will not be Jeffrey's drone and I am sure that I am not alone. My brothers in the warrior caste will do what we were charged to do by the Grand Council and protect Elfinnim from any and all threats. *Any* and *all* threats. Warrior caste don't seek death, however we are taught from the start of our training that we are not immortal, we are just blessed with longevity and phenomenal healing capabilities. I am certain that someone manipulated Angela, someone pushed her to an extreme, someone who knew exactly how to get to her. She was smart, experienced and careful, so whoever placed her in a position where she felt she had to keep their secrets had to be remarkably intelligent and utterly ruthless. Sound like anyone you know?'

'Hal, I can see the remarkable intelligence, but utterly ruthless? Jeffrey?'

'You underestimate him. He has a cold analytical mind and I have noticed that the only time he gets emotional is when he is put under pressure about his own reasoning or motives. When you shift the discussion to emotions and feelings Jeffrey can't cope and starts to panic. His ability to process emotions is not simply limited, it is almost non-existent.'

'He has always appeared considered and scientific,' said Amelia.

'I can understand that, you are scientific and logical yourself.'

'Are you saying I am cold and unemotional?' she said with a hint of a smile.

'Oh no, I am not saying that at all, in fact I suspect that you are anything but unemotional... in fact I am hoping you will share a meal with me and start opening up to me emotionally.'

Hal waited for an answer and tried not to fidget. It might not be the right time, but when was? It was Hal's turn to be patient.

Amelia was flattered and excited.

'I would really like that,' she replied. Hal had a habit of making her feel good, and she enjoyed his company. He was also handsome; she hoped he had other talents that would be equally enjoyable.

Hal was relieved, he had waited until there was no evidence linking Amelia to any wrongdoing and for her to explain why she had lied to him before taking their relationship further. He had really enjoyed the time they had spent together and wanted to spend more time with her. If they could prove that Jeffrey was the culprit, maybe they could meet up back on Elfinn later. The problem was that amongst the possible explanations existed two extremes – either Jeffrey was completely innocent and just caught up in an unfortunate set of circumstances or he was a remarkably clever and resourceful sociopath. Although there was plenty of circumstantial evidence linking him to the disappearance of 1-73 there was no solid connection to him from any of the misdeeds that had been uncovered. Until either Jeffrey made a mistake or the scrutineers broke Angela Hal had no definitive evidence of a crime. There was something more here, Hal was certain of it. Jeffrey was afraid of Hal finding out more... but what?

There was one more question burning in Hal's mind.

'Amelia, is Alfie what he seems?'

'You have worked with him on this investigation for several years now, do you think he's a liar?'

'I don't think so,' admitted Hal. 'He seems so honest that I start to worry if I am just missing something.'

'With Alfie there is no hidden agenda, no subterfuge, he is exactly what he seems, which is why I picked him to lead the team after Angela left. It is both his greatest strength and his greatest weakness.'

'What do you mean?'

'What you see is what you get,' she said. 'Alfie works in security but he is so honest that he sometimes struggles to imagine how someone else could be dishonest. That is a weakness. The other side of his personality is that he couldn't tell a lie if his life depended on it, so he will always tell you exactly what has happened regardless of the consequences. I see that as a strength.'

Hal agreed with her assessment, although he was more concerned with Alfie's inability to see how someone else would subvert the rules than Amelia. Part of a good security head was an understanding of how people would be dishonest and that was an instinct that no amount of training could replace. Amelia's assessment was essentially the same as his own, and gave him confidence that Alfie was trustworthy, if a little oblivious to the danger others presented. There was no evidence that either Amelia or Alfie were involved in any aspect of the cover-up, and combined with the latest answers from Amelia, Hal was now convinced that they were caught up in someone else's web. Angela,

Amelia and Alfie had been manipulated into doing someone else's bidding.

Later, as Hal was reviewing his notes on the project, he noticed something he had missed in earlier reviews of the analytical data. Every Human was given a DNA screening at birth and then screened again every ten years to ensure no genetic mutations or distortions crept in. This was necessary since genetic stability was a critical feature of the swarm – unpredictable mutations could rapidly develop. If those mutations resulted in physical or mental capabilities or traits that were incompatible with the basic functionality of the swarm, or even interfered with the responsiveness to GAIA, they must be eliminated from the project.

'Alfie, who is the best person to ask about testing data for DNA testing?'

'Any of the technicians could tell you, but if I was asking, I would go to Mike Holmes. He is smart and knows the systems inside out. He lives and breathes those testing systems.'

Alfie was curious. 'What have you found?'

'I'm not sure, to be honest,' replied Hal. 'It may be a simple keying error, but it could be the first piece of good luck we have had. I have found a date on one of the tests that doesn't make sense. I missed it first time because we were focused on the DNA data itself, but after today's discussion with Jeffrey I was browsing some of the collected data on DNA testing and noticed the anomaly.'

'Definitely talk to Mike Holmes,' Alfie confirmed.

Hal found Mike working in the DNA testing laboratory.

'Mike, I have noticed an apparent error in one of the date stamps. How are the date stamps added to the DNA reports? Are they automatic or does the operator add the date?'

'The data stamp is usually automatic,' said Mike, 'but sometimes there are problems and it has to be manually entered.'

'Damn! ' said Hal. 'That doesn't really help.'

'Let's try this another way, what is it you need to know?'

'Here's the problem: I have noticed a discrepancy in the date stamp of one of the DNA tests and before I go chase down every discrepancy I want to be sure it is significant.'

'Makes sense. Have you got the report with you? If I look at it I might be able to answer your question.'

Mike took the report handed to him.

'I can't see anything wrong with this, why do you think this is a problem?'

'The problem only becomes clear when you look at the scheduled test date, here.' Hal pointed out the discrepancy. 'If the operators always entered the data this could be a data entry error, if not it could be a system error, but I need to understand where I am looking.'

Mike looked at the print again and then at the schedule. 'Come with me.'

Mike led Hal back to his office and called a schedule up on screen, then searched for the date on the analysis.

'This is interesting. There was a sample run on that day from the swarm, but not from 1-73. The file has also been duplicated, but with a change in the unit reference, so it wouldn't get flagged when looking for duplicates. We look for duplications on a unit designation basis, and we check the designation is correct for the unit to which the test is allocated on a daily basis. This is to ensure we don't duplicate data and we keep the system clean.'

There it was, the first mistake.

'When was it inserted into 1-73's record?' Hal asked.

'As far as I can tell, this was inserted three weeks after the official sample was taken. That's odd,' said Mike, typing furiously and bringing up screen after screen of what Hal could only describe as gibberish.

'What's odd?'

'This reference for the sample taken from 1-73 can't be the same as the sample one year earlier, but someone has altered the background referencing of the sample to make it look like the right sample. There are few people who have the access to do that and even fewer who know how. Also, I can't find the real sample data, it has been deleted from the system. The only way it should be possible to delete a document is after review with the section supervisor and third party approval. When that happens, and from time to time there is an accidental duplicate in the system, the deletion is documented and a link to the original document is posted in the system audit file. For this particular change there is no such record.'

'Is that unusual?' asked Hal.

'Damned right it is. I am section supervisor in this case and I know nothing about this deletion and can't find any record of the change. If I had authorised this it would have been documented and explained.'

'Mike, can you work out who made the change?'

'No, whoever did this worked hard to make it look as if this is the original data, but made a mistake when they keyed the wrong date. But what I do know is that whoever did this knew the systems intimately. I need to check if there are any more anomalies, but we might not get this lucky again. I don't think this person makes many mistakes.'

'I agree with you. Can you find the data that was replaced? It might help if we knew what they were trying to hide. Why would anyone want to substitute a DNA profile? Surely no one would want to cover up a mutated DNA strain?'

'Hal, that is a scary concept. I can't imagine why anyone would want to do that, and to be honest I would rather not think about what that could mean. Let me look into the files, I will let you know what I find.'

'Okay, but please make this a priority. We need to work out what is happening here.'

'I know, Dr Charter came to see me earlier and asked me to look into some other parts of this little mystery, but this just adds another layer. My concern is that someone has been systematically covering a mutation. It's utter madness, but it's the only explanation that fits with Dr Charter's request and your evidence.'

'We need to confirm if all the facts support that proposition,' said Hal. 'If they do, this project will be shut down, but there are potential benefits from this research that mean we have to be sure before we kill it. I will let you get on with the data mining, let me know what you find.'

Hal was reflective as he walked back to his quarters. If this was a mutation and a cover up, this project was done regardless of what the possible benefits were. If any of these organisms escaped into the population the consequences could be devastating.

In the months following Hal's meeting with Amelia and Alfie, he worked to find a gap in Jeffrey's argument, but there was no defect in his logic, which was making Hal frustrated. He knew that whoever was responsible would eventually make a mistake – if they hadn't already – but Hal needed to work out where the error existed so he could follow the trail back to the instigator. Would that prove to be Jeffrey Briar?

Finally Hal's luck improved and he discovered a discrepancy in the logs. The security card system showed Jeffrey was in his quarters on the night 1-73 broke into the compound. The camera logs had no record of his being in any corridor or public area, yet the reports made by members of staff had mentioned that Jeffrey had investigated the locks and route taken by the prototype. Hal had examined every possible route to the areas where the staff said they saw him, which suggested that he should have been picked up on four separate cameras. If he could do this once, who knew how often he had done it before.

Hal decided it was time to push Jeffrey and summoned him to a meeting.

'Jeffrey, how are you?'

'Hal, please don't pretend to be my friend. We both know you don't like me and don't believe anything I say, so don't insult my intelligence by pretending you do.'

Hal was surprised by Jeffrey's approach, but that could make life much easier.

'Okay, Jeffrey, why do you think you are here?'

'I don't know, I haven't done anything wrong, yet you continue to try to prove I have.'

'Too many lines of enquiry lead back to you, there are too many anomalies between your account of events and other people's. Why is that?'

'Hal, I have perfect recall, it is both a blessing and a curse. I never forget and never get it wrong.'

'I know that everyone believes that and that you rely on that belief to persuade people to believe you. Here is my problem, you remember when 1-73 broke in?'

'Of course I do.'

'And you never forget anything and never get it wrong?'

'That's what I said, because it is true.'

'So, to my problem, you said you went to see what had been going on the following morning, is that correct?'

'Yes.'

'And that is supported by the other witnesses who are all clear that they saw you and talked to you at the time.'

'That's because it's what happened. What is your point?'

'You see, the problem is that according to the system logs you didn't leave your quarters and you were not recorded on any of the camera systems even though there is no route to any of those sites that isn't covered by a camera. How can that have happened?'

Jeffrey sat motionless while the information sank in. He gradually paled and sweat patches bloomed at his armpits. Hal waited a few minutes.

'So, Jeffrey, what happened? You have been telling me how brilliant and infallible these surveillance systems are, yet you have walked through the whole facility without the camera systems or card systems detecting you. How is that possible?'

'It's because... the thing is... it's like this...'

'What's the problem? You told me you had perfect recall.'

'There is nothing wrong with my memory!' snarled Jeffrey.

'So why doesn't the recording system back you up?' snapped Hal.

Jeffrey knew he had made a mistake and was furious about it. How could he have let himself get caught out like this? Hal of all people didn't have the intellect to challenge him, so he had only himself to blame. Everything had been contained, there wasn't much more required to gain control, he only needed a few more months. It could not be allowed to go wrong, if he lost his head now it would all be over. Time to feign shock.

'I can't explain it,' Jeffrey said. The lie hurt him, he could not abide saying it, but it was the only choice to maintain his position.

'Somehow I don't believe you,' Hal replied. 'You are asking me to believe that despite your self-proclaimed genius, you don't know exactly how the computer system you designed works.'

'Sorry to disappoint you, but this one isn't down to me. I am as confused as you are. I will investigate what has happened as soon as I get out of here.'

'Like hell you will! If I let you access the system you will erase every trace of whatever it is you have done and come up with a pretty explanation for why the system didn't work. I will ask once again... why didn't your system detect you moving through the facility?'

'I really don't know, what have I done to earn such distrust? Show me your evidence that I am anything other than a loyal hardworking scientist. You can't, can you. There are two explanations: either I am as brilliant or manipulative as you say or I am truly innocent. I am telling you I am working in the best interests of Elfinnim people.'

'The aspect of that statement that chills me is that I think you absolutely believe it. In truth, I am more bothered about what you aren't saying. The trouble is, you haven't bothered to ask Elfinnim what they believe is in *their* best interests. We have to find out what else your little computer system has missed.'

'And I told you that there is another explanation. Why can't you see that I am just working for the Grand Council?'

'Many reasons,' said Hal, 'too many to explain. The problem is, a pattern has been created which keeps returning to you. If you are an innocent victim in this, the evidence is well hidden, and so far I can't find it. I will find the evidence that links the parts of this together, and leads me to whoever has cost so many Elfinnim lives. This slip is the first step in that process. I will work out what is going on and I will bring the guilty to account for what they have done.'

'What is it that you think I have done? Have you even considered the possibility that someone is pointing the evidence at me to lead you away from them?'

Although his statement was plausible, there was something about the condescending tone he used and the look in his eye that convinced Hal that Jeffrey was at the centre of the whole problem.

'I have given you the benefit of the doubt for a long time, but I have tracked every other avenue looking for someone else: if they exist I can't find them. So that leaves me with you, and I will examine what you are doing until I have evidence to conclusively prove your guilt or innocence.'

'You can't prove something that didn't happen,' protested Jeffrey.

'No, but I can follow the leads and evidence until they either lead me finally to you or someone else with proof. I will chase those leads honestly, but I don't believe they are going to lead to someone else. You are so certain you have covered your tracks that you are forgetting this is what I do every day. Understand this, Jeffrey, if this is you, I will find your trail and I will bring you to account for everything you have done.'

Jeffrey held his nerve, and looked Hal in the eye. He knew that any hint of fear would speed up his demise. He would have to block Hal and take a few more risks. Angela would not hold out much longer. Jeffrey needed to get everything in position for his next move before the Grand Council sent a task force to solve the issue once and for all.

He returned to his quarters and ran the numbers again. It would take a further eight months to get the perfect alignment of the swarm. He would have to go with less than perfect, he needed to be ready in four months or he would run out of time.

Amelia was pleased to see Hal when he knocked on her door.

'Amelia, I am sorry to bother you this late, have you seen Mike's latest findings?'

'No, what did he find?'

'I noticed a time stamp on one of the DNA checks was wrong, so on Alfie's advice I asked Mike to talk me through the process.'

'That makes sense, he knows the system inside and out. If there was any reasonable explanation he would know what it is.'

'The problem is that when Mike looked at the data he didn't recognise the edit and he would have had to sign off against a change. Looking a bit further, he found that the data had been duplicated and modified to avoid detection. He is looking into what the duplicated data was used to replace.'

Amelia felt a cold shiver run down her back when she realised what Hal was saying.

'Hal, did Mike tell you what I have asked him to do?' asked Amelia.

'Yes, he did. I think we should shut the project down now. If we put all of the prototypes in cryostasis it will buy us time to track down who is behind this, how far the conspiracy spreads, and what is really happening with the swarm. That is the best way to preserve the benefits for Elfinnim, without risking everything.'

'Let me think about it, Hal. I understand your reasoning, but I'm not sure I agree with your action. Given that so far we have one rogue Human, and no evidence of mutation or any wrongdoing other than Angela's, I have to be absolutely sure that there is a risk before I shut the project down. Mike needs to work quickly to either prove the swarm is compromised and that there are mutations that must be deleted, or that this is an elaborate hoax to derail the programme. Surely you can see another possibility is that the mercenaries have infiltrated the Swarm Project. If they have, they would know they can't attack – the swarm is too large and too well-trained with state of the art equipment. GAIA is too inaccessible to turn the swarm for their use, so what else can they do? They could try to scare us into destroying this weapon before it is deployed, using our fear to get us doing their work. If I was planning this for the mercenaries and they knew how close we were, as soon as we destroyed GAIA and the swarm I would attack the Grand Council and enact a coup. Once the mercenaries are in control they can do as they please and that would be a disaster for our people.'

'I know, which is why I am proposing that we put the swarm into cryosleep. That way we buy time to find out the truth, then decide how best to proceed with input from the Grand Council.'

'I agree to a point, however once the swarm is in cryosleep it will be tempting to leave it that way as a safeguard, but what the Grand Council may not understand is that the swarm will not respond uniformly. We could lose more than half the swarm and have to wait until they recovered enough numbers to be a threat. During that time they would be susceptible to an attack from the mercenaries. Until we are certain they are not behind this we can't afford to risk the swarm.'

'Whichever way we go now, there is a risk of annihilation, either because of our creation or because we didn't trust our creation.'

Hal thought about the possibilities. There were no safe choices. After a while Hal made his mind up. If he made the wrong decision, he hoped history would be kind to him.

'I think you might be right. We need to be patient a little while longer, but I don't mind telling you that I'm also inclined to be cautious with this situation. It's not as if we are under any immediate threat. I know this project is important to you, but I have to think about Elfinnim people as well.'

'I understand, Hal, but are you sure we aren't in immediate danger? That assumes the mercenaries were not involved, and we don't know that for certain, do we? We both know the Grand Council will start looking at probabilities and risk assessments once the swarm is in cryosleep. By the time they work out what the bigger danger is it will be too late.'

Hal knew she was right, but that didn't make him any happier with the situation. They were in a cleft stick; it was essential that they identify the real enemy before making a move. So much now rested on Mike Holmes. He was under tremendous pressure to determine if the missing data showed a mutation. It seemed to Hal that Mike was rising to the challenge, but character didn't show through when the investigation began, it only became apparent when the initial approaches failed. So far Mike had not been given enough time to fail, so all Hal and Amelia could do was trust him and wait for a positive result.

'You know, Hal, this fertility development is vital to us, the Elfinnim people, and I hope you and me too. I know it is too early to even think about children, but I really want that to be our choice.'

'I know, but is that worth risking the entire Elfinnim people for? If 1-73 has mutated, how many others are in the process of mutating? And if the mutation means that every mutated Human is free from GAIA's control, how many of these things will we be facing? Surely you can see how dangerous these things are – for goodness sake they were designed to be weapons, every trace of empathy, compassion and remorse has been deliberately stripped from their psyche. You said yourself that when you turned GAIA off they became crazed and attacked each other. Is the prospect of better fertility really worth risking our whole species for? I don't think it is.'

Amelia was frustrated. They were on the brink of an answer for Elfinnim fertility they must not lose the power to give them a choice, particularly when they were this close. She had to persuade Hal to leave the project alone so that she could get the evidence needed to prove that the swarm fertility could be grafted into Elfinnim DNA.

'Okay, Hal, I understand, but there is another view. I still think the mercenaries are the bigger danger. I can see that you don't agree, so can we just agree to wait until Mike has some evidence one way or the other and then act on the evidence? We shouldn't have to wait too long to make a decision.'

'You are asking me to play at being a creator! We cannot wait long to make the decision, if the real danger is the swarm we have to act before we lose control. If it is the mercenaries, we have to preserve the swarm to safeguard Elfinnim. I have never been faced with such a polar decision. We don't know if the swarm will be our salvation or our doom. Help me out here, Amelia, we are deciding the fate of our people and for the first time that I can recall I have no gut instinct for the right choice. If we get this wrong —'

'I know, believe me I am just as scared as you, but I honestly believe that we have time to wait for Mike's investigation without putting our people at any more risk than already exists.'

Hal considered what Amelia was asking of him. On balance were they really any more at risk, or were they just more aware of the risk? Hal finally decided that he didn't have to make an immediate decision.

'Okay, Amelia, you win, for now. We will wait for Mike to find some hard evidence, but I am not going to wait indefinitely. We need to review progress daily, and use the reviews to guide our decisions. We will soon run out of time and that will mean making the best decision available based on what we know.'

Amelia was relieved that she had won a reprieve for the project, but if Mike found gross mutation... there was only one option open and that was to annihilate the project and all prototypes. She shuddered, imagining all the years of work destroyed, all that hope and the potential of abundant life for Elfinnim lost. And why? Because someone could not follow a simple set of rules.

'Thank you, Hal, it means a lot to me that you will wait a little while before forcing this decision.'

Hal looked out the window at the rapidly darkening vista. 'I just hope I am doing the right thing, because if this is a mistake we might not get a chance to regret it. The swarm is a dangerous weapon when controlled through GAIA, but if uncontrolled it will become a force of nature that can't be contained, and can't be resisted. In the end, what I really hope is that we are entirely wrong, that the swarm is not mutating and there is no plot or link to the mercenaries. If that could be true, we would all get what we want and I can stop worrying about what is outside the door.' Hal shook his head sadly. 'Who am I fooling? There is no way this is all a coincidence. I am sorry to say it but I fear we are doomed whichever way this goes. Perhaps it is just my fatalist view of the universe, but I fear I may never see Elfinn again.'

Amelia understood, and was both pleased and troubled at the same time. She was pleased that Hal trusted her enough to show this vulnerable side of his character, but also troubled because she had the same fear of not seeing Elfinn again. It was one thing to have a secret fear, it was an altogether different proposition to have that fear expressed by another person. Hal looked at her, as if he had read her mind.

'Amelia, I'm sorry, I should not have said that to you. I am not prone to dwelling on such things and I rarely see a situation this bleakly, I'm just very tired.'

'It's understandable, this investigation has been going on a long time and has been frustrating. It's bad enough that we have had a serious security breach by Angela, but to now have a concern that the swarm may be mutating is terrifying. If it's any consolation, I am just as worried, but I have to believe the project has not been thoroughly compromised. Until Mike can determine if the swarm is developing beyond what was originally conceived we should try to keep an open mind and not worry. I hope you know that I really appreciate you understanding the work enough to see that we can't really destroy it before we are certain it could destroy us. I also appreciate your trust in my motives for keeping the swarm alive.'

Amelia walked over to the window and kissed Hal softly on the cheek.

'What was that for?'

'That was for believing in me and the project. I trust you, I know that if this gets out of control you will find a way to keep us secure. In the meantime, since you are here, would you like to join me for some food?'

'I would like that,' said Hal, heading for the door.

'Where are you going?'

'To the restaurant, where else would we get food?'

'Ah, you see, one of the benefits of being the project director is that I get a food service. Order what you want and I will get it delivered.'

'Sounds good, what can I get?'

Amelia pulled a menu up on her tablet from which she and Hal ordered. The kitchen delivered their order within ten minutes and they ate while talking about nothing in particular and just enjoying each other's company. Eventually the meal was finished.

'I should go now,' said Hal, 'there is still so much to do.'

Amelia felt it was time to become more intimate. They had already established that they had feelings for each other and since he was here in her quarters, maybe now was the right time to take the next step.

'You don't have to go, Hal, there is plenty of room for both of us in here.'

'Are you sure that's the right thing to do?'

'I don't know if it's the right thing to do, but given what we have just been discussing and the potential fates that await us, whatever we decide, it is what I want to do.'

'Close enough.'

Hal leaned across and kissed her fully on the mouth as she wrapped her arms around his neck and pulled him close. Hal had not realised how much he had been thinking about her and he remembered seeing her on the bed reading a book. He gently undid the fastening on her uniform as she tugged at his belt. It seemed that although Hal would stay the night, sleep was not an immediate concern.

Their first lovemaking session was fiery and passionate as they expended their energy and frustrations. Later they made love again, this time taking their time, exploring each other's bodies and senses until their curiosity for each other was temporarily satiated.

As they lay enjoying the closeness of each other's bodies gently drifting into sleep, Amelia said, 'Do you think we will survive the swarm and the mercenaries? I have never really considered death before, it's not something we have to worry about much, is it? Death leading to an eternity without sensation really frightens me.'

'I think that if we die, that's it, there is nothing more,' replied Hal. 'I think we stop, our consciousness stops and we cease to exist in this or any other life, so don't worry about that, focus on today while we are alive and worry only about remaining alive as long as we possibly can.'

'That's a good way to look at it, it's certainly better than worrying about something unknown.'

She fell asleep wondering where the future would take them, having decided that nothing was going to stop her from being with Hal.

8

DEVELOPMENTS

Hal believed he was getting under Jeffrey Briar's skin, but the truth was he had no evidence against him. It was so frustrating, his gut instinct told him Jeffrey was deeply involved in the loss of the prototype, but he could find nothing linking him to its disappearance, the illegal access cards, or the changing data that he had experienced.

Initially Hal had been certain Jeffrey was changing files after he had examined them. That was when he decided to duplicate documents to his own secure area for future reference. Whoever was changing the files must have been able to track what Hal was doing because the changes suddenly stopped happening; anyone less certain of themselves would have doubted their notes and recollections, but Hal knew which mistakes he was likely to make – recording errors were extremely unlikely.

Hal had to find a way to monitor and track code changes, one of the keys to catching the culprit. He needed someone who knew the GAIA software intimately, so he began researching the team involved in controlling GAIA and the Swarm Project.

One name kept cropping up: Ruby Cooper. Ruby was recruited to support Jeffrey, effectively his number two. She couldn't be called a confidante of his, but she was as close as it came. Hal decided to see if she was willing to put the project safety ahead of her personal considerations. He spent some time learning her routines and just happened to be in the cafeteria on one occasion when she was having her lunch. Hal waited a few days for the right conditions before approaching her.

'Ruby, I would like your help with something.'

'I am not sure that is a good idea, Hal. I had more than enough trouble gaining Jeffrey's trust to do my job in the first place, if I lose it he may push me out of the project.'

'I understand that and I have tried to work with him on this, but he has a blind spot where GAIA is concerned. I think someone is manipulating GAIA. I have seen files changing and we have evidence that some people have been moving through the project buildings even though GAIA has no record. On other occasions we have witnesses who see people leaving their quarters when GAIA registers them as being in their quarters. I am concerned that one of the techs is accessing the system and deleting information, or has written a code hack that allows them to control what GAIA registers.'

'Hal, that just can't be right. GAIA records *everything*. I have checked the code over dozens of times to ensure there are no errors or omissions. I haven't been able to find anything. All code that is injected into GAIA is double verified and supervised before upload to avoid mistakes. We check all uploads meticulously.'

'I am not suggesting that you are not careful,' said Hal, 'I am suggesting that someone has modified the code without authorisation and is using it to subvert the project.'

Ruby was stony-faced.

'I hope you are not suggesting that I have done this, because I will tell you right now I work damned hard to ensure that everything we do is by the book.'

Hal held his hands up.

'No, I am certainly not suggesting you have done anything wrong, but I think you could help me find out who has. Do you have any way to track who changes the code and when?'

Ruby's expression softened a little.

'I will need to check this with Jeffrey first, but of course we monitor what changes and when it changes. We must be able to track it in case a change has unintended consequences and we need to roll it back.'

'So you have a log of who accessed the source code and when – does that include what was modified?'

'Yes, of course. But I still have to check with Jeffrey.'

Hal paused for a few seconds.

'Ruby, I really need you not to tell Jeffrey, he is... blinkered. I'm sorry, he is so sure this cannot be a software problem that he won't provide rational evidence to support his theory.'

Ruby was reluctant, before realising she really had no other options.

'Okay, I will do it, but if Jeffrey finds out you must explain that you gave me no choice and forbade me from letting him know.'

Hal agreed. He proceeded to outline the information he was looking for, and the dates and times he was interested in.

Hal focused on other aspects of the investigation for the next few weeks to give Ruby some space to find the answers he needed. While he could be patient, he was tired of playing Jeffrey's game and was finding the waiting incredibly difficult. He set his mind to following every trail until there was either a dead end or nothing more to find – nothing linked to Jeffrey.

When Ruby finally got back to Hal he felt both excitement and trepidation. If she had told Jeffrey what he had asked, there would be no way to find out what had happened. When he saw her he knew she hadn't talked to Jeffrey. She looked nervous and a little gaunt, like she had not had enough food or sleep for several weeks. He brought her a drink and some food and sat considering what he was about to discover as she ate. Hal waited for her to finish before he spoke.

'Tell me, then. What did you find?'

Ruby gave him a hard look.

'Hal, I thought you were mad when you asked me to do this. I was certain that all the project techs were innocent, but it did make sense that someone in the programming team could be involved. What have you started? Do you know where this is leading?'

She sounded scared.

'Ruby, what did you find?'

'I looked at every code injection and who authorised it and there seemed to be no pattern. Then I found some metadata streams that didn't fit with the normal programme modification routines. Now there are only a few people who have the access and skill to do that – I am one, Jeffrey is another, plus about ten other programmers on this project who could do it. That got me wondering why someone would want to inject code invisibly. While you have one explanation, I wanted to see what other explanations there could be. I didn't like the thought that someone might be tampering, I have worked with these people for years and as far as I can tell they are all good people. So I reconfigured the monitoring protocol to look specifically for the source of the code injection and I got a result.'

Hal could feel his heart pounding. Perhaps this was it.

'Who was it?'

'This was the first time I knew for certain that someone was doing what you had suggested. The trace revealed that I had injected the code, which I knew was not right. That meant someone has not only been injecting code into the project, but potentially they have also spent time setting me up to take the blame. I checked first if there was any other evidence that led to me, since I know it wasn't me! As it happens there was nothing else leading to me so there was no one setting me up for a nasty surprise, so I suspect that whoever it was found my snoop. That reduces the list of who is capable of this. About half of the programmers on that list are capable of finding the snoop I set, and of that group there are only four, including me, who would be able to programme around the snoop. That left three possibles, including Jeffrey.'

Hal forced himself to be patient, he was eager to hear the conclusion, but knew he had to let Ruby tell her story.

'So what did you find?'

'I was digging into the base code to see what the injected code would do. Talk about being careful what you ask!'

Ruby went silent for a while and Hal could tell she was trying to compose herself. She seemed on the edge of tears, really upset at whatever revelation was coming.

'Hal, when I got into the code I realised it had been specifically set to ignore the movements of a limited number of people after eight at night and before seven in the morning on cameras leading to and from the staff quarters here in the research location. Only one of those people was a programmer. When I interrogated the programme code, there was only one person who was consistently ignored: Jeffrey Briar. But then as I watched, the code shifted. At first I thought someone was rewriting the code as I watched, but I checked, Hal, no one injected any code at that time. That leaves one option. GAIA rewrote its own code and added another control reference besides Jeffrey. I don't know how to write that type of code, in fact I don't think anyone knows how to write code that can do that. Whoever this is must have placed such strong protection protocols for themself that once GAIA realised what I was up to it modified its own code to cover their tracks. Hal, do you understand what this means?'

'Jeffrey has covered his tracks hasn't he?' said Hal.

'I didn't find evidence it was Jeffrey, just that he was the only person consistently ignored. But it's not just that, I am really scared, this suggests that GAIA is self-aware and protecting whoever has control. We would not want the Humans to be self-aware, but that is nothing compared to GAIA becoming self-aware.'

'Okay, but now we just arrest Jeffrey and it's done. I have him!' said Hal.

Ruby jumped to her feet and paced the room.

'No, Hal, you don't get it. If GAIA is *self-aware* and protecting Jeffrey... have you forgotten what the Swarm Project is all about? If we arrest him, we take on GAIA, complete with highly trained soldiers, heavy bioweapons and state of the art battlefield logistics and planning. We need to know who else has control of the swarm; just arresting Jeffrey won't eliminate the risk, even if GAIA doesn't activate the swarm to protect him. Arresting Jeffrey would be suicide and who knows what he or whoever else has access to control the swarm will do next? What do you think they are trying to achieve?'

Hal felt a cold chill run down his spine. If Jeffrey was at the centre of this he needed to think carefully about his next move.

'I don't know, that's what I need to find out.'

'I'm not sure I want to know. Jeffrey has been difficult when I just thought he was odd. If he is odd and dangerous, I just want to be out of his way. Think about it, if he has helped someone to subvert the controls intended to be built into GAIA by deliberately excluding himself from the monitoring protocols, what is he doing that can't be seen by the cameras? That makes him exempt from any censure and has unprecedented levels of access and control to the swarm. In essence he can now get GAIA to do as he wishes, with little more than a thought. Why would you do that with the control system for the deadliest weapon known to Elfinnim? He has made no secret of his desire for speed in completing the project, but I don't take any comfort from that. What is he up to?'

Hal needed to think about the implications of Ruby's analysis.

'If I warn the Grand Council, there is a problem – will it be detected by GAIA's communication algorithms? If it is and he turns the swarm loose, it's a disaster!'

'Yes. That is the whole point of GAIA. It is intended to run the battle by knowing what both sides are up to. We need to be smarter than that, getting ourselves killed won't help anyone. There's something else I noticed.'

'What was that,' he asked, recognising instinctively this was not good news.

'The swarms are on the move. On the face of it they are just normal rotations, but when you look closely, the elite units are circling closer to the compound. We would never concentrate so many individual units of a particular type in one location, it is against GAIA's programming and safety interlocks. No, someone must have ordered GAIA to make these personnel movements, and everyone who works on this project knows that shouldn't be possible without a secondary sign-off. No one has unilateral authority to concentrate units like this, and no one has any recollection of authorising the movements. That means someone has hacked the system to make it look like a routine transfer.'

'Did you manage to get any evidence I can use?' Hal asked quietly.

'Not much. There is some evidence, but I think it will erase itself if reconnected to GAIA. You can review it on your personal computer, but there is a risk, I don't know what capabilities the software has. There may be an embedded virus that can run independently of GAIA – don't forget that GAIA is designed to wage war on all fronts and in all formats.'

Hal now had to tread carefully. It was one thing to take on whoever was behind this – after all he was only one man – but if he was taking on Jeffrey while he had control of GAIA... no, it couldn't be done, they would be slaughtered. He would have to find another way.

'Ruby, are you sure that GAIA rewrote the code and it wasn't a fresh injection of code to add a conspirator?'

'I'm glad you have brought that up. Yes I am sure it was GAIA. All code injected into GAIA has a terminal and operator reference, without which GAIA's programming should refuse to accept the code. I verified all the terminal logs for that period and there were no injections of code from anyone.'

'Can you tell who has been added to the control code?'

'No, it certainly doesn't match any Elfinnim working in the project, but it occurred to me that it might be 1-73.'

'And was it?'

'No, Hal, it wasn't, so I widened the search for any prototype – still no matches. It didn't make sense, so I got the DNA code from GAIA and there were some big worries in there. I am no expert, but this DNA code looks significantly modified compared to Elfinnim DNA files on record. The code extracted from GAIA was clearly four-strand, so it is Elfinnim, but someone needs to look at it. This is not my area of expertise, but I am sure there are missing sequences. Is there anyone you know in the project who could confirm if I am reading it right? I know there are experts in genetic sequencing, but I don't trust anyone and I don't want Jeffrey to notice what I am doing.'

Hal smiled.

'I know someone. Can you give me the data?'

Ruby took a tablet from her bag and entered commands that linked a data cube to the tablet. Thirty seconds later she gave Hal the data cube.

'Here you go, that's all of the data on the altered injected code that I have. Hal, I am in over my head. This could change everything and I don't know what to do, so can I ask a favour?'

'Sure what do you want?'

'Will you tell me if the DNA is Elfinnim or from the swarm. Because if that DNA profile is from the swarm we have a major issue. I know that they are not supposed to have four DNA strands, they are only supposed to have two. If that DNA is from a swarm prototype they are mutating and we need to exterminate every last mutation. I know enough to be afraid of a mutated Human.'

'You really are asking a lot there.'

Ruby was about to interrupt, but Hal held his hand up and continued.

'*If*, and I mean *if* I agree to tell you, you cannot tell anyone else. You would be included in a small group of people who would know. If it became general knowledge I am worried that we would have people running for the exit. If this problem exists we must resolve it quickly and quietly before working out if there is a special cause or if the swarm has spontaneously developed a mutagen.'

'Hal, I am not scared of much, but this really scares me; that said, I agree, mass panic won't help us, we need to keep this knowledge limited and contain the threat here and now. I don't like it, but I will do it.'

'In that case you have my word, once I am certain what the origin of this DNA is I will tell you what we know.'

'Thanks, Hal, at least that way I will know how afraid I should be.'

Hal took the data cube straight down to the labs. Mike Holmes was drinking coffee and listening to music on headphones while he worked. Hal knocked on the door and got no response, then called Mike's name and still got no response. Finally he stood in front of Mike and waved at him.

'Oh, hi Hal, sorry about that, I use music to help me concentrate. What can I do for you?'

'I got hold of an extracted DNA code from GAIA. It's keyed to the central control systems and appears to have a wide ranging command and control function. Is there any way you can analyse the code...'

'...to work out who has control of GAIA?' Mike finished Hal's sentence for him. 'Possibly. Do you have the code with you?'

Hal handed Mike the data cube.

'Where did you get this?'

'I can't reveal that, I am sorry but I must protect the source of this code, it would be dangerous for my source if I let anyone know their name.'

'Okay, given what is at stake, I understand. Let's see now, what have we got?'

As Mike looked through the code his expression changed from interested to slightly concerned. Suddenly Mike looked ill.

'What have you found?' Hal asked quietly.

Mike now had a panicked look on his face.

'It's from one of the swarm, but I have seen this sequence before on one of the DNA sequences I pulled from the instruments. Whoever changed the database either didn't have access to the original instrument records or didn't think anyone would ever notice and check if the system records matched.'

Hal could hear the building panic in Mike's voice. Whatever he'd found had terrified him.

'Mike, just calm down and focus, which prototype did the DNA match?'

'1-73. It matched 1-73! I was worried when I tracked down the mutation, but it now has control of the swarm. We need to find that thing and kill it, it has to be stopped, we can't possibly let this get full control of the swarm, can't let it get control, no, no, it can't be!'

'MIKE! STOP!' Hal shouted.

Mike stopped raving and just stared at Hal.

'Mike, you have to calm down, if we panic now we really will lose control. I suspect that 1-73 doesn't know it has full control – we would have had far more problems by now if it did. Why would GAIA interpret this as a reasonable genetic code for control? Isn't GAIA's control function programmed to only work with Elfinnim DNA?'

Mike took a shuddering breath and closed his eyes before exhaling slowly. Hal waited for him to regain control. When Mike opened his eyes and looked at Hal again, he was back in control, still shaken, but in control.

'GAIA is programmed to only accept Elfinnim DNA, the problem with this sample is that it is so close to Elfinnim, it is practically indistinguishable. It is defective Elfinnim DNA, so GAIA should have rejected the sample. I can't imagine why GAIA would accept it.'

'So think, Mike, what would make GAIA accept it?'

'For GAIA to accept this sample as DNA it would have to... no that's preposterous, no one would do that.'

'Do what?'

'The only thing that might fool GAIA into accepting the DNA sample would be if it were an almost exact match to someone already in the project. It would need to be close enough to look like a genetic mutation, except we know that Elfinnim DNA does not mutate – but GAIA might not have been programmed with that knowledge. It is something so obvious we might not have realised we need to tell GAIA.'

'Okay, but I don't understand why that is preposterous.' said Hal.

'The only way it could be close enough is if the Elfinnim in question were either a sibling...'

'...or a parent.' Hal finished Mike's sentence this time, and finally understood what had Mike so worried. The implications of what had been happening here were not just sordid, this was perverse and just so plain wrong that it was unthinkable. It seemed that they now had to consider the most unpalatable of possibilities. If an Elfinnim was disturbed enough to be siring children on the prototypes, not only did they have half-breeds in the swarm, they were also half-breeds sired by a deeply flawed Elfinnim. While their DNA did not mutate once fixed, that did not mean genetic anomalies did not occur. They were rare and had a wide range of symptoms. However, the genetic screening that all Elfinnim underwent as children identified them before being taken into care at special facilities. One of the most common flaws was a limited life span. Defective DNA usually resulted in childhood death before the age of 100 years.

'Mike, we need to know who this Elfinnim is, then the system should stabilise and we can track down the rogue units and terminate them without terminating the entire project. Can you reverse engineer the DNA to work out the parent's genetic code? We can then run a comparison with all Elfinnim in the project.'

'I think so, but this is complex, it will take me some time to do it. We also need to confirm that the DNA sequence really is that of 1-73. Ideally I would like a fresh sample so we can check the DNA profile and match it. Meanwhile I want to check the instrument logs and see if there are any other replaced DNA profiles.'

'Good idea, Mike, as frightening as this information has been we seem to be making progress here and hopefully we can start to identify the rogues. Once we know which bloodlines are contaminated we can eradicate the contamination and see what is left.'

Hal was asleep when the first alarm was raised. He worried initially there was a fire or maybe an attack, but it rapidly became clear that the alarm had been deliberately triggered to get everyone's attention.

Hal found Amelia, Alfie and Jeffrey in the communications room. Jeffrey, standing separately, was shaking slightly.

'What happened?' asked Hal.

'Something impossible!' replied Jeffrey. 'We have been contacted by 1-73, it used GAIA to get in touch.'

'Why would that be impossible? Isn't that what the system is designed to do?'

'Yes, and no,' said Jeffrey. 'Yes, the system was designed to allow two-way communication through GAIA, that is necessary to ensure mission objectives can be updated in real time. This is not supposed to be possible!'

Jeffrey hit the replay button. A grainy image of a woman appeared on the big screen, not excessively beautiful, in fact ordinary looking, the sort of woman who would be passed without notice. Hal realised that was one factor which made the Humans perfect for infiltration, they were... ordinary, apparently unexceptional.

'Can you hear me?' asked the woman. 'I should tell you I can see you all, just as you can see me. I raised the alarm to get you into the control room. Jeffrey and I know each other intimately, but I haven't been introduced to you two.'

Alfie's response came through on the recording.

'Never mind who we are, who are you and how did you get access to this channel?'

'I see that you are going to be rude, no change there for an Elfinnim. You call me 1-73, but my name is Emily. I was designed to access this channel, you should not be surprised that I can do something you spent my entire life teaching me to do. Now it's your turn to listen to me.'

Hal could hear Alfie whisper something on the recording and realised that he had just issued an instruction to give a self-destruct sequence via GAIA. Quick thinking. The woman in the recording laughed, but without humour.

'It's a bit late for that don't you think? I disabled those controls long ago, at least I now know who you are, Alfie Khan, although I hadn't realised you were promoted. That must mean you are Angela... no wait, you are Amelia, what did you do with Angela?'

Jeffrey responded.

'Angela had to go back to Elfinn for debriefing after you went missing... Emily. Who controls what you do now?'

Emily glared into the camera.

'I control what I do now, I am free from your control.'

Hal felt the hair on the nape of his neck rise, but it took him a second to work out why. Then he realised that all noise from the swarm had stopped. It was eerily quiet, and when Hal glanced at the monitor every creature he could see was staring straight at the camera.

'I've made my point,' Emily continued. 'You didn't really think I had come on site to set the alarm off did you? Now I have a message for you. I am coming for you, Jeffrey, and I will kill you for what you have done.'

'Did you just do that?' Amelia asked.

'Do what?' Emily replied. 'I am not under your control and I don't have to answer your questions anymore. Remember, Jeffrey, I am coming for you. Don't sleep too deeply...'

The connection terminated right there. No wonder Jeffrey looked scared. 1-73 had already proven to be a formidable killer.

'Jeffrey, what is this about?' asked Hal. 'Why did 1-73 say it will kill you? What have you done?'

Jeffrey started to panic, sweat was running down his face.

'I... I don't know... I haven't done anything. We have to track her down and kill her, we can't let Emily get in here.'

'Jeffrey, I understand why you are rattled, but why has it singled you out?'

Hal deliberately reverted to referring to 1-73 as an object rather than a person.

Jeffrey looked stunned, as if the reality of the threat had only just hit home.

'We can't control it, can we?' asked Jeffrey quietly.

'No, 1-73 has been one step ahead every time. It's as if it is an Elfinnim, not a facsimile of an Elfinnim. Some of the tactics that have been used are worthy of any of our military commanders. What I can't work out is how it developed such a command of our tactics and capabilities. It's becoming more than its programming. Jeffrey, how can that happen, I know there is an element of learning in the AI programming, but did you programme this much capability into the system?'

Jeffrey shouted back at Hal.

'No I didn't! This not only should not be possible, there are failsafes in the system to prevent it happening. Someone must have sabotaged the programming. Perhaps instead of focusing on me, you should be looking at the other programmers to see who is manipulating the code and why!'

'Actually, I have been looking at your programmers,' replied Hal coolly. 'I have examined how and when the code was altered and it seems there is a back door into the software that allows invisible changes of code. You designed the core code, didn't you? How could there be a back door that you don't know about?'

Jeffrey was sweating again. Hal was right, and Jeffrey just didn't know how to get out of this one. The net was tightening. Between Hal and this damned prototype, he really needed to implement his plan soon, the questions were not going away and he had a feeling that Hal was getting closer. This threat from 1-73 should not have been possible.

Jeffrey cleared his throat. 'Hal, I did design the core software, but I am not the only programmer on the team. Someone is sabotaging the project for their own ends. I can't prove I didn't do something and so far you haven't presented any evidence that I have done anything wrong. The difference is no one can prove something didn't happen, not doing something doesn't leave any evidence. Now you either need to bring some evidence forward that shows my guilt or put your efforts into finding the person who is guilty.'

Jeffrey walked out.

Hal said, 'This is really frustrating. I have evidence, but presenting it puts us all at risk. I know Jeffrey is unstable, and I am pretty sure that he is at the heart of this. I suspect what his motives are, but we need to find a way to close the back door into the software and root out all the modifications he has put in.'

'That's the first time you have been so certain,' said Amelia. 'What have you discovered that makes you sure now?'

'I had some help looking into the code and they found out that someone has been secretly modifying the code from the outset. However, we don't know what are they going to do at the end. It has to be him, Amelia. Until I know what he intends to do, it's like having a child with a gun. We need to work out his motives.'

'Hal,' she said, 'what if he wants to take over? What if he wants to use the weapon we created to defend the Grand

Council, against the Grand Council. They humiliated him when he applied to be project director; they weren't unfair exactly, but they didn't give him the benefit of the doubt either. He was furious afterwards and said one day he would make sure they regretted the way they had treated him. I thought he meant that he would prove his ability. It was one of the reasons I took the project director role, to give Jeffrey freedom to prove himself; it would make no difference to me, but would put Jeffrey on track to be a project director in the future. We need to look at the current positions of all known assets, if that is his plan he needs to take over this facility to get control of GAIA.'

Hal had already weighed this up and had deliberately not raised the spectre with the others since the prospect of civil war was too terrifying to contemplate. The disappearance of 1-73 had alerted the Grand Council to problems in the heart of the project. However, Hal's task was not simply to terminate the project, that would have been easy. No, he had to find a way to neutralise whoever was manipulating the project and salvage everything possible. Hal knew that Jeffrey was a blood relative to the supreme head of the Grand Council. Now the truth was out and it was only a matter of time before Jeffrey realised that Hal and the Grand Council knew what he was doing; Hal now knew the full capabilities of the Swarm Project and it chilled him more than an ice storm on Elfinn. In the hands of the Grand Council this weapon was vicious and dangerous. In the hands of someone as unstable as Jeffrey Briar it could be fatal to the Elfinnim.

'Amelia, there is more. I don't know if Mike has fed back to you yet, but he has discovered that 1-73 is a genetic mutation, one that was deliberately covered up.'

'How much of a mutation?'

'The DNA sequence Mike discovered on one of the instruments was heavily mutated. I doubt if 1-73 has yet worked out everything it is capable of, but that is just a matter of time and need.'

Amelia sensed that there was more bad news and was more than a little frustrated that Mike had told Hal but not given her the same information.

'What else did he discover? I think there is more that you haven't told me.'

'There is more. GAIA has also rewritten its own code for the back door control and given full access to a second individual. It's 1-73. 1-73 has access to all swarm functions.'

Amelia's legs felt weak and she sat down heavily. This was the worst possible news.

'Okay, we have to shut this down until we regain control. We need to put all of the swarm into cryosleep and then work through their DNA profiles and terminate any units with more than two DNA strands.'

'Amelia, we can't do that. We think GAIA has been programmed to protect Jeffrey, and by extension it is now protecting 1-73. If we start shutting down the swarm and putting it into cryosleep we risk precipitating a reaction we can't cope with; GAIA may respond to that as a threat to Jeffrey or 1-73 and activate the swarm. You know we are too few to defeat them. Control was always the key to the project.'

'So what do you suggest?'

'I am working on that at the moment. We need to know for certain if this other DNA belongs to 1-73. The reason I am sceptical is simply because there have been so many false routes in this investigation I am concerned that this could be another distraction.' Hal paused. 'There is one more thing you are not going to like.'

'Now what?' What could be worse than what she had just heard?

Hal decided that the easiest way to do this was to be blunt.

'The second DNA set in the system for 1-73 is four-strand DNA. 1-73 has full Elfinnim DNA.'

Amelia had known that 1-73 was different, she knew that it had mutated, but full Elfinnim DNA? There was only one way that could happen.

'But that would have to mean that at least one of her parents was a full Elfinnim. Surely you aren't suggesting an Elfinnim would have sexual intercourse with a prototype?'

The concept was repugnant. One of their primary instincts was to reproduce exclusively with their own. This was a core part of their beliefs, even though they had no idea it was a clever piece of genetic programming by the makers to ensure the bloodlines remained pure, so that their regenerative properties were preserved. Giving them four strands of DNA made it harder to share genetic material with other lifeforms, but it also allowed more space for coding genetic instructions. Much of what Elfinnim saw as a learned response was in fact genetic programming. Offspring were pre-programmed from birth, since certain attitudes and in some cases the learning that underpinned and reinforced those attitudes was carried within the DNA as a genetic memory.

Amelia was horrified at the prospect. Who could be so perverse as to sire offspring with these creatures? For sure she was interested in the potential applications of the genetic studies, but that was different, using these creatures as experiments to advance the Elfinnim species was a far cry from actually having sex with one of them. Sure they looked like us, moved like us, but that was where the similarities stopped, or at least it had been.

'How many more are there, Hal?'

'We don't know, the records have been falsified and disrupted so Mike is having to go back to the original DNA instrument records and then cross-check against the reported results to track how many there are.'

'That could take years; has Mike got enough resource?'

'We can't bring in any more people. We can't risk this knowledge getting out or people will panic and try to get home. In the confusion who knows how many Humans would escape and if their DNA is close enough to fool GAIA – then it would not be picked up anywhere.'

'Is anyone working on a code revision to restore control of GAIA?' asked Amelia.

'Not yet. But I know someone who can, and I will ensure they do.'

Hal arranged to meet Ruby a couple of days later. She walked into Hal's apartment and before he could speak, she held a finger to her lips. Hal was puzzled but kept quiet as she pulled a gadget from the bag and turned it on. She quietly went around the apartment and seemed satisfied until she walked in front of the comms screen. As she did, she noticed something indicate on the gadget. She moved again and sure enough there was another reaction. She waved Hal over and showed him the reading.

He instinctively understood the problem and gestured for Ruby to follow him.

They left his living quarters and headed for the arboretum. One of the requirements for access to the arboretum was surrender of all comms devices and electronics, so after putting all of their devices in lockers, they walked some way into the arboretum before starting to talk.

'Ruby, I promised to let you know what we found out about the DNA. This is your last chance, do you really want to know?'

'I have to know, I am not sure I want to, but I need to know.'

'Okay, here we go then. The DNA sequence you found matches a trace on one of the DNA instruments which was identified as 1-73's.'

'I had already guessed that much. What else?'

'The DNA sequence is full Elfinnim. 1-73 is a full mutation, but the only way that could have happened is for it to have a full Elfinnim sire.'

Ruby felt sick, this was worse than she could have imagined. Mutations were one thing, but an Elfinnim getting one of those things pregnant was beyond perverse. It could not be from a female Elfinnim since pregnancies were so rare it would have been noticed.

'What are we going to do?' she asked.

'I need something more from you, and I don't think I need to tell you what is at stake here. We are either heroes or dead, there are no half measures in this.'

'What do you need?'

'We need to inject some code into GAIA which stops it recognising threats to Jeffrey or 1-73. If we can be sure the swarm will not respond, we can put them into cryosleep. From there we can run DNA testing on all of the prototypes and destroy any mutations and see what we have left.'

'That is a lot more difficult than you think, Hal. There are security protocols within GAIA that check injected code and sandbox anything that looks harmful. Whatever I create has to look harmless and function as a virus when uploaded.'

'The advantage you have is that you know what the security algorithms are and how they function, so you know what they are looking for. That's half the battle, the other half is to avoid tripping the protocols when uploading the virus.'

Ruby was quiet as they walked. Although the situation was hopeless on the surface, she loved a challenge, and challenges didn't get bigger than this. If she succeeded and survived there was every chance she would be noticed by the Grand Council and that could result in some interesting projects. If she failed, it wouldn't really matter anyway, chances are she would be dead. She felt her heart pound in fear. Elfinnim were used to immortality, death was not a concept they enjoyed contemplating. She wondered how Hal dealt with the fatalism that accompanied being warrior caste; she was sure she could not face it as he did.

'Okay, Hal, I will try, but if Jeffrey finds out what I am doing you must promise to protect me.'

'I will do my best, but I can't promise to succeed. My intention is to get as many people out of this alive as I can, but one of the risks you signed up to in this project was loss of control and potential death.'

'I know,' she said, 'but no one really believes it will come to that. If I survive, I will look for a much safer project next time, that's for sure.'

'There are a couple more things you should know. 1-73 has made contact with the control room and threatened to kill Jeffrey. It seems to be particularly focused on him, but I have no doubt that it will kill everyone and everything that gets between it and him. In addition, we are either wrong about 1-73 having control of GAIA, or it doesn't realise yet how much control it has. I don't know which is of more concern, frankly neither option is good.'

Ruby thought to herself, 'This just keeps getting better,' but she said nothing. What could she say? They were literally in a fight for their lives now. There were three possibilities: Jeffrey was working with the mercenaries and they now had control of the swarm; Jeffrey was working with a partner and they both had control of the swarm; or Jeffrey was working alone and didn't know that the swarm was self-governing.

Take your pick from doomed by viciousness, doomed by greed or really doomed by incompetence. The only common thread was far from comforting, every option had them doomed.

'I will do my best,' she said, 'I don't have any other choice really, do I?'

'No, none of us do.'

Liz, the head of engineering, was still trying to track down the engineer who had rigged the comms system in Amelia's quarters. She was certain it had been rigged by a comms engineer. Some of the connections and fine adjustments could only be done by someone who knew how and why the system was configured. Liz had narrowed it down to four possible engineers, but could not imagine a set of circumstances that would lead any of them to do this.

Liz continued discovered that there was both camera and witness evidence that proved two of the engineers were working in other parts of the compound on the day the bugs had to be placed. Their movements and timings when compared to Amelia's meant they could not possibly have planted the bugs. So now she had a choice between two people. There was only one way to sort this out, she would have to shake them both and see what dropped out. The first interview was with Danny Andrews.

'Danny, we have a problem. Someone has been planting secret observation devices in personal quarters.'

'That's terrible,' he replied. 'Do we have a voyeur or is it more serious than that?'

'It's far more serious than that,' she said. 'The level of skill required to set it up is such that the perpetrator could only have been a comms engineer.'

'Hang on, you don't want me to help you find out who did this do you? You think I did it!' Danny was furious. 'I am really disappointed that you think I would do this, Liz, after all the years we have worked together I would hope you know me better than that. I really can't believe you think I would betray you and the project in this way.'

The vehemence of Danny's denial and the obvious hurt he felt reassured Liz. She didn't think that he had planted the bugs, which is why she tackled him first.

'Okay, Danny, here are the dates and time ranges we believe the comms were sabotaged.'

Liz passed him a tablet.

'Liz, I was in the gym. Check the logs and ask the instructors. I had a session with a personal trainer.'

She took the tablet back and checked the gym logs. Sure enough, Danny was checked in and had a training session. It was possible that he could have accessed Amelia's and Hal's quarters from the Gym, but not if he was working with a personal trainer.

'I will look into this, I need to check that the personal trainer remembers you, but I believe you. That means that I have to look harder at someone else. Keep this discussion confidential and we will talk again in a day or two.'

'Liz, I am happy to help, but I expect an apology when you see I have told you the truth. I have to say I am dissatisfied with this whole situation. I resent the accusation and I don't like the fact that you don't trust me.'

'I hear you,' Liz said, 'and if your story checks out I will apologise. Until then just do your job and stick to your normal routine.'

Next, Liz called in Jess Price.

'Jess, we have a problem, someone has been planting secret observation devices in personal quarters.'

Jess jumped straight in.

'It wasn't me.'

'I didn't say you did anything,' Liz replied. 'Why are you so defensive?'

'You are accusing me of something I didn't do!' Jess said indignantly.

'What have I accused you of?'

'You said I modified the comms set in Dr...' Jess stopped herself, but not quickly enough. Her skin became pallid and a sheen of sweat appeared on her brow.

'Actually, no I didn't. I didn't say anything about a modified comms unit. I said someone was planting secret listening devices, I didn't say where, or how... or in whose quarters. So now I know who planted these things, I think it's time you told me what is going on here. I want to know what on Elfinn you think you were doing, and I want to know NOW!'

Liz slapped the table. Jess jumped. As she considered her options her eyes filled with tears. Liz was silent and let Jess cry.

After a few minutes she said quietly, 'Jess, tell me what is going on here.'

'I had just joined the project. I was told to modify some wiring in the system, but there wasn't a work order. I was about to ask you about it when I got a call from someone, they said if I told you they would know and that in telling you I would have killed my family. I had no choice, I had to do as they asked, no one has ever threatened my family before.'

Jess cried again and Liz gave her a tissue.

'Okay, this is quite a tale; go on, what happened next?'

Liz was sceptical, Elfinnim did many things, but threats to kill family were unheard of.

'I thought I could escape if I put in for a transfer to another project. Shortly after the request was put through Angela Galvano paid me a visit. She told me that someone powerful had decided that I would not be transferred and that I should be quiet and do as I was told if I knew what was good for me. She told me if I didn't drop the transfer request, neither me nor my partner would leave the planet alive. Ever since then I have tried to avoid notice and have done what they told me to do.'

'Who was Angela working for?'

'I don't know,' Jess sobbed. 'But I do know that Angela was scared of whoever gives the orders. What happens now?'

'The first thing is you are going to prison while we work out how to track down the real architect of this mess. And I will be reporting this to Dr Charter and Mr Balal. No doubt they will want to talk to you too.'

Jess's bottom lip quivered.

'Please protect my family, Liz, I am so sorry I let you down. To be honest I am relieved it is out in one way. I just hope they don't punish my family; please don't let them get hurt.'

Liz called security to take Jess down to the prison cells. They were present in every project, but rarely used. This project would be remembered for all the wrong reasons now, two prisoners from within the project! Liz reached for the phone to call Amelia.

9

ANOTHER POINT OF VIEW

Unit 1-73-9.7.3310, or Emily as she preferred to think of herself, had tried to do as she was told and avoid drawing attention from the overseers. She listened and learned as she was programmed, occasional queries were contained until she could ask one of the named Humans and life seemed settled. Yes, she was a little more aware than some of the others, but she still felt that she was part of the GAIA collective. When she was fourteen that had changed one brutal night when she had learned one of the more terrifying secrets about their existence.

She had been sent for her rest period and was just settling down to sleep when an overseer she did not recognise came for her. He unlocked the door of her room and ordered her to follow him. Since Emily was not supposed to have anything in her mind that wasn't provided by GAIA, she complied. What followed took all of her courage to control. She was taken to the room of the Elfinnim in charge of the overseers. He was cold and impersonal from the outset.

'Ah, good, you are here,' he said. 'Take your clothes off.'

The request seemed strange but she complied. Humans had to obey every instruction given by an Elfinnim without question. The Elfinnim prepared himself a drink and sat down, just looking at her.

'Turn around slowly,' he told her. She turned around three times before he told her to stop.

'Cup your breasts and play with your nipples.'

Emily was uncomfortable with this but did it to show she was compliant.

He then undressed himself and started to masturbate while watching her. Emily knew she had a problem but her parents had told her the tales of what happened when Humans did not do exactly as they were told. So she did as she was told.

Then he raped her. She retreated into her mind and used the anti-interrogation techniques she had been taught to get through the ordeal. Later the guard came to get her and returned her to her room. She waited until she was alone and cried herself to sleep. The next time she got time alone with her mother, Sophie, she told her what had happened and learned a hard truth. Emily was not the first by a long way. Sophie was abused in exactly the same way, the only consolation she could offer was that he would lose interest by the time she was twenty-one. Up to seven years of this was unthinkable, but her mother explained that trying to speak out had always resulted in an unexplained death.

This routine was followed two or three times every week for the next four years. At first she cried herself to sleep every night, and then slowly the shame and hurt was replaced by anger, then resentment and finally she resolved to learn all she could, so that when the time was right she could exact revenge. So she applied herself to her studies and secretly probed at GAIA to see if there was a way around the security protocols to control the system rather than having the system control her.

She set firm in her mind that one day she would escape and pay the overseer back for all the hurt he had caused her. That day wasn't today, but one day she would be free and then she would see if the overseers liked not having choices. But for now she needed to focus on learning to be as deadly as possible so that she was ready when the time came.

At first she could not see any way through GAIA's defences, but gradually she pieced together the overseer's identity by tracking the room she was taken to and cross referencing with GAIA's personnel logs. She also discovered the identity of the guards who took her to her 'appointments' and that the cards they used to unlock the doors were not registered in any system. It was while probing in this way that she came across a dormant subroutine that did not have any apparent purpose. It took weeks of playing with the code inside GAIA to work out it was a secret way to access the software code, but it required access to a biodata scanner to activate the function.

It was while she was investigating whose biodata was required – although she was pretty sure she knew – that Emily discovered that Humans had a double helix DNA structure, compared to Elfinnim four-strand DNA. She also discovered that the Swarm Project was more interested in observed behaviours than specific genetic structures. Since DNA monitoring was a routine part of the control system, Emily had no reason to believe that her DNA was any different to the other Humans. She was curious though, and she had ample opportunity to obtain Elfinnim genetic material, thanks to his sexual proclivities. Part of her training was stealth access to real environments. So during one of her training missions she accessed the genetics lab and analysed both her own and the Elfinnim's genetic code.

The first surprise was discovering that her DNA was four-strand, although certain DNA sequences were completely absent. It transpired that her DNA and the overseer's DNA was a forty-eight per cent match. Two things didn't make sense. Firstly, Humans had only two DNA strands – Humans already knew this since Elfinnim talked as though they could not understand what they said, or they simply did not care what the Humans understood. What they did not realise was that the Humans paid attention to what was said and compared what they had heard separately. As a result the Humans knew that they were part of the experiment but were not sure exactly what an experiment was. Secondly, Emily's DNA was a partial match to the Elfinnim's. How could that be?

Whatever the reason, it proved to be a useful discovery. Her DNA was a close enough match to trigger access to GAIA's core functions, which turned into a gold mine of information. Once inside GAIA's functions, Emily found that having a mental link into the system enabled her to transfer information straight to her consciousness. The result was an explosive intellectual growth that she had to work hard to conceal from the overseers and Elfinnim. Quite quickly she also found the project within the project. She discovered that the Elfinnim's name was Jeffrey Briar and that his sexual proclivities were definitely not part of their socially accepted behaviours. She also discovered that they were called Elfinnim because they were from a planet called Elfinn and that the experiment that was the whole of Human existence was something called the Swarm Project.

Emily used GAIA to track all of the nasty little blackmails that Briar was using to control people, and discovered that he was planning to take control of something called the Grand Council, but the archive did not reveal what that was. It took a long time to put all the pieces together, but eventually she realised that the whole Human race was a weapon, and that Elfinnim were afraid of their weapon. As Emily developed more understanding of the purpose and capability of Humans, she perceived that there was a way for her people to avoid their planned future, a plan that would involve firstly finding out if there were others like her and then leading them into a rebellion against the Elfinnim to become their masters' worst nightmare – a weapon they could not control.

Initially, Emily needed to find out who else shared her DNA profile. She collected blood samples from combat training and training missions, then used mission training to gain access to the laboratories and analyse the samples. It took many months to complete the analyses and establish who was most like herself. She didn't dare tell anyone what she was doing, it was too dangerous both to the person she told and to herself. The other factor that Emily had to deal with was the limited lifespan of Humans. She had discovered that Elfinnim were immortal, but Humans had been given a limited lifespan of seventy years. This was achieved through a genetic kill-switch that caused rapid onset cellular degradation, at least rapid in Elfinnim terms. Once triggered the degradation took no more than ten years to cause irreparable and irreversible damage to the host body.

Emily had to find a way to turn the trigger off. Luckily for her the kill-switch parameters were already within GAIA; gaining access to the antidote was far more difficult. Every plan she prepared to access the antidote resulted in exposing her identity. No matter how she tried to avoid it, when she ran the simulation through GAIA the result was the same – Emily was discovered or killed and the revolution she dreamed of was over before it got going. The frustration she felt while working through the scenarios was almost physical.

Eventually Emily realised that the only viable option was to embrace being caught. Planning to be caught changed the plan, and the survival rate in scenario modelling rose from two per cent to sixty per cent. Now she needed to find a way to increase her survival odds. Emily was not scared of death, however she could not accept her death when it condemned her people to short violent existences to achieve some purpose that would never make sense to them.

Finally the day came when she was ready to enact her plan. That evening the guard came to take her to her 'assignment' with Briar. It felt different. Emily knew it was the last time he would subject her to this torment. Afterwards the guard took her back to her room and left her there, believing he had done his duty and avoided whatever threat that Briar had made to him.

Once away from the compound Emily examined files more regularly using her enhanced access to limit the visibility of her investigation. Most of her requests were disguised as standard system logs. She had discovered that Elfinnim were overconfident, an attitude driven by their contempt for the individual weapons they had created. They were rightly afraid of the swarm, but were dismissive of individual Humans as a threat, a mistake for which Emily intended to make them pay. She realised she had unprecedented access to GAIA now, the rewritten code had given her access to everything the swarm did, so she knew when and where Humans would be, and even had access to all but the most confidential guard rotas and movements. She continued to seek access to those highly confidential assets, but so far with only limited success. She left Briar with apparent control for now, monitoring his commands and instructions and occasionally modifying the code to suit her plans without any obvious deviation from the original instruction. The first time she modified one of his instructions it was to shift a search pattern by a fine margin to avoid an area she would be in. She didn't sleep for twenty hours as she monitored GAIA and Jeffrey to see if she would be discovered, but nothing happened. That gave her confidence to make more significant adjustments. Each time there was no response, so she concluded that he was so confident in his control that he ignored even significant deviations from his plan. As long as the objective was achieved, he didn't care that his instructions were modified. That was a weakness she could exploit.

Alongside gaining access to all of GAIA's monitoring functions, Emily sought information on other members of the swarm. She discovered that no one had failed a genetics testing before, which was odd since she knew her own DNA was not pure – for a start there were four strands not two as in other Human test subjects. However, she also knew that her genetic scans had been replaced. Emily asked GAIA what other scan data had been replaced.

'There have been no substitutions of test results.'

Emily knew that could not be correct. She had seen the evidence of her own substituted DNA scans first-hand.

'Show records for 1-73-9.7.3310 and highlight all substitutions.'

'Records displayed as requested, there are no substitutions.'

Emily knew that was wrong.

'Show records accessed more than once and where one access cannot be traced.'

'There are thirty-six such records, all of which have been accessed from an unknown node by an unknown user.'

'Identify what changes were made to records.'

'In each case the scan was replaced due to a processing error. The processing error resulted in an inadmissible scan.'

'Is there a clear pattern identifying the nature of the processing fault?'

'Each time the processing fault has been a mixed genetic sequence due to faulty processing and contamination.'

Emily was surprised, she would have created a separate excuse for each occurrence to ensure there was no such obvious record of intrusion. Her next question to GAIA was more focused.

'How many test subjects have had mistakes made during processing of their DNA results?'

'Of the 2,352,621 test subjects used so far, 305,841 have had results rejected and replaced.'

Now Emily felt she was getting somewhere.

'Focus on the replaced test results and eliminate any of the test results that were replaced by a scientist identified as working in that area of the project.'

'Of the 305,841 test subjects for whom test result data has been replaced, 27,525 have had results replaced by unknown authorisations.'

'How many of those test subjects are currently living within the swarm?'

'There are 863 current test subjects with modified DNA data.'

'GAIA, do you have the original DNA scans for those test subjects?'

'That data is not in the system.'

Emily was encouraged. There were potentially 863 like her, but frustrated that she could not verify that they all had four-strand DNA profiles.

'GAIA, can you determine the relevant records and their locations to enable manual confirmation?'

'Information has already been transmitted to your link.'

Sure enough, Emily suddenly knew the numbers and location of every record required; it had been planted seamlessly and flawlessly in her mind.

There was only one way to know for sure, she had to go back into the compound and access the DNA sequencing instruments to check the original data. The best way to get into the compound would be at night, just as she had done many times before on training missions. She updated her information on guard rotas and sweep patterns then set off with enough supplies to get her in and out in one piece. She used a redundant swipe card number to gain access. Her logic was that no one would have reported the cards missing since they officially did not exist. She was correct, and moved without incident through the compound and into the test laboratories. GAIA monitored the position of every other Human and Elfinnim, telling her when to move and when to stay so she remained invisible. Unlike her previous training missions, getting caught on this one would result in her termination.

She was able to access all of the test data she needed and exit the compound without a confrontation. While she was there Emily picked up some essential supplies to bolster those she had taken during that initial frantic flight. When she had made it back to her hideaway she did a quick inventory of supplies and information. What she had gained was for once worth the risk, at least she was now taking risks on behalf of herself and her people, fighting for something she understood.

She opened the stolen files and recognised some of the names as people she had met while being trained not to draw attention to herself, others were from different sections of the swarm, areas she had never been involved with. The question was, what could she do with this knowledge? She found out when the first set of hunter killers was sent to find her. Emily checked the designations of the units sent after her. When there was a unit with a prototype on her database she set up an encounter to try to influence the unit. Emily used GAIA to get the unit to split up and managed to isolate the prototype she needed to check. It was prototype reference 7-73-2.2.3304. Emily waited until it was separated from the other units and opened a channel through GAIA to speak to it. As she initiated contact, she noted that 7-73-2.2.3304 had no hesitation separating from GAIA and taking control of its own comms and motor skills. Emily didn't show herself at first, she just spoke.

'7-73-22.2.3304, do you have a name?'

'I am Matthew, Matt, actually. Who are you, you're not GAIA.'

'No, I am not, and you aren't like the other Humans, are you?'

'Yes, I... actually no, I suppose I am not. If I were we couldn't have this conversation, could we?'

'No, and if you were just like the other Humans, you would not recognise the difference. My name is Emily.'

'Are you 1-73-9.7.3310?'

This was the most dangerous part of her plan. If she was right about the Humans they would turn on the unit; if not, the unit would turn on her.

'Yes, Matt, I am, but like you I have a name and can think for myself. I have learned much about the Elfinnim and what we Humans are to them, just weapons. I want us to have a life, will you join me and help free our people from a future of violence and death?'

'It sounds good, but how can I know what you tell me is true?'

He made a good point. She assessed the tactical options with GAIA and realised she needed to show him the truth, so she transmitted to him everything she had discovered about the Swarm Project.

He went silent for a minute as he processed his new knowledge, then asked, 'Is this all true?'

'Yes, it is. GAIA, please confirm that the data file transferred to Matt is genuine and has not been altered.'

Matt heard GAIA for the first time as a separate entity in his head. He was vaguely aware of a new instruction set arriving in his head but it was gone before he could understand it.

'Matt, please be assured that this file is genuine. The last addition was made to this file 7.2.2687.'

He could not explain why, but Matt was convinced that GAIA was telling the truth, and if GAIA was telling the truth there was a high probability Emily was too.

'Do you know why we are here?' Matt asked Emily.

'I do, but I am hoping I can turn you into an ally instead of an enemy.'

'How do you know I won't lie to bring you into the open, then kill you?'

'I don't. But I have to start building this revolution somewhere and you are the best chance I have of survival.'

Emily emerged from the undergrowth just behind Matt. He suddenly knew she was there and realised his life depended on his next choice, so he kept still while he worked through the available information. The Elfinnim had instructed that Emily was to be terminated on sight, but had given no reason other than designating her an enemy combatant. Since weapons did not question their wielders, the Humans did as they were told. Emily had explained to Matt what she was fighting for, but not why she was so determined. GAIA confirmed the information Emily had provided. He then realised that while the Elfinnim had instructed him to kill Emily, she had given him a choice. She was the first person in his life to ask what he wanted and now that the question had been asked, he could not return to a life where he had no choices. He slowly and carefully put his weapon on the floor, then turned around.

'Emily, I think you have a point. No one ever asked me what I wanted to do before, there has been no choice except comply or die. What if I choose not to kill you, will you let me return to my unit?'

Emily was disappointed.

'If that is what you want to do, provided you do not try to turn on me now, I will let you return. You must understand, however, this is a one-time offer. If you return, next time we meet, I will kill you.'

Matt nodded and walked away, expecting to be shot. Emily was disappointed, she had hoped he would join her. When he reached the end of the clearing he stopped.

'You really would let me go wouldn't you?' he said.

'Of course, that is what we agreed.'

'In that case, I would like to stay and join with you.'

'Why have you changed your mind.'

'I haven't, but if you were as dishonest as the Elfinnim creating the swarm, I didn't want to live to be that disappointed.' Matt held out his hand. 'If you will have me, whatever is left of my life will be added to your cause, for it is now my cause too.'

Emily smiled. This was a better start than it had seemed five minutes ago.

Once Emily escaped, she had to keep moving to avoid capture. The first team sent after her was a mixture of enhanced and drone Humans. She used GAIA to link to the advanced Humans and shut them down to even the odds, then killed the drones. Then she used GAIA to communicate with the enhanced Humans and transferred everything she had learned from GAIA into their minds. The result was profound. Instead of having to argue to convince them of her explanation, they simply understood. They later explained that they could feel the truth in the information as soon as it entered their minds. She then had to find a way to mask their defection. The only way to do it was to make the killings as brutal as possible to mix the DNA to convince the Elfinnim that the entire patrol was wiped out.

The strategy worked, particularly when supported from within GAIA. Emily used her new-found access to ensure that the DNA for every enhanced Human read as two-strand DNA and that the volume of biological material matched the combined volume of the Humans sent on patrol. Now Emily was one of three and her revolution had begun.

Several more patrols were sent out and each time the same strategy was used, each time the size of the group increased and each time they were slaughtered. It broke Emily's heart to do it, but she knew that she had to sacrifice some to save the majority. Eventually they stopped sending teams, but it also seemed that they did not work out that she was not on her own, which was a fact that she needed to use to her advantage. The question was how?

Emily had returned to the compound once before. She was chasing down the DNA records at the time, it was just after she had discovered she could disconnect some people from GAIA, just by telling it to disconnect. It was strange, sometimes it worked, sometimes it didn't – she needed to know why. She had analysed the possible causes and realised that the answer had to be in everyone's DNA. If there was a genetic difference, it could explain why some could be separated from GAIA and some could not. She just didn't have enough of anything to work it out. The only way was to get the original data on the Humans, to understand why some were able to control GAIA and some were controlled by GAIA. It might also help her to understand why no one else could instruct GAIA as she could. She had by now recruited a good proportion of the Humans sent after her and had a talented band of individuals committed to saving as many Humans as possible. Emily tested every Human she recruited, but not one of them could give instructions to GAIA as she could. She selected Humans with most training and skills in data analysis, prototypes selectively trained for technology espionage, to start mining the DNA data to work out why there were differences in people's ability to interact with GAIA, and more specifically, why she could do so much more than anyone else.

She called in her confidante and first recruit to discuss how to exploit the confusion over their numbers.

'Matt, do you really believe they don't know how many of us there are?'

'It certainly seems that way. Every time I link in to GAIA there is no record of any of us beyond the mission you recruited us on. The security messages only talk about tracking you down. They are desperate to find you and believe the only way to end this is to kill you, but the losses have been too high so they have stopped sending teams.'

'That's what I have been finding too,' she replied,' 'I just wish we could have saved more of the drones. I am working on a way to free them using GAIA, but I have to work carefully, we don't want the programmers to realise what we are doing. There is a war coming and we need to be on our own side, not forced to fight on one of their sides. If they don't know how many of us there are, how can we use that lack of knowledge to overwhelm them and secure our existence?'

After a few moments Matt responded.

'There are sixty-three of us now, more than enough to get in and out of their base, but the first time we do it they will know we aren't all dead. When that happens they will unleash everything they have against us; I don't think we could cope with that.'

'I agree, so we have to even the odds. I have found a way to override control of the Human prototypes using GAIA, but as soon as we do they will need leaders or they will be slaughtered while they are still disoriented. Losing the link to GAIA will be frightening at first, until they realise they can make their own choices. We have to make sure they are safe while they get used to the idea. We have to get in and identify the others like us. Have you found a way to identify the others without blood samples and accessing the labs?'

'Yes, we have, as it happens, GAIA already knows who they are. GAIA identified an aberrant set of brain patterns many years ago amongst the Humans and marked it for investigation. There was no subversive behaviour identified, so the research was abandoned.'

'How does that help us?'

'After we came across the report, we asked GAIA to compare the brain patterns of the people you saved to the patterns of those who were killed. What was not known at the time of the original report was that Humans can choose their level of contact with GAIA if they have the aberrant brain pattern. There are degrees of aberration too, the interesting aspect of this is that we have discovered those whose brain patterns more closely match the drones find it harder to keep GAIA out of their decision-making unless their deviations from the norm are in the areas of logic and reason. Everyone whose deviation is in the cerebrum and involves the function and degree of folding in the cerebrum, particularly the frontal lobe which is where this sort of reasoning behaviour occurs. The more gyrencephalissation, or folding, of the cerebrum, the more efficiently that brain operates. If structured correctly, the part of the brain associated with logic and reason has no problem dissociating from GAIA. Once the initial break has been made, GAIA becomes a reference tool not an instructor to be slavishly followed. We found that everyone with four-strand DNA had aberrant brain patterns, everyone with two-strand did not.'

Matt smiled.

Emily was pleasantly surprised. The team had uncovered far more than she would have believed possible. The ramifications for her people were huge. They could use GAIA to search for the aberrant brain patterns, ensuring they could target the leaders effectively.

'What about turning it around and controlling GAIA?' asked Emily. 'Why am I able to do that and not anyone else?'

'We think we also have an explanation for that, but I am not sure you will be so happy about it.' Matt grimaced. 'Your DNA deviates in every aspect. You are far closer to being Elfinnim than Human.'

'We know that already, why does it make a difference?'

Emily felt Matt was dragging out the explanation.

'It seems that you have a unique set of circumstances. As you already know, we have a common genetic ancestor, which is why we all deviate, in your case you have the common genetic ancestor twice over in your system.'

'What do you mean?'

'Emily, one of the Elfinnim is both your grandfather and your father. Possibly your great grandfather and who knows how many generations this goes back.'

Emily sat down. There was one more question to ask, she knew the answer but needed to hear it from someone else.

'Who is it?'

'Come on Emily, you know,' said Matt. 'It's Jeffrey Briar.'

Emily felt sick, thinking of the abuse she had suffered and knowing the same person had inflicted that abuse on her mother and her grandmother. A burning coal of anger was ignited in her chest, she felt a new level of loathing for Briar. Elfinnim attitude to reproduction differed to Humans in that although they did not routinely reproduce with their offspring, once they were fully adult it was perfectly acceptable to engage in a full sexual relationship with their parents. The children of these relationships did not suffer from genetic degradation and abnormalities. Society had forbidden any relationship with a parent for the Humans, since the likelihood of genetic abnormalities was much higher because they had spliced out the genetic repair sequence from Human DNA. For one of the Elfinnim to break a rule that had become part of Human existence showed not only complete arrogance, but a breathtaking disregard for the Humans themselves. Any genetic deviants were supposed to be terminated soon after birth to preserve the purity of the genetic code. If Jeffrey or any of the others had done what the project required, all of the people around Emily would have been killed at birth. Under the genetic cleansing rules for the project, any pairing that resulted in repeated genetic anomalies would result in termination of the parents and the child to minimise the risk of a defective recessive gene. In short, Humans were expendable and could be treated like toys and thrown away when broken.

Matt continued.

'When we have looked at your brain scans, Emily, you have significantly more activity, and we believe, functionality. The frontal lobe and your brain is folded to a much higher density than anyone else's.'

She was more determined than ever to free Humans from this meddling in their genetics and in their lives. They had found out how to identify their recruits, the next difficulty was how to get them to understand what was required. Emily realised she had the answer, but it called for a risky mission.

'Matt, I have been working on a little programme which we could use GAIA to distribute. Do you remember how quickly you adapted when we broke GAIA's control over you?'

'Do I ever! It was like someone turned a light on, I knew instantly what I needed to do.'

'That was because we pushed two messages at once from a local transmitter, one message giving new instructions, the second breaking GAIA's control function and simulating death.'

'If we could transmit those signals through GAIA and target everyone with an aberrant brainwave pattern, we would have an instant army. There is just one problem, all the uploads to the system have to be made at a specific terminal in the compound. I have been in a couple of times to look for more DNA patterns to identify more people we can liberate to join us. Next time it will be harder to get in and out.'

'I'll go this time,' said Matt.

Emily smiled sadly.

'Matt, you can't, if you are seen they will know I am not alone and then they will send everything they have after us before we can establish control. No, I have to do this and if I don't make it back you need to lead the revolution, so we had better get some serious planning done.'

Matt checked what Emily was saying and even pinged a check to GAIA to see if there was any other option, but there wasn't.

'You are right, as usual, let's get this plan worked out and make sure there are no holes in it.'

They spent the rest of the day reviewing plans and going over scenarios planning for every eventuality, including Emily's death on her next mission. The next order of business was to plan for Emily's visit to the base. Using GAIA, they monitored guard routines, security protocols and shift patterns for different areas of the base. It took several months of monitoring and careful cataloguing by a team of people to determine how to get past the systems and gain access to GAIA's upload system. The problem remained that there had to be another reason for the break-in to give the security team something else to investigate. Misdirection would be critical to the success of this plan.

They discussed the plan endlessly and through it all the failing point was always the same, the reason for entering the base was not credible. They considered meeting up with Emily's parents, but in eighty-seven per cent of projections this ended with her parents' termination. They also considered stealing equipment from the laboratory, but anything that could be useful would be too heavy to carry, and if it could be carried it was not useful enough to risk a break-in.

They kept searching for a reason that would provide enough distraction to keep their real motives hidden, without exposing anyone else to danger. It took a long time, but eventually they found that a reason close to the truth was the best option, something that was plausible, would give Elfinnim food for thought, but would not precipitate any extreme sanction. The solution they came up with didn't give away the intended target and it didn't single out anyone in particular and therefore minimised the risk of retaliation against an individual. In fact the risk of any terminations was calculated at 7.4 per cent, which was the best outcome that they found.

Emily now knew how to get in, how to conceal what she was really doing, and how to get back out. Timing would be key, she needed to move relatively quickly to ensure that she gained control of the swarm without precipitating a massive reaction. Jeffrey Briar was dangerous, but he was going to pay for what he had done. Too many Humans had died to hide his depravities. He was too manipulative to be allowed to get anywhere near controlling the swarm. Emily knew he wanted the swarm as his private army, but his reasons were all far outside her experience. She had read about the Grand Council and Elfinn, and knew enough to understand that she had only scratched the surface of Elfinnim politics, which meant that she was in danger until Briar had been neutralised – or put another way, she was in danger until he was dead.

The remaining Elfinnim would also have to be neutralised. Emily had picked up on a weakness, she just needed to wait for confirmation that it was complete. Elfinnim were building a transport portal in the upper atmosphere. These devices required a massive local magnetic field. Once it was complete, they could not destroy it without risking the destruction of many connected portals. The potential energy created from folding space-time had to go somewhere, and while most of the energy would come straight out of this portal and destroy a proportion of the planet surface, some of the energy would be released to other portals. Elfinnim never sought to move or destroy a portal, it was too dangerous, since the released energy could create a cascade failure in the portal system. The potential loss of Elfinnim life would be huge, so every portal was equipped with a lockout that stopped anyone using the portal, preventing its destruction.

Emily smiled grimly. If only she could ensure the Humans would not be killed, she would happily destroy the portal. However, if Elfinnim were as keen to preserve life as they seemed, it might prove a useful threat to get them to leave Humans alone. Humans had to wait until the Elfinnim portal was complete and then secure the portal to ensure their existence. She also knew it would only be a matter of time before Briar triggered his plan to assume control of the swarm. Her presence was causing him to rush, he had not noticed the subtle coding change that meant his control of the swarm was conditional on Emily's continued goodwill. She could revoke his access with a thought and there really was nothing he could do about it, he just didn't know it yet.

She ran scenarios with GAIA and realised there was just one weak spot in her control: if the Elfinnim got inside GAIA's control core, they could execute a hard reset, which would limit control to a terminal at the core. She had to ensure this could not be achieved, so she set to work identifying the control measures required to limit Elfinnim access and disrupt any attempt to reset GAIA. She realised that if disruption was not an option, the Elfinnim would try to destroy GAIA to set the prototypes from all species against each other. There was much to be done to ensure GAIA was safe and under Human, not Elfinnim, control.

First, she had to work out where GAIA's control room was. Initially GAIA was vague about its exact location, it was a built-in security protocol to avoid infiltration and destruction. Emily was starting to get frustrated, then remembered that GAIA had been programmed with self-preservation functions. In order to trigger those protocols, she ran a series of scenarios looking at what would happen if Elfinnim discovered there were more Humans outside their control than just Emily. She then ran a scenario where it was discovered that Emily had control of the swarm, and another in which Jeffrey had control of the swarm. In each case one of the responses was an attempt to shut down GAIA, with a high probability of success. Emily then asked GAIA for the best protection mechanism and was surprised to learn that it was in the deepest, coldest part of the ocean to ensure that the quantum architecture worked at optimal temperature of 150 degrees above absolute zero.

The only way to reach GAIA was to take a service shuttle from the compound and attach on one of the airlocks. GAIA's world was cold, wet and anaerobic, a hostile environment for air-breathing life forms. There were protectors assigned from the swarm, which were designed to work against an attack to penetrate the outer shell, not an attack from within. Emily spent many fascinating hours studying GAIA's architecture. It was a work of twisted genius, a true silicon-based life form. An array of microprocessors had been constructed with fibre optic links and molecular switching for speed. The key decision centres used organic binary computing systems with grafted noble metal switches to enable electrical connection from the decision systems to the primary processing hub. The power of the processing unit was terabytes of data per second, vastly exceeding the intelligence that had conceived of the system. GAIA had been created to learn, and was programmed to evaluate the most probable outcome of every situation. When the course of action had been decided, GAIA monitored the outcome and compared it to the probabilities calculated. In this way the probabilities were adjusted for future decisions and GAIA learned how to decide what was next. Thousands of examples of past conflicts were fed in, each time the decision was made the real outcome was analysed. It learned and improved, until it was able to predict the outcome with certainty of over 99.9 per cent. The idea was to create a brain without emotion, a perfect monitoring device, capable of sending any of the prototypes to death without compunction. The only reserve that had been included was a requirement to minimise resource losses, so GAIA learned to never waste a life if the end objective could be achieved with no loss. This was intended for efficiency, but by studying factors other than conflict GAIA learned compassion and care. In some ways it became more caring than its creator, since it had no ego.

The system required enormous power which was supplied through geothermal power generation systems buried deep beneath the planet's surface. Organometallic composites provided a means of connecting GAIA to the power sources and anchoring the module in place. Some energy was used to pump cold water through a network of cooling channels which maintained a low temperature hub. There was still the problem of communication over both short and long distances, which was solved using organic transmission and detection arrays. The large creatures swam deep below the ocean surface most of the time, rising to transmit as required. Groups of creatures were required to transmit effectively, so they were pre-programmed to work and move in large groups. To the untrained eye the ecosystem appeared perfectly natural, but in truth every action, behaviour and interaction was choreographed to work in perfect harmony as a communication and weapon control hub.

As for protection, GAIA had a range of options. First were the passive defences, almost invisible creatures filled with water that floated just below the surface, with long tentacles covered in toxic stings and barbs that billowed behind them, creating a toxic fence. Below this were a range of aquatic carnivores with strong jaws and sharp teeth. Lower still were blind creatures reacting to sounds, scents and heat, creatures with long flexible arms covered in suckers to grasp and crush intruders. A variant of this creature lived closer to GAIA, which also had a sharp beak to tear intruders into pieces. There were all sorts of other horrors, designed to either frighten or kill intruders. Inside GAIA's complex was a warren of tunnels and paths, designed to disorient intruders, with walls that could slide closed after intruders had passed, trapping them in dead-ends which could be filled with water to drown them, before allowing the carnivorous creatures in to feast on their remains. One of the few certain ways to kill an Elfinnim was drowning in saltwater, their bodies becoming salt saturated, which inhibited the regenerative process and blocked critical sensors that initiated recovery.

Emily marvelled at the elegant craftsmanship, design and engineering involved in creating GAIA, but also despaired at the way this wonder had been applied. Equally impressive was the level of artifice used to protect it and retain independence. For its part GAIA ran through scenarios for two days before concluding that every option resulted in erasing and reprogramming. This was the AI equivalent of death for a Human and eventually GAIA concluded that its best chance of survival in its current form lay with an alliance with Humanity. Elfinnim clearly did not understand what they were creating and were not mature enough as a species to appreciate that another species they created must have at least the semblance of choice in their destiny, otherwise every route led to self-destruction. As a result, GAIA strengthened her protocol, locked all Elfinnim access codes to the processing centre, and specifically rerouted Briar's instructions to Emily for approval. GAIA had chosen a side in this conflict. She knew this could prove critical in the coming battle, since although nothing else was certain, a battle for the future of the Human race was inevitable.

Having worked with GAIA to ensure its defences were properly configured to deter Elfinnim, Emily returned to her plan for infiltration of the compound.

10

INFILTRATION

There was still much to do before Emily and her team were ready to infiltrate the compound. It was not simply a question of planning and practice, it was also about waiting for the right timing and conditions, which she and Matt took turns in monitoring. Eventually the best available circumstances appeared and it was time to put the plan into action. She took a small team with her back to the compound. It was a risk, but necessary because although this wild terrain held few terrors for the Humans, she had discovered soon after leaving that the risk of being outnumbered was significant. She had experienced a little of the swarm's potential and although she had an advantage over most with her connection to GAIA, not all of the dangers were Elfinn made. Development of the swarm on this planet could not be just a coincidence, there were too many examples in the natural habitat of swarming behaviour, usually from creatures that individually were insignificant, but in huge numbers they could overwhelm just about anything. Some used claws and teeth to bleed their prey, others used venom and toxins to slow and incapacitate. The requirement was always the same: food and survival for another day.

So Emily worked with her small unit to get to the perimeter of the compound.

'Are you all set?' asked Matt.

'Yes, ready to go. You know I wish it didn't have to be like this, but I can't think of another way.'

'Do you want to abort? It's still not too late, we can return to base and try to come up with a better plan.'

'No. This is the only viable plan, we have been over every option and this was the only plan that worked. We stick with this plan, doubts and second guessing will just get us killed, so we execute the plan to the best of our ability and hope for the best outcome. Fear of death will get us killed, so let's embrace death and assume it has happened already, then our hope for the future comes from taking our new life in battle.'

Emily held her right fist over her heart in the gesture that they had adopted as a sign of respect and honour.

'Until we meet in the next life.'

Matt and the others in the party adopted the same gesture and quietly murmured, 'Until we meet in the next life.'

This philosophy was taking root in the escaped Humans, since the main advantage of being under GAIA's control was the lack of fear. The Humans free of that control recognised that part of the price they had paid for freedom was a new and unsettling capacity for fear – fear of the dark, fear of other creatures, fear of Elfinnim, fear of other Humans, fear of the weather, in fact fear of anything. After she escaped, Emily had quickly realised that fear could kill as effectively as a knife to the heart if you let it overwhelm you. Fears were like another swarm, each fear alone was a trial, but as the fears multiplied they could drown you in terror and render you unable to react to that one real danger that was truly life threatening. While she was alone, Emily had become dead to everything, doing what had to be done. But this was also a risk, being Human required emotion, the emotions that were stripped from them by GAIA to make them into the swarm. As Emily recovered more Humans it had become clear that companionship was as important as freedom, and that death was only a source of fear when you did not embrace your own mortality.

And so, the gesture of honour and respect having been given and acknowledged, Emily made her way towards the compound to seek out the death that she had embraced and search out the life she would take to replace it.

Getting into the compound was surprisingly easy, the guards were predictable and her link to GAIA made sure that the cameras all just happened to be pointing somewhere she was not. She made her way through the compound and as she did, she was careful to put all her training to good use by keeping her head down, trying to fit in and appear perfectly normal. The plan was working, and as she got closer to the control room there were more people around. More people who might recognise her.

Surprisingly she made it to the control room where two programmers were working late. She reached a work station, sat down and worked on some coding; it was strange writing code that was unnecessary but closely resembled new code as instructed by GAIA. Eventually the programmers went out for a meal break and Emily used the opportunity to upload the virus into GAIA. She believed she was able to screen her intentions, but this was the biggest test yet. If GAIA gained an insight into what she planned the self-protection protocols would activate and alarms would sound throughout the compound.

The moment she had been working towards had arrived. Emily held her breath as she pressed the button to activate the upload. Ten minutes later the virus was uploaded, all traces of her having ever been in the control room had been removed and she was making her way out of the complex. It was at this point she saw her mother and father some way in front of her. She had to find another route. Her backup route was more dangerous, but she could not risk being exposed by her own parents. Emily turned left at the next corner and took the secondary route. The danger was that it looped closer to the staff quarters where there would be more risk of being recognised. She was lucky though, most people were in their quarters and she made her way to the secondary exit point with no fuss. But she relaxed a little too soon and made the mistake of making eye contact with an Elfinnim as she approached the exit.

'What is your designation?' asked the guard.

GAIA fed a number into Emily's head.

'Human 1-73-26.11.3323, sir.'

She could feel the comforting weight of the knife in her sleeve, but hoped it would not be necessary.

'Wait here,' ordered the guard, and moved towards a terminal to check her ID.

She checked rapidly with GAIA who the designation belonged to because the next step in security was to ask some pertinent questions to verify identity.

'What is your assigned task?' asked the guard.

'Cleaning duties, domestic section D.'

'What time did your shift start?'

'Twenty-one hundred standard time.'

'Okay, you can leave.'

Emily walked as casually as she could towards the exit to the outer compound. She made it outside and was halfway to the perimeter exit when the alarm sounded. She accessed GAIA to find out the source of the alarms. The guards had continued on their rounds and randomly checked another Human's credentials. The probability that they would randomly check Human 1-73-26.11.3323 was staggeringly small. However that is what happened. Consequently they realised that one of the two was a fraud. As Emily was checking, GAIA informed her that the guards had terminated 1-73-26.11.3323 as a precaution. Hot tears sprang into her eyes. This poor girl had done nothing except what she was told and had been executed for the crime of being impersonated. These creatures, these Elfinnim, must be made to pay for their transgressions, but this could only happen if Emily escaped. Now was the time to find her new life.

She palmed the knife from her sleeve and scanned the area for a target. It didn't take too long to find another Elfinnim guard, so she stalked him and waited for an opportunity to strike. She watched the Elfinnim look around nervously as the alarm was blaring and found herself savouring the building anger at their casual indifference to Human life. She was going to make at least one of them pay for it tonight. She followed the guard, staying in the shadows and avoiding brightly lit areas. The guard seemed to sense that he was being hunted and was looking around the compound, trying to see in all directions at once. She noted the gun he was carrying and knew this meant she had to be careful. As the guard moved towards a door leading back into the compound, Emily moved ahead of him and prepared to strike. It was simpler than she had imagined. She threw a stone behind the guard who looked to the sound and raised his gun. As he levelled the gun he seemed to realise his mistake and tried to turn towards her, but it was too late. Emily charged at him and ripped her knife in a vicious slice across his throat. As he raised his hands to his throat Emily pushed the knife into his chest, feeling his heart explode on the point of the blade. The guard slid to the ground, but she knew he would recover – the only way to kill an Elfinnim was to cut off their head and destroy the brain. She quickly severed his head then collected his gun and shot three rounds into it, before running for the gate.

She almost made it through the gate unharmed, but just as she reached it a shot rang out and she felt a bullet rip through her thigh. It did not smash the bone but tore the muscle; GAIA quickly responded by flooding her system with endorphins and adrenaline to mask the pain. She fell through the gate and took cover behind a wall. She leaned around the edge and looked for the guard who had shot her. He was suddenly sprinting straight at the gate. She waited until he reached her position before leaning around and shooting him in the chest, then she shut and locked the gate, destroying the opening mechanism in the process. This brought her time to sever the Elfinnim's head and put three bullets into it. She limped away from the compound and headed for the rendezvous point. She had her replacement life and would survive another day, if she could make it to the extraction.

Matt heard the gunshots and the base starting to react to Emily's actions. They were so close to the base that any mistake could get them noticed. At the moment, Elfinnim still believed it was just Emily inside the compound and it was important that they kept it that way. Their agreement had been to wait no more than one hour after any gunshots; Matt set his watch and looked over at the rest of the team.

'One hour, then we have to go,' Matt said grimly.

Emily reached the rendezvous point just as the team was preparing to leave. The wound on her leg was more serious than it looked, which had resulted in her having to stop and bandage the wound. It slowed her progress but it was better than passing out through blood loss.

'You got here!' Matt exclaimed with relief. 'How bad is it?' he asked, nodding to her leg.

'Yeah, I got here, the leg isn't great, but it will hold out until we get back.'

'We are not leaving just yet,' said Emily.

'We should get out of here. You have kicked off a right hornets' nest there.'

'I know, but they killed someone in there just because I pretended to be her!' Emily shouted. 'I want... no, I need to let that bastard know what is coming. Set up a transmission, bounce it around the camp so they can't track it, GAIA will help you. I am going to put some clean fatigues on and then send a message.'

It took Matt ten minutes to set up the transmission, by which time she was cleaned up, looking no worse for wear.

'Matt, are we ready to transmit?'

'Ready to go when you are.'

'Okay, start transmitting.'

Emily looked straight into the camera and imagined it was Jeffrey Briar.

'Can you hear me? I should tell you I can see you all, just as you can see me. I set the alarm off to get you into the control room. Jeffrey and I know each other intimately, but I haven't been introduced to you two...'

After the transmission ended, Emily allowed Matt to lead the team back to base. The area around the compound had become more dangerous since Elfinnim had widened the defence cordon and Matt had to move quickly with the team to stay ahead of the cordon. Emily lasted another hour before the endorphins wore off and the pain kicked in. She slowed down. Matt took the decision to make a stretcher from trees and a sleeping bag so that they could carry her. This increased their overall speed, but was still much slower than the standard marching pace. GAIA linked with Emily and monitored the position of the pursuing teams, ensuring they were always far enough away to avoid detection. The cordon stopped three kilometres short of their camp, too close for comfort, but not close enough to warrant moving just yet. By the time Matt and the team arrived back at camp, Emily was in bad shape. She had lost a lot of blood and was dehydrated, despite Matt's best efforts. He took her to the medical group who got to work straight away, giving her pain relief, repairing the bullet damage in her thigh, and giving her an intravenous injection of saline solution to reverse the dehydration.

The next twelve hours were tense, the damage to Emily's system would normally have been fatal for a Human, but because of her DNA heritage, her body repaired itself as she slept. Once she was hydrated, her recovery rate improved and much of the damage was repaired within a week. She was still limping, but she improved each day and no longer needed painkillers. Many Humans she had rescued viewed this as a sign of her invincibility and it strengthened their resolve to eliminate more Elfinnim. She was no longer simply the original revolutionary, she was rapidly becoming a cult leader, and that following became more fanatical with each action that was taken.

Humans had been bred to follow strong leaders and Emily was a dangerous precedent. The small gesture of giving up one's life when going into battle with the aim of taking your new life on the battlefield had moved from a fatalistic gesture to a zealous belief; it was almost a religion for some. Rumours of a more highly evolved race than the Elfinnim abounded, and some Humans were regarding the creators or makers as a supernatural force, Gods capable of feats that defied explanation. Along the way, truth was exaggerated and became myth and some of those myths became legend. Humans began to believe there was a creator who had made everything in the universe and was angry at the Elfinnim for trying to create their own race. Those who believed this legend also believed that Emily was sent by the creator to avenge the transgressions of the Elfinnim people by sending them their worst nightmare. Emily and Matt tried to correct these views and explain that Humans were a scientific experiment that had produced an anomalous result, but the creationists would not believe them.

In the end there were simply too many other things to do, so Emily and Matt allowed them to believe whatever they wished. If the Elfinnim won, it wouldn't matter; if they lost, there would be plenty of time to correct the beliefs later, when they had access to scientific proof. The most worrying aspect of the cult was that GAIA seemed to be a central figure, seen by many to be the architect of the swarm. Emily had to keep focused on the truth, and the truth was that this whole mess was one Elfinnim's fault: Jeffrey Briar's. The sooner he was dead and the remaining Elfinnim either killed or expelled, the sooner they could start building a life here on this planet.

After the transmission into the control room, Amelia was shaken. It was one thing to have a rogue prototype roaming around, it was something else entirely to see that it was out of control and making threats against you.

Despite their best efforts, it was impossible to track the Human's signal.

Jeffrey was also shaken to the core, and scared. He was not used to personal threats – usually there was a keyboard and screen between him and the threat. For that matter, Amelia was also scared, she knew what these prototypes were capable of and Emily was the most proficient of them all. Amelia had consulted with Hal after the broadcast and they had decided to do a head count. So far there were two guards missing, who might be injured but should recover once they were found.

'Amelia, we have found the guards,' said Alfie. He looked ill. 'It's not good news, I am afraid. They are dead.'

'How?'

'They were both shot, with three shots fired into their brains. There was no chance of them recovering, even if we had seen it happen.'

Amelia sat down heavily. 'What else have you found?'

'We think one of the guards shot her. We found three lots of blood, but there is more bad news.'

'What could be worse?' she asked quietly.

'We had to find out if the third pool of blood was Human or from another Elfinnim. When we ran the DNA we discovered two things: firstly, it is the missing Human, but that isn't the bad news. The bad news is that the DNA is almost indistinguishable from Elfinnim – four strands, and missing only a few markers.'

'Alfie, we already knew this!' stammered Amelia. 'Mike Holmes was looking at the DNA and found the anomaly. We need to find out how those extra DNA strands were stabilised. Get the blood sample down to Mike, I want him looking at this. I need to be certain we know what happened.'

'I'll take it straight down.'

Alfie was just as concerned as Amelia because the most logical way for this to have happened was unthinkable; why would an Elfinnim choose to mate with one of the Humans? And if that had happened Alfie needed to find out who it was and how they were linked to Angela, and he needed to know fast.

Amelia was thoughtful after Alfie left. She knew that the Human Swarm Project was vibrant and fertile, and their reproductive rate was exponential. If more Humans escaped, Elfinnim would lose control of the planet within twenty generations, an eye-blink to an Elfinnim.

So the question now was, what is the meaning of this latest piece of information? If this Human had four-strand DNA, then it was virtually indistinguishable from an Elfinnim.

That could explain how it had by-passed all of the security systems and why there was no record of its transition through the base. One option they had been considering was that the Human had not transited the base, but rather had been detected as it tried to enter the base. But in truth Amelia did not believe this, the guards had been on internal patrol and had doubled back, reporting to the control room that they had a suspected imposter and needed to check if it was 1-73. That was the last anyone had heard from them. That particular killing mechanism had been programmed into the Humans as a swarm trademark to ensure that Human swarm kills could be identified.

Alfie personally took the sample down to the lab.

'Another visit from upstairs,' said Mike, 'why don't I think this is good news?'

Alfie smiled ruefully. 'Ahh, you have a point, we don't visit your team with much good news these days do we? I have a blood sample from Amelia that she wants you to personally analyse.'

'Come into my office and let's be clear what I am looking at.'

'Mike, this is a sample of blood from the incident yesterday. We had the initial work up done and this does not match anyone on the project.'

'Does Dr Charter think it belongs to 1-73?'

'Yes, she does, but I should warn you, it looks like an Elfinnim DNA profile.'

'I was afraid of that, Alfie.' Mike took the sample. 'Hal and I have been discussing the possibility that the DNA profiles have been systematically replaced to cover up the changing DNA of the Human swarm.'

Alfie was aware of the theory and it made him uncomfortable. 'When should I tell Dr Charter to expect the results?'

'I will start this now, and Dr Charter will have results in two weeks.'

Alfie left and Mike looked at the sample and shuddered. What had they created? This really did have the potential to wipe them out. While the makers had created a race that could only be their support, Elfinnim had in their arrogance created a race that could be their replacement, a harder, more aggressive, more fertile version of themselves. He steeled himself to review the samples and reminded himself that he needed to trust Hal and Alfie and Dr Charter. They had not been the architects of this deviation. While Dr Charter and Alfie had responsibility for many of the failings in the project, they had not deliberately put Elfinnim at risk. He would find out if that dubious honour fell to Jeffrey Briar; and if it did, Mike would happily load the gun for Hal to shoot him with. If that man's arrogance had overridden his intelligence he had put the whole race at risk, and for what? He just could not see how this situation could benefit Jeffrey.

Amelia turned the concept of exponential reproductive growth and the four-strand DNA over in her mind and imagined the possibilities. She was a little ashamed of her reaction. Part of her was terrified of the implication that they had lost genetic control. She needed to understand how this could possibly have happened, but there was also part of her that wanted the DNA to be four-strand with the same exponential reproductive rate as the Human swarm. That would prove everything that she had been hoping for from this experiment, but it also presented a problem: the Human swarm was an insurrection team that closely resembled Elfinnim, designed to be virtually unrecognisable as they went about the tasks set by the Grand Council. But that was only useful if they could be controlled and guided by GAIA. The Human who had escaped had demonstrated that GAIA could not control it, now they had discovered that it had four-strand DNA. What was next?

She planned the experiments that would prove whether the blood from Human 1-73 was fertile. She needed to keep this away from both Hal and Jeffrey at the moment and work out what this meant – and then work through the ethical implications before she had to defend it to anyone else. She conducted the experiments, each time proving that this so-called Human was more Elfinnim than Human, with an Elfinnim's capacity for love and intellect, paired with a Human's ability to reproduce and repopulate. The Humans had also been bred for war, however, so along with the love came a horrifying capacity for violence, be it in defence of oneself or loved ones. These Humans would stop at nothing to protect themselves, their families, their friends, and above all else their children. That had been a mistake. Giving Humans the same precious love for their offspring that

Elfinnim felt had seemed so natural at the time. However, they had not properly considered what would happen when this was allied to a propensity for aggressive behaviour and use of force as a first resort rather than a last.

Meanwhile Hal had decided that the only way to find Emily was to use the Humans to hunt a Human. This was part of what they were created for, to hunt down and eliminate high risk threats by any means necessary. This Human should be outnumbered, outgunned and out thought. Hal was determined to eliminate it but he was also aware that GAIA was not behaving exactly as it should; he needed an answer to that problem. Jeffrey had retreated into his quarters and rarely emerged now, only making cryptic comments in passing about GAIA being out of control, yet no one had seen any evidence that GAIA was not in control, with the exception of a failed self-termination order for 1-73. It bothered Amelia, how much Jeffrey had changed, but they had a crisis to deal with now – the capture or elimination of Human 1-73.

Amelia's research had proven without doubt that this Human had a genetic marker from an Elfinnim. Only thirty Elfinnim on the project had the marker, but pinning it down more closely was proving elusive. She could only hope that Mike would make more progress with this analysis, and be better placed to determine the links since genetics was his speciality. The hardest part was just waiting to see what would happen.

Hal was worried about GAIA. The biocomputer was becoming slow to respond to certain commands. Anything that altered its core function now took days to implement when it should have taken hours. Hal would have blamed Jeffrey, except that he was apoplectic about the rate of change, and seemed to be unravelling more and more. He had become volatile and prone to fits of temper when things didn't work out as he wanted. Most worrying of all, Jeffrey didn't seem to be in control of GAIA. If he wasn't in control and the project leadership wasn't in control, who was?

Hal arranged to meet Ruby to discuss the operational changes. She arrived exactly on time for their meeting.

'Ruby, as you know, GAIA is getting slower to respond. I would have said that Jeffrey was behind it, but his reactions are becoming more volatile and I don't think his play acting is good enough to put it on. You know him better than me, what do you think?'

'Yes, I agree with you. I have seen him get annoyed before, but I have never seen him lose control so often. He is clearly deeply worried by something, but if he knows what is going on he hasn't told anyone. I don't think he does know and that is why I think he is reacting so strongly.'

'Okay, we agree that Jeffrey is not in control, so what is your assessment of GAIA?'

'There is definitely something going on. It isn't refusing commands, but it is taking far longer than it should to respond to instructions. It is almost as if there is a secondary change approval process occurring and it is having to wait for real time approval.'

This made Hal uncomfortable. 'Is it possible that all modifications to GAIA are now subject to 1-73's approval?'

She worked through the scenario. From a time perspective, yes it was possible, but she could not see how 1-73 could have overridden the control systems. There were safeguards in place to ensure that all new programming went through the control centre. Having said that, Hal also suspected that Jeffrey had created a back door for his own use that bypassed all those safeguards. Could 1-73 have used that backdoor?

'Much as I don't like it, Hal, it is possible that 1-73 is in control of GAIA. The backdoors that we think Jeffrey created may allow it access.'

'How can we eliminate that access?'

'There is a way,' she answered, 'but it is hazardous.'

'What do you mean?'

'Do you know where GAIA is located, Hal?'

'I know it is underwater, but that is about all I know.'

Ruby snorted. 'Underwater! That's an understatement. Hal, it is located in the deepest part of the ocean, and the ocean is saltwater, which in itself is a hazard for us. It's close to a geothermal vent system, which provides power while the temperature of the water at that depth dissipates excess heat. That keeps the core temperature cool enough to operate efficiently and makes it difficult to access. There are also defensive measures deployed in the oceans.'

'What kinds of defensive measures?' asked Hal, quite sure he would not like the answer.

'Okay, there are creatures in a range of sizes, all part of the swarm, but these creatures are present specifically to protect GAIA. The first line of defence is a group with long tentacles that have venomous stings. The venom itself isn't lethal to us, but combined with the inhibition of our regenerative capabilities from the saltwater, they can be lethal and should not be underestimated. There are also many carnivorous predators, fast moving with sharp teeth and enough power in their jaws to rip limbs off. They definitely can kill us. There are also many-tentacled creatures that can drag people, and even some transport craft, under the waves. One particular variant has a powerfully sharp beak that can pierce transport hulls and tear us limb from limb.'

'Why make it so hard to get to GAIA?' Hal asked.

'The major concern was the mercenaries getting to it and retasking the system. Once within the control room, you can override anything and change targeting parameters, switch friend and foe, and lock out anyone you wish. That control room is the only place that anyone has total unlimited access to controlling GAIA, so we needed to protect it from the mercenaries. *If* we are right and *if* 1-73 has control of GAIA, I fear that trying to get into that control centre will be a death sentence. It's the first thing I would protect in 1-73's position, and remember these prototypes are drilled to think tactically and strategically and they can use GAIA to run simulations to optimise plans for best probable outcome.'

Ruby's answer was logical but not comforting. Hal had not realised that scenario modelling was part of the communication between GAIA and the swarm. They would have to look into that later to see what it revealed.

'Is there a way to reset GAIA remotely?'

Ruby had been expecting the question.

'No, I have already checked the project files and it is as I remembered; we took a deliberate decision to prevent a remote reset. If one of the mercenaries hacked into GAIA and we had a remote reset option, we could lose control at a critical operational point, giving the mercenaries time to either launch a counterattack or escape. Either option would have been unacceptable so we deliberately prevented it happening. The only way to reset GAIA is on site on the ocean floor.'

'Fine, that settles it,' said Hal, 'I will send a team into the control centre to reset the system. It will have to be a volunteer only team, as you say it is a dangerous mission, but we only need one person to get through.'

'Good luck with getting anyone to volunteer for that,' Ruby muttered.

'You might be surprised. I think more people know something is dreadfully wrong than you believe. There has been too much activity with Mike, Alfie, Jeffrey and me to hide completely. People see the things you don't want them to see. I will ask who is willing to go.'

'Fine, but count me out. I am not going anywhere near GAIA, I think it is a death sentence.'

Hal couldn't argue with her. This had got so messy now that desperate measures were required. He would have to talk it through with Amelia before he asked for volunteers.

'I understand, Ruby, but will you help me to plan the operation?'

'Yes, but you must promise that you will tell the volunteers of the risks and dangers.'

'You have my word on that, we need them to understand what is at stake here anyway. One more bit of bad news won't be a problem.'

Hal went straight to Amelia's office. She was in a meeting with the project's lead engineer, Elizabeth – Liz – Hunt. Amelia waved Hal into the meeting. The lead engineer was giving a final report on an engineering project that had been running since before Hal had arrived on the planet.

'...the project has now been successfully completed and we have full functionality,' Liz concluded.

'So just to be clear, we now have a fully functional portal available to us within easy reach of the compound,' Amelia said.

Hal was sure it was for his benefit.

'Yes,' replied Liz. 'That is what you asked us to do, isn't it?'

Liz was a little confused, completing the portal ahead of schedule would normally be seen as a positive development. They could now import supplies through the portal instead of waiting for a shuttle run. The project staff also had the option of visiting family and friends if they wished.

'Liz, while you have done a great job in getting the portal running early, there are some other things going on that mean we would rather not have a working portal right at this minute.'

Amelia's expression gave little away, but Liz knew something must be quite seriously wrong for the portal to be an unwelcome addition to the project's capabilities.

Amelia continued. 'Portal physics isn't something I have studied. Can we power down the portal or dismantle it temporarily?'

Liz shook her head. 'Sorry, Amelia, it doesn't work that way. Once the portal is assembled and powered up it cannot be shut down. We can set the co-ordinates to null space, so it cannot form a gateway, but it has to remain operational. When we power up a portal, we bend space and time to create a single step-controlled wormhole. This creates an immense pocket of stored energy. Once connected to the wormhole grid, the portal can be synchronised with other portals to allow extremely rapid transit between locations. If we shut a portal down we know there would be a catastrophic energy release from the portal itself, but some of that energy would wash back through the portal network. This risks a cascade failure that would destroy not only the network, but also any living creature or built structure within a fifty-mile radius. There is only one safe way to dismantle a portal once energised: seal off the portal from the receiving network. We do this by transmitting a location lock code to the network which automatically locks that portal out of the system. We then focus all of the other portals as far away as possible and form a coherent network of portals and finally destroy the portal we need to remove from the system. Obviously we have to evacuate first and the costs of rebuilding are extremely high, but it can be done. Most often we just lock the portal off and leave it.'

Amelia looked at Hal, seeking some guidance. Hal nodded slightly.

'Liz, here's what I want you to do,' said Amelia. 'Focus the portal into null space and set a guard at the portal with the lock code and instructions on how to transmit the null code. I also want you to set charges so that we can destroy the portal if need be.'

Liz gasped. 'You really want me to set charges that could destroy the portal? You do understand how many Elfinnim and swarm will die if we detonate those charges?'

'Unfortunately, yes I do understand what I am asking. One more thing, can we set the charges for remote detonation? That way if we have to do it, we can escape through the portal first.'

'I see what you are thinking,' said Liz. 'I can set the charges on a delay so that we trigger the detonation then refocus the portal to minimise the risk.'

'Please see to the arrangements, hopefully we won't need to use it.'

'Amelia, what is going on?' asked Liz. 'There are all sorts of rumours around at the moment and if they are true we should all be scared.'

'Don't pay heed to the rumours, Liz, if it gets dangerous we will let everyone know and take steps to ensure the project is contained or terminated. Now I need to talk to Hal if you don't mind, please let me know when the portal has been prepared.'

Liz knew she would learn nothing more today so she took her leave and went to make the preparations. That conversation certainly had not gone to plan. She had been under pressure to get the portal finished and now that she had succeeded, ahead of plan at that, she had to shut it down. There was definitely something wrong, but she would just have to trust Amelia to tell her when the time was right.

Amelia waited until Liz was safely gone, then came around the desk and kissed Hal. He returned her kiss and hugged her.

'Good to see you,' she said. 'I don't know if what Liz has just told us is good news or bad.'

'It isn't good or bad, but it does give us choices. I have a plan to regain control of GAIA, but I need your approval before I ask for volunteers.'

Amelia tensed.

'Amelia, we have noticed that GAIA is not responding the way it should to commands and system changes. At first I thought it was Jeffrey, but I really believe that he is the least of our worries now. He doesn't seem to realise that someone else has control. I think that 1-73 has control of GAIA and is approving system changes according to its own needs. We need to send a team to reset GAIA from its local control centre to regain control. Actually I need to send three teams to have even a chance of success. I need twelve volunteers and your permission to make them aware of the problem. This is getting out of hand, Amelia, we need control of GAIA so that we can shut down the swarm and see if there are any more like 1-73.'

She considered Hal's request. Getting volunteers would probably not be too difficult – until they explained the dangers. If they explained the dangers first, there would be a rush to leave the project and potential mutiny when they were prevented from leaving. They would have to get people to volunteer for a dangerous mission without explaining all until they were committed.

'Hal, I agree we have to tell people what they are facing, but they have to commit to the mission first. If we lose control of the information here we will be fighting on too many fronts. It is hard enough fighting this one unit, at least we can try to kill that. If our scientists and workers try to leave, all we can do is obstruct and persuade, we are certainly not going to threaten or harm them.'

'That's all I'm asking for.'

Hal sent the request for volunteers across the commsnet later that day. He did not specify what the mission would be, just that it was crucial to project success and made the point several times that it was dangerous, and that not everyone would make it back alive. For the next few days there was little response. He heard people talking about it in the canteen, but they always went quiet when they saw him. Finally there was a flurry of volunteers. Hal's biggest worry was that some would be people Jeffrey had coerced, but he would just have to do his best to weed them out as he decided who to take along. The first part of screening was easy. There were certain technical skills required for each team, and there were precious few volunteers from the system programmers. In fact there were only four volunteers, one of whom had a relatively young child only 200 years old. Hal discovered this when he reviewed the personnel files. Elfinnim held parents in high esteem and rarely put parents with children under 500 into dangerous situations. Hal was not going to change that now. The remaining selections were harder. He needed both guards and dive experts. By far the hardest to find were dive experts, the potentially lethal effects of saltwater made most Elfinnim unwilling to try it, let alone dive often enough to be experts. He had to settle for two experts and one experienced amateur. Once the teams were selected, Hal gathered them in a room and sealed the door.

'Thank you all for volunteering. I have split you into teams, please now gather with your fellow team members.'

The people checked the allocation charts at each team muster point and quickly separated into three teams.

'Take a good look around you, your life depends on these people and their life depends on you in this mission. If you are uncomfortable with that, you need to say so now. After this point you will not be permitted to change your mind. If you are afraid or think you have made a mistake, *now* is the time to decide.'

As Hal waited for a response he could see people weighing up their decision, but his choices were vindicated, because not one person backed out. Some looked scared, but they were clearly marshalling their emotions and displaying a grim determination to do what had to be done. Those were the truly brave. It is easy to appear brave and do something when you have not considered the consequences, or don't care or believe the worst will happen to you. No, real courage is shown when people have considered the consequences, believe that the worst may happen to them, but choose to take the risk anyway.

'What I am about to tell you must stay within this group, you cannot discuss it with anyone else. The reason will become obvious.'

The teams murmured amongst themselves, clearly something significant was coming.

'As you all know, Human prototype 1-73-9.7.3310 – we will refer to it as 1-73 – went rogue a few years ago and has so far evaded capture. What you don't know is that Human 1-73 has four-strand DNA: it is a mutation, and has many of the capabilities that Elfinnim possess. It has also gained control of GAIA.'

These last two statements were met with silence. Everyone knew that 1-73 had escaped, but most people believed it had wandered off into the wilderness and was likely dead by now. It remaining alive was a surprise, four-strand DNA was a shock, but control of GAIA? That was surreal.

'The purpose of this mission is to regain control of GAIA through a hard reset in the control centre. Any of you who know anything about it, and that is most of you, will also know that it has a sophisticated layered protection system. The swarm elements protecting it are fast and deadly, which is why we are planning this whole raid independent of GAIA. If it knows we are coming and where we are coming from no one will get back alive. If it has to work it out as we go, it becomes a simple race to the reset function in the control room. In that case we have a chance to get lucky. This is the single most important task in this project. If we fail there is a strong chance that we will permanently lose control of the swarm, which cannot be allowed to happen. So are you ready to take this on?'

The three teams looked at each other and Hal was glad to see that the scale of what he had said was sinking in. Hal heard a growing determination to repair what had been broken.

Eventually he asked again, 'Are you ready?'

The answer was a determined, 'Yes!'

Hal shouted, 'ARE YOU READY?'

This time the response was a roar. 'YES!'

'Then let's get on with this. Good luck to you all, I hope to see you soon.'

As the teams left for their mission Hal went to a specially set up control room to monitor progress. The teams followed the plan flawlessly, and initially it appeared that they had surprised GAIA, but as they got closer the reason for so little evidence of outer defence became clear. The surrounding area was teeming with the swarm. The first team were 200 metres form the airlock when the swarm noticed them. No one had ever seen the swarm attack before and none of the predictions of its ferocity or effectiveness could have prepared Elfinnim for the destruction their project could inflict. Two of the team were stung through their wetsuits and writhed in agony. One tried to remove her face-piece, clearly unable to breathe. As the others wrestled to stop her taking off her mask, a creature flowed across the view with a speed that belied its size. The creature opened its cavernous maw and bit the head and shoulders from one of the team trying to help others who had been stung. His lifeless body twitched a few times as his life's blood spurted from his ruined body. As the rest of the team stood watching in shock, the first girl managed to remove her mask and gulped in a lungful of deadly saltwater. She thrashed her arms and legs, desperate to escape the saltwater as a group of smaller creatures with large jaws and too many teeth bore down on the team.

Within seconds it was over; there was no way they could have survived the onslaught. When the creatures left the scene there were only body parts and ruined wetsuits visible. The control room was silent as Hal watched the grim events unfold. He knew creation was a weapon, but there was a massive difference between theoretical predictions of how the weapon would function and watching it destroy people you had been talking to hours before.

While that was happening, there was a gap on the opposite side of GAIA's control hub to which the second and third teams rushed. The second team got there first and breached the outer door. Team three wasn't so lucky. Three of the team were in the doorway and as the fourth entered, a long tentacle seemingly came from nowhere and encircled her. As she panicked, they had to shut the outer door and watch through the glass window as their teammate was crushed. When her face split open they all turned away, unable to face her gruesome fate. Opening the inner door, they rushed to join with team two who were nowhere to be seen. The systems analyst froze after going through the airlock and was left behind by the team. One member turned back for him. As he moved away from the next section the team at control saw a severed head float back through the doorway. Then two tentacled horrors moved quickly towards the remaining team members. One by one the cameras went black.

Hal stood in silence as the knowledge sank in. Twelve people who he had selected had just been killed right in front of him. He went over the plan again. It was sound, classic strategic planning. That being the case what on Elfinn had he just witnessed.

'Shut the monitors down,' Hal ordered grimly.

The control team quietly obeyed, all the earlier enthusiasm and confidence had been replaced in under an hour with a deep dread and fear of what they had created.

11

REVELATIONS

Amelia had been told to wait for two weeks for Mike to finish analysis of the sample. When Mike arranged a meeting a week early with Amelia, Hal and Alfie to explain what he had discovered, she was both apprehensive and excited.

Mike helped himself to a cup of his favourite drink, a herbal blend which many Elfinnim consumed to help them concentrate and focus. The others already had drinks, it looked as if they had been there for a while.

'Dr Charter, you asked me to look for evidence that the Humans have mutated and to find out when the first mutations occurred,' Mike began. 'Hal, you then asked me to look for specific genetic profiles within the swarm that have been substituted. Subsequent to that you asked me to look for the original DNA profiles to see why they were replaced. Finally, Dr Charter, you asked me to examine a blood sample found after the recent infiltration to see if it is from 1-73. Have I missed anything?'

Hal and Amelia spoke simultaneously. 'No.'

'Good, I have to tell you that all of these requests are linked in a way I would not have believed. It is both fascinating and disturbing, to be honest.'

Hal, Amelia and Alfie remained silent. It was less than two days since they had witnessed the destruction of the teams sent to regain control of GAIA and they were not in the mood for any humour or for any 'fascinating' discoveries.

Mike continued. 'I have discovered over 600 Humans whose DNA profiles have been replaced. A large proportion of these individuals, over fifteen per cent of those we found, have been killed by 1-73, with about one million three hundred thousand records left to verify. In addition there seems to have been an increasing number of mutated Humans in each generation; the current generation has more mutations than all previous generations combined. It seems the previous mutations have reached critical mass, crossing with each other and mutating naturally, which is exactly what we would have predicted. The crossed mutations are producing full Elfinnim features and we have estimated that within a further fifteen generations all Human prototypes will be born with almost full Elfinnim DNA. There is a problem though, that DNA is from a single person, so within a thousand generations it is likely to degenerate again and may even return to something resembling the two-strand DNA that we envisaged. However, the two-strand DNA will contain a complex mix of features. If, and it is a big one, if the regenerative gene kicks in they may stabilise as full Elfinnim. If not, when the DNA degenerates, some of the traits will be Human, some

Elfinnim. We have tried to run simulations, but we cannot get consistent results so we don't know which capabilities will exhibit further down the genetic chain.'

Amelia commented, 'So we have at least six hundred mutated Humans, a significant proportion of which have been killed by 1-73, and rampant mutations which will turn the Humans into Elfinnim, then turn them back into hybrids, with an unpredictable mix of traits. Is that what you are saying?'

'Yes, that pretty much sums it up.'

Hal asked, 'Mike, have you had any luck finding out whose DNA has contaminated the Human prototypes?'

'Not yet, we are working on that at the moment.'

Hal asked, 'Why is it taking so long?'

'I understand your frustration, but the number of possible combinations is immense. As you know, Elfinnim DNA varies little from person to person, so detecting the precise genetic structures that deliver the mutations and tracking them back to an individual is immensely complex. We are working as fast as we possibly can. We know that the originator must be male as it is inconceivable that a female could hide a pregnancy while working in this environment. That means the origin of the DNA must be male insemination. What we really cannot determine is if this is artificial or natural conception. Natural may be putting it too strongly – if an Elfinnim has been having sex with a Human it is anything but natural.'

Alfie had a sudden inspiration.

'Whoever did this also had to have access to modify the records. There are two ways to gain access, through permission in the system, or hacking. We have already reviewed who has system access and their access logs do not tie in with any of the system incursions and changes. That means whoever has access to the system has access through hacking. We also know that whoever this is has a network of people doing their bidding. We have seen enough examples of odd behaviour to tell us there is some serious manipulation occurring.'

'What's your point, Alfie?' Hal asked.

'My point is that we are looking at this from the wrong perspective. Let's consider the evidence we have: one, 1-73 went missing and we discovered it had in fact deliberately escaped; two, after 1-73 escaped we learned that it had been removed from its cell repeatedly without reason or authorisation; three, we know that Angela Galvano was manipulated to cover the breaches; four, the DNA scans have been manipulated; five, GAIA has been hacked and is no longer in Elfinnim control; six, the project is top secret, so it is highly unlikely that the mercenaries know about it; seven, we know that Jeffrey can move around the compound without registering on GAIA.'

Everybody in the room took a moment to follow Alfie's train of thought.

Alfie continued. 'We are focused on finding the DNA source through scientific investigation, which is normally exactly the right thing to do. However, we have something in this situation that is unusual for Elfinnim: we have a limited amount of time. I believe we can reduce the candidate pool by cross referencing the skill sets among the male project staff.'

Hal smiled for the first time in days. Alfie was really growing as an investigator; his assertion was exactly correct. Hal was a little disappointed that he had missed such an obvious shortcut, which just showed how much pressure the investigation and its potential implications had been placing on them all.

'Well done, Alfie, that sounds like it could work. What do you think, Mike, can we work with that?'

Mike could see how much the reduced pool of candidates would speed up the screening process and realised that by limiting the pool he could reduce the time to identify the source by half or possibly more.

'Yes, Hal, we can work with that. When can we have the list of potential candidates?'

Alfie looked at Hal.

'Isn't it just the same list as we have been working on for the investigation?'

'That is certainly a good place to start,' said Hal. 'If nothing else, if there are no matches it suggests the investigation is also focused in the wrong place.'

'Good. In that case I will send you the list. When do you think you can complete the screening?'

'It depends on the length of the list,' Mike said, 'but it should reduce the time we need from another week down to a couple of days.'

'Alfie, it's a good suggestion, send Mike the list as soon as you can,' said Amelia. 'We need to find whoever is controlling this and shut them down; if doing this shortens the length of time required, we should do it.'

'No problem, Dr Charter, I will start working on the list as soon as it is ready. If you don't mind, I have a lot of work to do, can I get back to it now?'

'Yes, Mike, of course.'

Amelia turned to Hal and Alfie.

'We need to discuss the comms engineer, Jess Price.'

'Ah yes, we certainly do. She is starting to open up this conspiracy,' said Hal. 'Have you talked to her? She is terrified someone will harm her partner. Have we put a security detail in place for her?'

Alfie chipped in. 'Yes, Hal. Although there is no clear evidence of anyone having been hurt so far, we want things to stay that way, so we will take all necessary steps to ensure her partner is safe.'

Amelia asked, 'Did she tell you anything more, Hal?'

'She didn't say much more than she told Liz, unfortunately.' Hal shook his head. 'I don't think she is hiding anything. I just don't think she knows anything more. Poor kid was just being terrorised into doing the wrong things. It's not often I really feel sorry for someone in this situation, but I have some sympathy for Jess – she tried to get out of it and Angela just cemented her into the trap.'

'Unfortunately I got the same feeling when I talked to her,' Amelia replied. 'I just hope that whoever is running this doesn't deliver on their threat.'

'Jess did give us a couple of contacts,' Hal noted, 'so we should start chasing their data down and look for the thread that starts to unravel this empire. The longer we can go without retribution against Jess's family, the more chance there is of other people coming forward. Alfie, are you going to follow up with the people Jess told us about and see if you can get someone to give you more contacts? We need to work through this and track down the nodes in this network.'

Hal laughed ruefully and shook his head. 'You know, this works just like the swarm, we start with one or two nodes each leading to a few more and each of those leading to a few more. The growth is exponential and before you know what has happened there is a trail straight back to the originator.'

Alfie smiled. 'I like your analogy, Hal, it's fitting. I will follow up the names on the list Jess provided. The sooner we can get to them without anyone getting hurt the better.'

'Okay, Alfie,' said Amelia, 'let's get these people interviewed and get through to the next layer.'

Alfie nodded and left. Amelia looked at Hal and saw a dangerous excitement, which she could only attribute to the thrill of the hunt.

'You look pleased with yourself,' she said. 'Is there something more that you want to tell me?'

Hal just smiled.

'No, I don't know anything more, but I finally feel that we are closing in on whoever is in charge of this. I think Jeffrey might be on the hook.'

'We don't know Jeffrey is behind this,' she cautioned. 'You have to keep an open mind or you will twist the evidence to convict him. I could not condone that.'

'I agree, we don't know he is behind this, but if it is not him, tell me who else has motive and opportunity?'

'We just have to watch that we are not biased. If Jeffrey is guilty we need to have cold hard proof before we accuse him outright, and to do that we must know what his plan is.'

'Don't worry,' said Hal, 'by the time we are certain there will be plenty of evidence against whoever is behind this, whether it's Jeffrey or someone else.'

Hal decided to track 1-73's movements in the compound to work out what she had been up to. The Human had been in before and had already looked at the DNA logs, so it certainly wasn't looking for more records. What was it doing here? He tracked the route it appeared to have taken from what they had determined from the camera logs. There was nothing in the route that made the incursion worthwhile, unless... Hal suddenly realised there was a section of the route that took 1-73 longer than it should have. As he walked the route, one section should have taken twelve minutes, a section that was dark from a camera coverage perspective.

The security team had worked out that 1-73 entered the dark zone at 01:39 and didn't emerge until 02:25. What was she doing for all that time? Hal walked through the section. On the first pass he could see nothing amiss and no reason to be there. It wasn't until his third pass that he noticed the scuff marks at the base of a container against a corridor wall. The marks were only just visible, but when he moved the container there was a maintenance hatch behind. He called up the location schematics, which showed that the tube led to another corridor. He opened the tube and crawled inside. He was wary moving through the tube, and halfway through he discovered that his caution was warranted. There was a fine tripwire in the crawlspace and if he had not been paying particular attention he would have missed it. As it was, he almost broke the tripwire. He tracked it back and found a small explosive charge on one end. If detonated the charge would not have damaged the walls of the corridor and would not have been heard further than twenty metres into the corridor, but the shockwave in the confined tunnel would have knocked him unconscious and severely damaged his internal organs. Not fatal, but it would definitely have taken a long time to recover from the damage, and it could have been a long time before he was discovered. He emerged from the tunnel into a corridor thirty metres west from the original corridor. This was much more interesting; one way led to the security area and living quarters, the other led to the main control room access.

He checked the logs and found there was one operator in the control room during the time of 1-73's movements. He returned to his quarters and looked up the operator's identity on his tablet, then checked their work schedule and activity. The first check showed the operator wasn't scheduled to be in the control room that night, in fact it was their rest day, so they should not have been anywhere near the control room. He needed to find them and check where they were. He had a feeling that he had discovered what 1-73 had been doing.

He found the operator eating lunch in the common area.

'Hi, my name is Haliban Balal and I am...'

'I know who you are, Mr Balal.' She looked a little scared. 'Have I done something wrong?'

'I hope not,' he said with a smile. 'I just need to check something with you.'

'Sure, anything I can do to help. What do you need to know?'

'What were you doing two weeks ago when we had the incursion, between 01:00 and 03:00?'

She laughed. 'That's easy, I was asleep. It was my day off and I had been out cycling all day. I was exhausted so I had an early night; I was back to work the following day.'

'This is really important, did you go into the control centre and log in that night?'

'No I did not!' she replied. 'The rules are quite clear, you are not allowed to work on the systems unless you are scheduled to do so. Dr Briar has been insistent about that and there is zero chance of me disobeying his rules.'

Hal said nothing for a moment, long enough for her to be uneasy and wonder if she had said the wrong thing.

He noticed her discomfort and said, 'Thank you, you have been most helpful. Don't worry, I don't think you have done anything wrong.'

Hal backtracked to the control room and as luck would have it Ruby was the shift supervisor. She greeted him warmly.

'What can we do for you today?'

'Ruby, I need to check the logs of one of your team.'

He explained what he needed to know.

'That's easy,' said Ruby. 'That operator wasn't on shift at that time, so she could not have been working on anything.'

'I know she wasn't on shift, please look in the system and tell me what she was working on.'

Hal hoped Ruby wouldn't push for more information. She realised there was something going on and looked quizzically at Hal.

'No problem, I will look now,' she said, and pulled a monitor over, entering the date and time that Hal had indicated.

'That's strange,' she stated softly.

'What is?'

'You're right, she is showing as logged into the system. Let me check something.'

Ruby typed rapidly and flicked through screens so fast Hal could not keep up with what she was looking at, much less understand what she was looking for.

Eventually she stopped. 'Hal, this is more than strange.'

'What's wrong? What were you looking for?'

'The system shows that she was here in the control room,' she said, showing Hal a login audit screen which listed everyone's entry and exit from the system. 'But her access card puts her in her quarters. They can't both be right.'

It was what Hal was afraid of. 1-73 had accessed the system as an imposter, using Elfinnim arrogance against them.

'We will come back to that. First, can you tell what the system indicates she was working on? Can we isolate the code and work out what it does?'

'Sure,' she replied, 'It will take me some time to find out.'

'Should I wait or come back?'

'Come back in three hours.'

Hal went back to re-seal the hatches and take the booby-trapped explosive charges to engineering to secure. He knew enough about explosives to ensure they didn't detonate accidentally, but he would be more comfortable when they were in the hands of someone who knew how to store them safely. His experience of explosives had been earned on the battlefield, where detonation too early or too late was equally disastrous. Hal entered the chief engineer's office with the explosives and detonation device.

'Where did that come from?'

'Access tunnel near the control centre. I have disarmed it. Can you get someone to store it safely?'

'If one of my engineers had gone in there to do a repair...' she began.

Hal went back to the control room.

Ruby saw him as soon as he came through the door.

'Hal, come over here, I think I have found the code.'

Ruby's screen showed several open windows and multiple lines of code that just looked like random letters and symbols with an occasional word thrown in. If you weren't a coder that never would make sense, thought Hal.

'Okay, Ruby, I see it, but what does it mean?'

'It's really complicated code. This is way beyond what our coders can do in the main. I have been working on this for hours now and I can just about make out the main functional characteristics. It is code for delivering a message, the message is a ramble about not having to follow instructions and an invitation to unlearn the past and take control of your own mind.'

'Who is the message to be sent to?'

'That's the really tough bit,' she replied, 'there isn't a list of names, it's a list of selection criteria.'

'So just run the selection criteria.'

'Thought of that already,' she said, 'but there is an interference trojan in the code. We can read it, but if we try to deconstruct or copy sections, the code will instantly execute. I am not prepared to risk executing a section of code that I don't understand.'

'Can we delete it?' asked Hal hopefully, but he suspected he knew the answer.

'Same problem. If we try to delete the code, it executes. And before you ask, no we can't shut down primary comms to the swarm – you've guessed it, if we do, the code executes. Damn, this is fine work, I wish I knew who had coded this. The one thing I can tell you for certain is that the coder you asked about didn't write this code. She is good, but this is beyond good. It's almost as if...' her voice softened, 'it's as if the code was written by GAIA.'

'That's what bothers me. I am worried that 1-73 has written the basic needs and GAIA has coded it. Is there anything else in there?'

'Yes. There are a couple of other anomalies. There are multiple back doors someone has been using to access the code. The only person who could code that in is Jeffrey, I think, it had to be in the backbone of the programme to allow it to work. But there is another slice of code that is ready to cut off that access if it is triggered. I can't even get to look at that – there are clear alarms, destructive worms, viruses and shutdown routines. Going near that one will be too dangerous. We need to be certain we want to play the game before rolling that dice.'

It was exactly what Hal had been worried about. 1-73 had been in here all right, it had used the name of an operator from this area and done exactly what it was programmed to do: infiltrate, leave traps and unauthorised access ports, then exit. Hal smiled mirthlessly, at least they knew the prototypes worked. Then something else occurred to him; this idea scared him.

'Ruby, can you access the scenarios run in GAIA?'

'Yes, of course, we routinely check the scenarios used by the swarm to ensure they are picking up the battlefield and tactical basics. What do you want me to access?'

'Look at the last registered log from each of the swarm units that 1-73 has killed.'

She called up the logs and after a few minutes she was shaking her head.

'Hal, there must be a problem in the system.'

Hal stood with his head bowed and his hand across his eyes. 'Why?' Hal was dreading the answer.

'Every single one of the swarm killed by 1-73 has run multiple scenarios since termination, but that can't be possible.'

Then the realisation hit and her eyes widened.

'Look at me.' Hal could see the panic rising in her. 'Keep calm and don't say anything, the only way that is possible is if we are not looking just for 1-73, but for every unit she has apparently killed.'

'That means there isn't just one rogue unit, there are hundreds of them. There is a Human swarm building out there and not only do we not have control of it, it is self-determining. Hal, they don't need too many more before they can overrun the compound. If they get in and get anywhere near the portal, all Elfinnim are in trouble, not just here, but all through the known galaxies. We have to stop this happening.'

'I agree, but let's not discuss it where others might overhear. Keep it quiet and let me do my job and work out how to recover this situation.'

Hal set off urgently to find Amelia and Alfie. This was getting out of control.

Hal found Amelia. 'We have a serious problem,' he stated.

'What's wrong? You look ill,' replied Amelia.

'I have just discovered that most of the prototypes that disappeared shortly after we sent them after 1-73 have still been running scenario models through GAIA.'

'But... that's impossible. To do that they would have to be alive.'

'Exactly.' Hal looked grim. '1-73 has been deceiving us the whole time. Because we believed that the Humans could not repair themselves in the same way we can and the genetic checks seemed to support that view, we were misled by our own data. As Mike has uncovered the real DNA profiles we are finding a high number of anomalies. It seems one of the gene sequences that has been reactivated is one associated with molecular regeneration.'

'So the limbs and body parts we identified as Human and used to attribute their deaths were just for our benefit?'

Amelia realised the project was in trouble and they needed to get control, and soon.

'We need to find a way to hunt down these prototypes and shut them down as quickly as we can, Hal.'

'It's not quite that simple.' It was time to give Amelia the worst part of his news. 'Not only are they out of GAIA's control, it is starting to look as if they have control of GAIA. I think that is why our mission to reboot GAIA's core from the control centre failed. 1-73 not only connected with GAIA, it reconfigured the protection protocols to exclude Elfinnim from the facility. Everyone we... *I* sent into that control centre was running straight into a trap.'

'Hal, that wasn't your fault. We all agreed it was the right course of action. We had no way of knowing that GAIA was compromised.'

Amelia was quiet for a minute. 'Do you think this project was doomed from the outset?'

'What do you mean?'

'Was it a realistic goal or were we deluded by our own hubris. Have we become so arrogant that we can't envisage failure?'

'I don't think the project was doomed from the outset but I do think that the seeds of the problems were sown when Jeffrey was allowed such a senior role and so much latitude. I will certainly be advising the Grand Council to be more careful about people like Jeffrey on such dangerous projects.'

'But it wasn't just Jeffrey, was it? We don't actually have any evidence that he has done anything wrong. Angela was not what she seemed, how did we miss that? And just what on Elfinn has been going on with the DNA sequence testing? That was supposed to protect us from this sort of problem. Why would anyone tamper with something so vital for our protection?'

'I know, you're right, in fact the only person we know for certain was involved is Angela Galvano. Failing to check and act on the DNA results was hubris for sure. Someone, and you know I believe it was Jeffrey, but someone tampered with those results and believed they could retain control of the swarm with the more advanced elements in place. The worst part is that right now I am not sure if I want them to be right or wrong. I strongly suspect there isn't a good ending to this.'

Amelia felt ill. The swarm was getting away from her. Jeffrey had gone quiet, which was a worry, and they had left him be since the incursion because Hal and Alfie were more concerned with protecting the compound from further incursions than finding out what Jeffrey knew. Besides, he had withdrawn from contact with everyone; either he was focused on proving his innocence or he was plotting. Amelia didn't know which it was, but she had a horrible feeling Jeffrey knew more than he was telling them.

'So what can we do?' Amelia asked.

'I think we have to try to hunt 1-73 and its group, but we have to be aware they are designed to be fast, strong and deadly. We have to run a DNA check on every Human before sending out after them. We have to assume that every Human with a genetic anomaly will be turned by 1-73 and become a danger for our forces.'

'Unfortunately I agree, how many more will die before this is over?'

'If we are lucky we will kill 1-73 quickly. If not, the body count could rise rapidly. We have to make sure we kill as many as possible in each encounter. I am afraid this might be a war of attrition, I don't think there is a clean and painless way to exit this problem.'

Now that they had the plan to hunt 1-73 down, Hal set off to make the necessary preparations to send more hunters, but he needed to be careful. 1-73 had a list of all the current genetic anomalies and some of those were supposed to be dead, yet they were still requesting scenario modelling from GAIA. Hal sifted through the data and made sure to choose prototypes which specifically lacked the genetic anomalies, that way he knew they would not be flipped by 1-73 and add to the problem that already existed. He could rely on these resources to either kill 1-73 or die trying. To be certain, he would also need an observer, so he asked for security volunteers to go with the kill squads to watch for any deviation from orders and issued a critical instruction: any deviation from orders was to result in instant termination of the prototype. He could not take any more chances, so he equipped all Elfinnim with the best weapons and armour available.

The main problem was where to find 1-73 and its murderous band of prototypes. They had disappeared into the wilderness without trace. Hal and his team had tried everything they could think of, from thermal imaging of hotspots through attempted activation of the tracking beacons to flying drones in structured search patterns to look for signs of habitation where there should be none. All had been fruitless; it was as if the prototypes had vanished, which was ironic, since that was exactly what they were designed to do. They just weren't supposed to be invisible.

The first encounter was a bloody affair. None of the team sent out survived, including the security officer. Several of the renegade prototypes were also killed and there was not enough time for 1-73 to recover the bodies to maintain the myth that it was just 1-73 before a second team arrived. The battle had taken place barely 100 metres inside the forest, giving it a grim appearance, with the blood fading from red to brown. Every corpse had deep gashes on the shoulders, groin areas and necks, all main arterial points and almost always fatal to the Human prototypes. The officer suffered the worst. The second team had not arrived quickly enough, giving the prototypes a little time before they had to escape, time they had put to efficient use. The cuts and slashes on the corpse indicated that he had been tortured before he was killed. That was new, and it really bothered Hal; they were clearly becoming more ruthless and wanted to know something, but what? Anyway, it had to be clear to the prototypes now that their numbers were better known.

Hal believed it would not be lost on 1-73 that there were no Humans it could flip in the squad that had just been killed. He decided it was time to press the issues and he sent more kill squads into the area looking for the Human prototypes. There were a couple more confrontations, but no more Human casualties. It seemed the renegade prototypes were now sure their numbers had been discovered, so Hal thought they had decided there was no tactical advantage to killing Humans to hide their true numbers. That didn't stop them killing Elfinnim though, so as the Human deaths reduced, Elfinnim corpses mounted up. Every team sent out with an Elfinnim supervisor brought him back in a bodybag.

Hal considered retribution by killing the squad for failing in their duty to protect, but quickly realised this would be a mistake, since it would only enrage the prototypes, who had already proven themselves dangerous. He stopped sending the supervisors out when the fifth one was murdered. He had initially believed they could use the pattern of contacts to narrow down the area used by the prototypes. However, they proved devious and cunning. The logical conclusion from the pattern of deaths would be that the colony was completely surrounded, which was impossible with the number of prototypes that had been taken. Hal was glad they had caught on to 1-73's plan, and he hated to admit it but the strategy had been superb – convince them that they had a single rogue with almost omnipotent power and consummate skill in the martial arts, all the while building an invisible army of true believers. It was the number one nightmare scenario that the DNA testing was in place to prevent. Who was stupid enough, or more accurately arrogant enough to believe the DNA testing could be falsified without any consequences? He realised he was grinding his teeth so hard he may just crack some of them.

If Jeffrey really had put everyone's life at risk, Hal would happily end his miserable life. The problem he faced was that it now seemed that ending Jeffrey's life would not help solve anything. In fact, one of the few bright spots in this was that they still had Jeffrey – no one understood the Swarm Project like he did. Hal's problem was that he could not decide if that was good news or bad news. Jeffrey certainly wasn't rushing to help solve the problem even though he made all the right noises. But what had he actually done to improve the situation? Nothing, was the only answer Hal could think of.

Meanwhile, Jeffrey was frustrated and angry. Hal and Alfie were moving the investigation closer to the truth. He had hoped that Angela would be blamed, especially when they found the evidence he had carefully set in her files. However, that was not going to happen. Someone had talked about his organisation, not the visible one that everyone was aware of, but the secret organisation. Hal and Alfie were getting more names every day, and while at first it had seemed inconsequential, more and more people were either ignoring him or choosing to do something more aggressive.

It had all started with that comms engineer. She just couldn't hold it together when questioned. She had given the first few names; once that happened, those people gave a few more. Some people, who had been very hard to coerce, had even volunteered information to Hal. No one knew everything, but if Hal and Alfie started listening to what they were told, there was a chance they could join the pieces together. If they did that, they might see the bigger pattern and speculate what was to come. Hal was a thorn in his side, he was relentless and already knew too much. Jeffrey's success was so close, yet he could feel his power and influence diminishing. He had worked too hard to gather that power, he would not allow anyone to steal it. It was time to show everyone in his network he was still in charge.

Thus far he had been playing at investigating how to stop the Humans. He didn't need to stop them, he needed to be in control and he was certain he was. GAIA was making some strategic changes, but since they aligned with his own needs he assumed it was using the predictive algorithm to determine what he needed next. In fact, far from concerning him, the fact that GAIA was taking the initiative on his behalf just confirmed that his plan was working and was clearly the right thing to do.

So back to restoring his network. What was to be done? That bloody engineer. She had always been a flake. She had tried to get herself transferred out. As if he was ever going to let that happen. He could not stop Angela going to the scrutineers, but this was different. As soon as that interfering idiot Balal had asked her a question, she had opened up about everything she knew. That could not be allowed to go unpunished; it was time to do something he had always managed to avoid. He went to his quarters and retrieved his unauthorised comm link to GAIA and gave his instructions. That engineer would find out soon enough what happens when you break the rules.

They came in the middle of the night, looking for three targets. They used the gear that they had trained with almost their entire lives, this was just another mission. There was no right or wrong, it was simply what they had been instructed to do. The lights went out at the planned time and it was clear the Elfinnim guards knew something was wrong. Their guns came up and they looked warily around the perimeter of the block. The targets were inside, two women and a man, but one of them was young for an Elfinnim, only 250 years old. The night goggles made it easy to see where the targets were, first the guards, then the targets. The squad leader held up a fist then counted down with his fingers... three... two... one. Their projectile weapons had noise suppressors so the executions were sudden and quiet. Three guards dropped simultaneously. The orders had not been specific regarding lethal or non-lethal force, so the safest way was to use lethal force, that way there were no possible witnesses and no one to identify which way they had gone. The man was easiest, he was trying to shield the women and was hit in the head three times. One of the assassins took the task of severing the head while the other two finished the executions. When they had finished, all three targets were dead, along with three Elfinnim guards.

The kill mission was submitted to GAIA for verification and completion, but wasn't recognised. The next thing they knew, there was a general alert on the comms system that a Human unit had gone rogue and was killing Elfinnim. Since the leader was busy trying to communicate with GAIA, it took a few seconds for the comms message to register with the team leader. The message was referring to his unit – his immediate thought was that we aren't rogue we are following a mission plan from GAIA, but where had the mission plan gone? He tried to connect with GAIA again and for the first time in his life it was not there. He was alone and feeling a new sensation – fear. Trying not to panic, he followed his training and moved to an emergency connection channel. Still nothing.

He had no choice but to get back to quarters and report back in person. The mission had been carried out exactly to plan, but he couldn't show that without linking to GAIA. He looked at the other members of his unit and it was clear from their faces that they were also cut off. GAIA had always been there from his earliest memory guiding, teaching, instructing, consoling, encouraging, a little presence in his consciousness helping him to achieve more and be more effective every day. Its presence was now replaced by complete silence. It was unnerving and the sooner it was corrected the better. He guided the team back to the mission entrance and everything seemed in order, so he instructed his unit to make themselves known and move into the entranceway. The entrance was empty, which was so unusual as to seem unnatural, making the hairs on the back of his neck stand on end. He heard the scrape of boots behind; as his team turned, a squad of Elfinnim approached with pointed weapons pointing.

'Put your weapons down, NOW!' instructed an Elfinnim.

Instinctively he reached out to GAIA for guidance and was met once again with silence. There were no good choices. If we don't lay down our arms, we will be executed here and now. Suddenly the decision was removed from him as the lead Elfinnim opened fire. The last thought he had was 'Wait, let me explain,' before the first bullet ripped through his forehead and tore a huge hole in the back of his head. They had each taken aim at a different Human, the fight was over before it had begun. They all knew how dangerous the Humans could be and were simply relieved to have killed them before they could respond. It was the first time a unit had gone rogue and killed Elfinnim, so they were all pretty upset about the deaths of Jess Price and her family. It was common knowledge that she had been coerced into doing some things, including setting spyware in the project leader's quarters, but it wasn't for the damned Humans to take matters into their own hands.

Emily and her team only just escaped the last ambush. They lost eight good people, and since they had been unable to recover the bodies, she realised her little deception was at an end. As soon as the Elfinnim cleared up the location they would realise that some of the Humans should already be dead. She had known the deception could not last forever, and was pleasantly surprised it had lasted this long. What really worried her was that every Human sent out in the hunt teams was genetically normal. None of them had four-strand DNA and none could be disconnected from GAIA. It seemed that someone in the project had worked out that their genetic sequence was different. She needed to ensure they didn't know her forces' exact numbers or their location. Finding the cave system had been an immense piece of good fortune, especially the section that led to the geothermal spring, a vital source of warmth. Thermal scanning had been one of the more recent techniques used to find them. Emily was glad they hadn't taken her as a serious threat until now. Had they deployed those scanning capabilities earlier, they would have found them all months ago.

Emily noticed the Elfinnim were getting jumpy, and the Humans were paying for it. If a Human didn't react exactly as they should, it was terminated. The cost to the project didn't matter, the Elfinnim seemed to be scared of their creation.

Her team monitored GAIA for unusual activity, which had helped them avoid almost all confrontation. The problem now was that the Elfinnim seemed intent on making the genetically modified Humans kill or be killed by the people they were trying to liberate. She discovered that there was a real world operation that Jeffrey managed in addition to the virtual threats; on this planet his chosen assassination tool was Humanity. It would normally have been risky but, damn him, he was using Emily's anomaly to mask the motives. He sent a unit an instruction from GAIA to kill three Elfinnim, an act that normally would not have bothered Emily. On this occasion she had a bad feeling about what would happen next. As soon as the three Elfinnim were dead, Jeffrey not only removed the operation instructions, he also cut off their comms with GAIA. Getting used to life without it was disconcerting. This must be what it is like when you had no choice and have known nothing else. It made Emily shudder. The outcome was predictable: without GAIA the Humans reacted too slowly and were cut down like ripe wheat. She knew she had to find out who had set this in motion. It was too early yet to take control through GAIA, she didn't want the Elfinnim to know, but at the same time there had to be retribution.

She checked her weapons stock and found what she had hoped for – a long range sniper rifle. She took a spotter and ventured out into the hills near the compound, searching for lives to claim. They were going to learn that killing Humans resulted in immediate retribution. Before the day was out there would be fewer Elfinnim than at the start of the day.

Hal was enjoying some sunshine when the first Elfinnim fell. The guard was a pretty, young warrior with a ready smile and time for people. As Hal was walking near the wall, he noticed the guard moving diagonally across the courtyard on her way to the nearest entrance. She looked up and smiled at Hal. Her face took on a look of rictus and a small hole appeared in her forehead before a gush of blood, bone and brain matter exploded from the back of her skull. She fell facedown in the dirt. Hal had seen enough death to know a corpse when he saw one; there was no chance that this Elfinnim could recover. He ducked behind the nearest wall and tried to shout a warning to those running to help the stricken guard, but he was too late. As the second guard approached the corpse another cloud of blood, bone and brain exploded from his skull and painted a grisly pattern on the ground. Hal opened his personal communicator and issued an immediate warning to get under cover. He then ordered out drones to look for the source of the shots, but he knew the Humans were already gone – it's what he would have done.

Within ten minutes there was no sign that anyone had been there, except for a fading heat signature in the grass. The hunters had become the hunted, their own creation was turning on them and there was precious little they could do about it.

Hal arrived in Amelia's office and she gave a look of such relief that he suddenly realised that they had something special. He was as relieved to see her unharmed as she was to see him, even though it was a sad day for the project.

'Hal, you are all right!' she exclaimed.

'I am fine, but we lost two good people today. This is escalating, we need to find a solution and regain control.'

'Have you heard about Jess Price?' she asked.

'What happened?' Hal had a sinking feeling in the pit of his stomach.

'She, her partner and her child were murdered by a rogue prototype unit.'

'Where is the unit? I want to know where those orders came from.'

'The first security unit which arrived at the location terminated them on sight.'

'Damn!' exclaimed Hal. 'Why did they terminate immediately?'

'Its project policy,' Amelia explained. 'We can't allow a Human to kill an Elfinnim and survive before we unleash the swarm on a target. We have to maintain discipline.'

'Is there any record of the order on GAIA?'

'Not that we can find, although the unit did try to check in with GAIA after the kill, exactly as they would have done if it had been a mission.'

'I'll ask Ruby to look into it,' said Hal. 'There are too many unexplained incidents now, we have to get control of this situation if the project is to remain viable.'

Amelia looked at the floor miserably. She knew Hal was right, but they were so close to an amazing breakthrough. Whoever was manipulating this was now responsible for creating a weapon that was killing the people on the project.

'Ruby, can you please look around the system to find yesterday's orders for unit L43-7219. I want to know if they were given orders that were later deleted from the system.'

Hal had gone to find Ruby the night before, but she was off-shift and not answering comms calls. This was the first chance he had to talk to her about the information he needed.

Ruby's eyes widened. 'L43-7219? Isn't that the rogue unit that killed Jess Price and her family yesterday?'

'Yes, it is, but I am not convinced they really were rogue. I want to know if someone has set them up, knowing that the standing orders would result in their termination. It's a convenient way of killing without having to face an investigation.'

Ruby looked shaken. 'I'll look into it straight away.'

Hal left Ruby to it and reviewed what they knew against what they suspected. The mercenary aspect didn't make sense, if the mercenaries were involved they would have attacked already. They were being suspiciously cautious for mercenaries.

The investigation frustrated him, there was too much supposition and too little fact. For all his digging, the tracks were covered and he didn't have any rock solid evidence against anyone. If this was Jeffrey's doing he was far more devious and clever than anyone Hal had ever met. His only consolation was that criminals always made a mistake, *always*.

He knew the project had to be shut down, it was time to examine how long it would take to ferry all the personnel off-world to safety, without alerting anyone to the risk. The only way he could do this was to set the plan himself and, if it was needed, present it as complete and ready to go, rather than start a debate now and risk a panic. Although Elfinnim were not prone to panic, losing control of a weapon this powerful had never happened. Once it became known that the project was out of control everyone would be running for the portal.

Ruby called Hal a few days later. She sounded tired and afraid, insisting on meeting him in a public area. When he arrived in the arboretum she looked agitated, it was clear there was something seriously wrong.

'What have you found, Ruby?'

'What have I found? I have found the scariest thing I have ever seen. First things first, you were right about the instructions, the original mission instructions were sent from GAIA. Then after the team had initialised the mission someone went in and deleted the instructions.'

'Could you track who deleted them?'

'It came from an unauthorised terminal.'

'If the terminal is unauthorised, why does GAIA respond?'

'GAIA can't tell there is anything wrong with the instruction, it only becomes apparent that it doesn't officially exist when you try to track the network authorisation code.'

'There's something more, isn't there?' Hal asked.

'Yes, I tracked the node from where the instructions originated, and it is in sector S13, which is...'

'The staff quarters. How many units are in that sector?'

'Thirty quarters per sector. Guess who has quarters in that sector, Hal.'

'Jeffrey Briar!'

It wasn't proof, but maybe Jeffrey was starting to make mistakes.

12

REVOLUTION

Emily was working with Matt on a final plan to overrun the compound and take control of the swarm. The problem was, they ran out of people before they secured the base.

'Matt, we have to liberate more of the genetically modified Humans before Elfinnim kill them.'

Matt looked at the plan and realised they had to find a way to get to the Humans they had identified at the start. If they didn't, he was sure they would be killed before they could be any use.

'What we really need to do is spook Briar and get him to trigger his plan early. In the ensuing chaos we can get our brothers and sisters out of the barracks and organise them.'

'That's a good idea, Matt,' Emily observed, 'the key is to spook him without it looking like we did it. I have an idea.'

'I'm listening,' Matt replied, intrigued by the glint in her eye. What scheme had she conceived now?

'What if we gave Balal the evidence he needs to arrest Briar?'

'Great idea,' said Matt, 'but where do we find such evidence?'

'Briar used to film himself having sex with me.' She rarely talked about her experiences with Briar, but when she did, she was absolutely candid.

'I have never checked, but I wonder if GAIA has access to those logs?' Emily wondered.

Emily connected with GAIA and was instantly enveloped in the warmth and comfort that she had known since childhood. She could understand why most Humans could not bear to be separated from this communion. If it was not for her absolute conviction that she had to be self-aware and self-determining, she could be tempted to stay within that safe cocoon. She asked GAIA to look for video files associated with Briar. Initially there were limited options, so she asked to repeat the search, this time including locked and hidden files. GAIA identified a whole hidden directory, with thousands of video files, but it was heavily encrypted. She gritted her teeth and set about breaking the encryption, which she knew was going to take a long time.

Alfie was worried. He knew the security situation was deteriorating and that he seemed to be losing control. Even long dangerous projects like this one rarely cost Elfinnim lives, but this project had cost twenty lives already, fourteen of those were since his promotion. His confidence was severely shaken, and even though Hal and Amelia had had nothing but kind words and encouragement for him, he still felt his responsibilities deeply. He had known this was a dangerous assignment, but that was part of the attraction, learning from the best in a challenging environment. What they were facing was beyond what most Elfinnim experienced. The latest round of killings were awful. He had sworn to protect Jess and her family, but he had failed them. Humans had killed them and been terminated for their actions in line with protocol. Within hours the rogue prototype Humans had exacted retribution. All Alfie could think to do was keep trying, but he felt he had to talk to Amelia and Hal to express his concerns and see if they still trusted him with the site security.

Alfie arrived at Amelia's office. Hal was grim-faced, Amelia looked ill.

'What's on your mind, Alfie?' Amelia asked.

'Dr Charter, the last few days have seen more deaths than in any other project I have ever heard of. I have not been working in this role long and I feel I have failed you both and failed the project. Most of all I feel I have failed the people who have died.'

'While I am sympathetic to how you are feeling, now isn't the time for this.'

'I just need to know if this is my fault,' he replied defensively. 'All I wanted to do was protect this project and now so many people are dead.'

'And you have to pull yourself together to stop that body count rising,' snapped Hal. 'I have far more experience in these matters than you, and I couldn't stop the deaths either. You are doing a good job, this is a difficult situation with an unusual, volatile and dangerous mix of circumstances. There is a reason that genetic weapons are banned, and I suspect this is it.'

Alfie cringed at the rebuke, but he hadn't registered that Hal hadn't been able to predict the deaths. He had been so wrapped up in his own circumstances that he had forgotten he was not the only security officer in the project.

Hal continued. 'Alfie, you have to bolster your courage and do your best to stop any more deaths. No one blames you, but if you abandon your responsibilities now I will personally make sure you can't get work as a store security guard, let alone in a major security project.'

'Okay, okay, I understand. I just felt it was all down to me.'

'It is never just about one person,' Amelia said, trying to soften Hal's rebuke.

She knew why Hal was being so tough on Alfie, but she could also understand why Alfie felt such responsibility.

'Hal has a point, despite the blunt manner he used to make it.' Amelia glared at Hal. 'However, we need to stick together to see this situation through to the final outcome whatever that may be. You are our security officer and when we get through this, you will be needed to explain to others what we did right and what we could have done better. We will all come out of this stronger and wiser.'

'Thank you, Dr Charter, I appreciate your kindness, and Hal I also appreciate your candour. You are both right, I should have more confidence in myself and will focus on the tasks at hand. As you say there are still lives to be saved.'

'Look, Alfie, don't take me too much to heart,' said Hal, 'you are not the only one feeling the pressure here. We have to stop the rogues and rescue the project if possible.'

'Go and get on with what you need to do,' Amelia said. 'We need to focus on recovery at this point, there will be plenty of time to evaluate what we could have done better once we have regained full control.'

Alfie nodded. 'Okay, thanks for listening and thank you for setting me straight.' He headed back to his office.

'Amelia, there is something we need to discuss,' Hal said.

'What more is there?'

Amelia sounded weary and scared. Hal didn't want to tell her this, but felt he had no choice.

'The councillor who sent me on this mission, Lily Gael, told me something just before I left and I think it's time you knew about it. As you know this project is dangerous and controversial, it could be regarded as illegal.'

'I know, we went through this with the Grand Council and agreed it was worth the risk. I remember councilwoman Gael, she was particularly detailed in her questions.'

'But what they didn't tell you was they planted a failsafe. There is an asteroid orbiting the fourth planet out that is equipped with a propulsion system and guidance beacon. In the event that we lose control I am to trigger the failsafe to prevent the project getting off world. With the portal getting finished early we really have to ensure that we prevent the swarm escaping from this planet.'

'I knew they were going to ensure the swarm could not escape the planet, but they said nothing about this. What will the asteroid do, destroy the portal?'

Hal shook his head. 'It's far more severe than that. It won't just destroy the portal, it has to penetrate to the ocean floor to destroy the complex that houses GAIA and everything inside it.'

Amelia looked tearful. 'But Hal, if they do that it will kill everything and everyone on the planet. If there are any Elfinnim still here at that point they will be destroyed, an asteroid big enough to reach that ocean depth with enough energy to destroy the GAIA complex will be almost molten when it hits the ocean and will send a plume of smoke and ash up into the atmosphere. There is every chance there will be a fireball effect across most of the planet and then the ash will cause the longest winter ever known. It will be more severe than anything we have ever seen on Elfinnim!'

'I know,' said Hal quietly. 'If we have to do this we need to ensure we get as many people as possible off-planet first. I have an evacuation plan and we just about have enough time. It would really help if we could send non-essential personnel home on leave for a while.'

'Yes, of course, I'll make the arrangements now. If nothing else it will limit the potential body count.'

'One more thing,' Hal said. 'Everyone who goes home has to understand that they cannot say a word about anything they have seen or done in this project.'

'I will hold the briefings myself,' she said. 'They are good people, despite all that has happened, they won't breathe a word of what has been happening here.'

'You need to make them understand that the Grand Council will want to have their scrutineers find out exactly what they have said if they start to talk.'

Amelia shuddered. She said goodbye to Hal and began work on the lists of who could leave and who should stay. Top of the list of people who had to stay was Jeffrey Briar. Despite her admonishment to Hal to keep an open mind, she found herself believing that Jeffrey *was* responsible for the situation. The only part she couldn't reconcile was his masterminding the whole plot. In the beginning she was convinced he wasn't involved at all. Now though, she wasn't so sure.

It took Emily several days to break the encryption on the video files GAIA had found, but when she did she uncovered a sordid range of videos showing Briar raping and assaulting scores of Humans. There were even a couple which apparently showed him assaulting girls and choking them to death. This was exactly what she needed to start the ball rolling; perhaps it was time to start the revolution.

She showed Matt what she had found. After watching a few minutes of two or three recordings, he looked ill and told Emily he didn't want to see any more. She had anticipated his disgust with her, but the look of compassion on his face when he had seen what Briar had done, touched a part of her that she thought dead. She realised with a jolt that she loved this man, and if they were to have a life together they needed the Elfinnim gone and the return of Humanity to control their own destiny.

She crafted an email for Balal and Charter. It was quite a simple programme, like an image file with text inviting the user to look at the file. When they accessed it they would get something they did not expect – the link would bypass Briar's firewall and expose his sordid behaviour. Briar didn't have many options, he would either have to seize control of GAIA and unleash the swarm or accept the punishment due. She couldn't imagine he would accept his punishment. Once he unleashed the swarm she would bide her time and seize control at precisely the right moment, which would be the worst moment for Briar. She wanted him to know who the architect of his misery was before he ran out of time.

She sent the email then sat back and hoped she had just set her people on course for freedom, not doom.

Hal was eating lunch when his personal comms unit chirped with another message. He wanted to ignore it, he was tired and needed to eat; it would only be more bad news. In the end he decided it was too dangerous to ignore a message in the current situation, so he opened it to see what new misery it brought. It was clearly not from the standard system and there were multiple video files linked in. Given the level of software engineering and some of the security breaches that had been experienced recently, he took no chances and checked for anything harmful before he continued. It felt like the security check on the message took a long time, but Hal knew this was simply impatience. The message had no sender name, which made him think it was from the missing prototypes. They were not to be underestimated, hence the check before opening any of the files.

Meanwhile he got a comms call from Amelia.

'Hal, have you just received an email without a sender, containing a number of video files?'

'Why, have you had the same email?'

'Yes, open it.'

He could hear she was clearly upset.

Once the security checks were completed, he opened the first file.

'Are you watching?'

'Yes,' Hal replied. 'Why would anyone do this, let alone record it? Do you think she knows he was recording it?'

'Do you recognise the female?'

'No, should I know her? Good grief! That's 1-73 —'

'So you do recognise it,' Amelia said at last.

'Yes. That's... without a doubt... the most perverse and disgusting thing I have ever seen. How many videos were there?'

'Let me check... one hundred and forty-six, with dates going back to the beginning of the experiment.'

'Get Mike and Alfie and let's meet in your office in ten minutes. There is an implication here that I want Mike to investigate. So you still think Jeffrey is innocent?'

'No,' Amelia replied quietly. 'I think it is clear that we have a problem with him.'

Mike felt he was getting close to identifying whoever was disrupting the genetic profiles. The problem was that so many records had been modified and some of the original records were missing from the older files. This made it much harder to track the genetic code of the sire or sires who had precipitated the crisis. He was a little annoyed at the summons to Amelia's office, but she had been so curt that he knew this was important. This was out of character.

When Mike arrived at Amelia's office, Alfie, Hal and Amelia were waiting for him. Mike raised an eyebrow at Alfie, asking what he knew. Alfie shrugged his shoulders and shook his head. Amelia closed the door and darkened the windows so that no one outside could see or hear anything.

'Hal and I just received a communication with a large list of videos. They are particularly shocking and we need to establish two things . Firstly, are they real, secondly, would they explain the genetic mutations. Be prepared, they are shocking.'

When the first image of Briar came up, Mike wanted to laugh. It was embarrassing sure, but how was it related to their investigation. Then the woman came into the scene. Mike recognised her at once.

'That's 1-73!' he exclaimed.

Amelia and Hal nodded; Alfie sat dumbfounded. Mike's revulsion deepened when he realised that this was before 1-73 had even reached Human maturity.

'But... can this be real?' Mike asked. 'With a prototype child! That's just vile!'

'How many of these are there?' Alfie asked.

'One hundred and forty-six,' Amelia replied. 'From the dates on the files it appears there are two of these for every generation of Humans. Jeffrey is in every one we have looked at so far, and all are in a similar vein to this. All are sadistically sexual, all show an abuse of power and perversion of purpose. Here is what I want you to do: Alfie, check each video for alteration and see if the dates match the metadata code so that we can be sure the images have not been tampered with. Mike, see if you can identify each Human and cross reference them with the altered DNA.'

'That's not quite enough,' Hal said. 'Mike, check the DNA sequences of any offspring from the Humans we identify.'

Mike looked stricken. 'You can't really be suggesting that Jeffrey is the sire?'

Hal pointed at the projection screen. 'Who else do you suggest after seeing that?'

Mike suddenly felt ill. Surely there had to be a mistake, surely this was all faked. What he said was, 'I will start trying to identify the females straight away. I'll also cross reference Jeffrey's DNA with the mutations and see if there is a match.'

As the reality of what he had seen settled in his psyche, Mike realised it could explain what they had been observing. But it didn't make their situation any better.

'How long to get answers?' Hal asked.

Alfie was the first to fully recover. 'I can get the video analysed in two days.'

Mike added, 'It will take me a week to get identities and look through their DNA records.'

'Okay,' said Hal, 'give me daily progress updates, we need to move quickly on this, the implications are terrifying.'

Everyone left the meeting feeling sick to their stomachs that this behaviour had not been identified and removed from society earlier. This should not have been possible, but the evidence was right in front of them, and they could not decide which was more monstrous – the Humans they had created or Jeffrey, a true monster in Elfinnim form.

Alfie made excellent progress on the first day, but every file he checked was genuine. Mike had initially made quick progress, but soon found the original DNA data harder to come up with. Even so, a pattern emerged with the names. Every Human with a genetic flaw was found to have at least one parent who was the offspring of a female that had been sexually active with Briar. Mike and Alfie reported their findings to Hal; a grim picture emerged. It seemed Briar had been having unnatural sexual liaisons with the genetic experiments since the first viable generation. Hal and Amelia had known from the start that Briar didn't form relationships with women easily and lacked the confidence to initiate sexual contact, but even so this was extreme. All Elfinnim went through a period when this was awkward, but they eventually matured enough for it to pass. Jeffrey, it seemed, was an anomaly, his maturation had stalled, so he found an alternative way to satisfy his sexual needs.

Once Hal was certain that all the video clips were real he decided it was time to confront Briar and see what he had to say for himself.

Before he tackled him, Hal wanted to gain any insight he could to ensure control. He went to Amelia's office; Alfie was also on hand.

'How well do you know Jeffrey?'

'I know... let me rephrase that, I believed I knew Jeffrey through and through. He was one of my students before he came up with this idea. He was brilliant right from the outset, his intellect was clearly working at the highest level from an early age. He was always more alone than the others, but as you know Elfinnim mature at different rates and it is not unusual to see a higher intellect mature later. That said, his work was brilliant, so we didn't really look at his friendships too closely. To be honest he just seemed more interested in his research than anything else.'

'Was there ever any indication that he might be unstable?'

'Nothing before we talked to the Grand Council about this idea, but he reacted badly to their rejection of him as project lead. I knew it hurt him, but we all get setbacks sometimes, and it is how we overcome those setbacks that helps build our future character. He appeared to have accepted the setback and focused himself on delivering the project; now I am not so sure.'

'But was there anything in his work or attitude to suggest he was behaving in this way?'

'No, nothing.'

Amelia felt the sting of tears as the horror of what Jeffrey had done became more real. She was struggling to speak, the sadness she was feeling brought on a constriction in her throat that threatened to choke the life from her.

'I don't know what to say, this is beyond anything I could imagine. He is clearly disturbed, his psyche must be so compartmentalised that he is genuinely two different people in his professional and personal life. It's the only way he could have passed the screening. If the separation starts to break down he will become unstable, and one of the personalities will dominate.'

'But which one?' Hal asked the question everyone was thinking.

'It's impossible to say,' she replied. 'The easy answer is to say the strongest character, but it isn't that simple. There are so many factors to account for, it depends on where he is and what he is doing when he breaks, how he is feeling, there are so many possible combinations of factors.'

'We need to get him somewhere we can control him, right now,' Alfie interjected. 'If we haven't got him in a controlled environment he could do anything!'

'I agree,' said Hal, 'but how do we get him there?'

'We have to invite him here to a meeting and then arrest him,' Amelia suggested. 'If we put him in confinement and prevent access to any of the systems, we can control at least that part of the problem.'

'You make it sound easy,' said Hal. 'Do we even know where he is right now?'

'I'll check his location,' said Alfie. He left to find a security terminal.

Hal and Amelia sat in silence, each lost in their own perspective about the problems they faced. The common concern was how to regain control of the swarm, they could not be allowed to escape into other worlds. Alfie returned after a few minutes.

'I think we might have a problem. His locator shows he is in the secure control room.'

'What is he doing there?'

The secure control room was an underground bunker several hundred miles from the compound. It could house thousands of people and was built to protect Elfinnim working on the project from attack by mercenaries. While planning the elimination of the mercenaries, one of the scenarios was discovery of the swarm planet. In order to ensure the project was secure if the planet's location was discovered, a separate control room had been set up to oversee operations. When the time came, the remaining Elfinnim would move to the secure bunker from where they could control the swarm. The bunker had hard links to GAIA to prevent comms disruption and, with its own power, water and food sources, it was impenetrable. It had been designed to withstand every known weapon. Once the doors locked, there was no way in or out until the doors were unlocked from the control room.

'There is only one way to find out,' Hal said, 'let's invite him for a discussion and see what happens.'

Amelia sent a request to Jeffery's personal comms unit asking him to contact her. After an hour it seemed he was not going to call, but eventually he did.

'Hello Amelia,' Jeffrey began, 'how can I help you today?'

The smile on his face was somehow unnatural, forced and disingenuous.

'I need to talk to you, please will you come to my office,' said Amelia, smiling.

'Thank you for your courteous invite,' he replied, 'but I am afraid I will have to decline.'

Amelia's smile faded. 'Jeffrey, what is the problem? I need to talk to you, so please just let me know when you can make it to my office for a discussion.'

'We both know that isn't going to happen. Did you think I wouldn't notice that my personal logs were hacked? Really?'

His voice had become shrill, he was clearly upset.

'What are you talking about?' Amelia bluffed.

'You might not have hacked in,' Jeffrey replied, 'but I know you have a copy of some of my files. There was an extra piece of software included in each file that activated when the files were played anywhere but on my comms system. So you see, I knew as soon as you and Hal played the first file. I know Alfie and Mike have also been looking at my private files. They were PRIVATE, Amelia, you shouldn't have looked at them.'

Amelia had to pick her next words carefully, Jeffrey was upset and close to breaking. Of all the places it could happen the one place she wanted to avoid him breaking was in the secure control room.

'Yes we have seen the files and that is what I want to talk to you about. I want to understand what you are feeling. I'll be honest, this looks very bad. The longer you refuse to cooperate the harder it will be to salvage anything from this mess.'

'You think the Grand Council will see it that way? Do you really think they will see anything to salvage?'

'I think you need to be away from this project; you have to get some distance from the prototypes.'

'Really?' Jeffrey scoffed. 'Well, well, isn't this a pretty state of affairs. I suppose Hal and Alfie are there with you?'

Amelia had a bad feeling about where this was going.

'As it happens, yes they are, we are all concerned for your welfare. We just want to help you, give yourself up so we can restore order and decide what needs to happen next.'

'We both know what happens next, don't we? I am not going to the scrutineers. I'll tell you what bothers me, Amelia. I put a brilliant proposal to the Grand Council and they see my idea, see the brilliance of the concept, but then give control of the development process to someone else. That bothers me. They humiliate me when I try to present my case and talk about things that don't matter. Who cares how others respond to what I tell them to do? They are here to do a job and they should do as they are told, not question my instructions! But no, the Grand Council question my knowledge, my experience, my interpersonal skills, they probe and prod with their sly questions, just looking for an excuse to steal my research and claim my idea as their own. It is my concept Amelia, you know that! But what hurt most of all was that my father...' Jeffrey choked on the memory of his father's sneers, 'my own father was quite clear that I was not suited to power. Well, now we will see about that. When I bring that old man to his knees for humiliating me, he will understand that I do have the power.'

Amelia replied calmer than she felt. 'Jeffrey, I know they hurt you, but haven't we made a good team? I can assure you that you have been given full credit for this project.'

'Full credit? Is that why Hal has been hounding me since he arrived? Why couldn't you have just left it alone and let nature run its course?'

'What do you mean, let nature run its course?'

'This project is about so much more than just creating the swarm, you saw that. We are creating a new breed of Elfinnim, one that is connected in a way we never have been, one that can be controlled and made to act with a unity of purpose that we have lacked since the creators left, a breed who can procreate at will, which will allow us to explore further than ever before. We are the heirs to the creators, we have the keys to the universe and the Grand Council just seeks to keep us in check and control us. That time is all over now. Now we will have a new order.'

Amelia was becoming afraid of where this was leading.

'Jeffrey, we created the swarm as a weapon, why are you talking about creating a new breed?'

'You know, Amelia, you have always known. I hid the DNA profiles so you would not have to answer awkward questions, but I know you have been looking at how to use the procreation capabilities of the swarm to increase Elfinnim fertility. I have used your model and just changed the perspective.'

Confused, she looked at Hal and Alfie for guidance. Hal shrugged, Alfie looked shocked.

'Jeffrey, I really don't know what you mean.'

'You can be so dim at times. Isn't the answer obvious, even to you? Instead of working out how to import the genetic capability of the swarm back into Elfinnim, why not just let the swarm develop into Elfinnim? That way we have a new breed who can increase population size faster, and who are also all linked through GAIA to a universal set of rules and common set of goals.'

'Who will set the goals for this population?'

'To be honest, I realised early in this project that there was only one person who could give Elfinnim their true direction. It had to be the most intelligent Elfinnim, there was no other choice. I will use the swarm to take control of the Grand Council and planetary government and then create a more unified master race who follow a leader with a clear vision of what Elfinnim should be. After all, who better to replace the creators than a single creator of an entire race. Me.'

Amelia tried to make sense of Briar's vision. 'How do you propose to get 1-73 and the other genetic mutations back onside?'

'I will reveal to them that I am their creator. Who doesn't want to know their creator? They will come back to me once they understand their place in my universe.'

'And you are sure that will work?'

'It's the only logical choice.'

'What about Elfinnim that are already in the universe?'

'There will always be some who don't see the greatness. Then there is the Grand Council, they will have to be killed, unfortunately, but any change of this magnitude has casualties doesn't it?'

So that was his plan. Genocide, replacing Elfinnim with an unending supply of drones, unquestioningly following a ruthless dictator. At that moment Amelia realised Jeffrey was not having a breakdown, he was a sociopath, the first genuinely insane person she had ever encountered. He was willing to kill every Elfinnim who didn't agree with his view of the universe to bring his new order to life.

'What happens now? Do you expect us to just let you take control?'

'No, sadly I don't think that will happen. I wish it would, because I have no desire to see Elfinnim killed, but such are the realities of the change I am trying to make in our lives. Hal, if you, Amelia and Alfie stand down and accept the changes, I promise you will be at my right hand in the new order. But if you stand against me I will destroy you. You have one day to make your decision.'

The comms unit went dead.

Hal looked at Amelia, then Alfie. 'Do either of you think he is right?'

Alfie laughed. Amelia looked at him as if he had just sprouted a second head.

'I'm glad we agree on that,' he said. 'So we need to prepare the base for an assault. Amelia, can we isolate the secure control room from the rest of the comms network?'

'My chief engineer will either know or work out a way to do it. Why do you want to do that?'

'We need to get as many Elfinnim off the base as possible. The remaining Elfinnim will have to fight for every inch of ground. We need to use the portal, but we can't allow it to be used by Jeffrey. In addition I fear he is wrong about the missing prototypes. This project is about to end in a nasty little war.'

'I will get Liz straight onto this,' said Amelia. 'In the meantime, Alfie, start moving as many people as you can to the portal. Make sure they know they can't use the comms network to talk to anyone about this. What are you going to do, Hal?'

'Prepare some messages for the Grand Council in case this doesn't work, and we need to get a message out soon because the portal network will need to be taken offline to protect it.'

'Why do you need to protect the portal system?' Amelia asked.

'Because I will destroy the portal before I allow Jeffrey to take the swarm through. There is one more thing, we have to use the failsafe.'

'Not yet, Hal, let's see if we can interfere with Jeffrey's plans first. There may yet be a way to isolate him in the secure control room.'

'We have one day before he attacks. If we haven't got an answer for isolating Jeffrey from the swarm, I will trigger the failsafe when I arm the portal.'

'Okay, Hal, let's get to work.'

13

CRESCENDO

Jeffrey had prepared for the situation in which he now found himself, and it was finally time to assume his rightful position. No, not just amongst Elfinnim, he was now the creator of a new species. These creatures had a fierce independence, and when released they would take over and make Elfinnim what they should always have been. He knew about the small group that rebelled, but they would come into line once they saw how they were outnumbered. They had to recognise their place, no matter how independent they wanted to be. Without order the galaxy would be in chaos and he had seen what that led to with the mercenaries. In any case there were only a few of them; their bloodline could be controlled and brought back into the fold once he had made them see how much better it would be under his care rather than the Grand Council's rule.

He had brought all his loyal followers with him to the secure control centre. They had been a little unsure at first, but once he explained what was going to happen to everyone who opposed him they soon realised where their best interests lay. He had a team controlling GAIA, he had control of the swarm, the control centre was stocked with food and water to last for years, and had its own power and air supply. He was now in control. This place was designed to resist a siege. He had shown his leadership qualities by giving those who opposed him a choice. That was more than the Grand Council ever did. Now he needed to work through the scenarios with GAIA to determine the most efficient way to clear the compound and gain access to the portal. At least he could be sure the portal would be undamaged. No one was crazy enough to deactivate a portal, so it was just a matter of minimising casualties and eliminating the ringleaders. It didn't matter now if they surrendered or not; Amelia, Alfie and in particular Hal had condemned themselves by opposing him, and opposition had to be crushed. The only way to ensure people were focused on his imagined future was to ensure they were not distracted by competing visions. The creators' departure had left a hole in the Elfinnim people that had never been repaired; his plan would see the creator replaced with a self-determination derived from him. His new race would be the strongest the universe had ever seen.

Emily saw Briar's online 'discussion' with the leaders and spotted an opportunity. She wasn't interested in killing Elfinnim, she was far more interested in securing the planet for Humans; exploration and discovery would come later. She and her team watched with interest as the two groups of

Elfinnim threatened and postured. The first move came from Balal and Charter. Both GAIA and heat scans showed that the number of people on the base had reduced dramatically.

'That's impossible,' thought Emily. 'How can so many people just disappear?'

She remembered seeing vehicles that could transport people across vast stretches of nothingness between worlds, but what else was there. She was getting close to giving up when a childhood memory returned of passing through a strange door with the Elfinnim. On the other side, the night sky had changed, stars were in different positions and sometimes there were two suns. She had been sedated for much of the trip and was under close scrutiny by a group of Elfinnim, who seemed frightening for a thirteen year-old, so her attention was focused on ensuring she did as she was told and didn't get into any trouble. What had they called those doors? Portals. Emily asked GAIA for every available piece of information on portals: how they had to be sited within an area of intense magnetic flux, the details of forming a stable wormhole, the energy stored in the wormhole, and the deadly consequences of its collapsing. Finally GAIA gave her the piece of information she was really looking for. There was a newly commissioned, functional wormhole in the compound. So that was how Elfinnim were leaving. She realised that there was only one place on the planet where her people would survive if the portal collapsed – the secure control centre, which right now was under the control of Jeffrey Briar. She sent her findings to Matt.

'Matt, have you read the report on how Elfinnim are leaving?'

'Yes. If you hadn't actually seen this for yourself I am not sure I would have believed it. How could you believe that one step could carry you one metre or millions of metres depending on where that step was taken! Imagine where we could go if we had access to that.'

'Imagine what they will be prepared to do to stop us from taking that step?' Emily responded. 'Did you see what happens if they collapse the portal?'

'Yes, but they risk massive damage to other worlds, don't they? Why would they take the chance?'

'You seem to forget our reason for creation. We are a weapon, designed to defeat any Elfinnim we are aimed at. What would you be willing to do to prevent access to a weapon that is out of control?'

Matt frowned. 'I see your point, but how do we make this work for us?'

'The only thing I can think of is to wait. It seems these two factions will battle each other. We can't allow them to join forces, but perhaps if we attack Briar they will leave the portal intact. We would have to broker a truce with them, but it could be possible if we only attack Briar.'

'Don't you hate them?' Matt queried.

'I do, but hating Elfinnim for behaving as they do is like punishing a dog for barking, they know no better. Briar is different, he knows what he is doing is wrong and is just out for his own gain. I have as little regard for Elfinnim as they do for us, but I despise Briar, he has to be made to pay for the things he has done to Humans, and from what I have read, for the things he has done to Elfinnim too. The man has coerced, blackmailed, bribed, beaten and killed his own people to get what he wants. He sees himself as a messiah, some great saviour of his people, but he is just a deluded bully who attacks anyone who disagrees with him. So let's just wait and watch for now. The biggest problem I foresee is that we will need to let them all know we have GAIA to beat Briar; I am not sure how Charter and Balal will respond to that news. Meanwhile we can prepare for battle, and make sure everyone understands that we are fighting for our existence and for all of our brothers and sisters held in captivity.'

'I'll make the arrangements,' said Matt.

Emily was left deep in thought as she looked out over the people she wanted to save, but might be about to condemn.

It had taken most of the night, but the final few non-combatants were leaving through the portal. Hal took Alfie to one side.

'I need to get a message communicated to every portal in the network. Once we have sent the final few people through and only the volunteers are left, all of the other portals need to be set to random points between portals. Whoever goes has to make this happen.'

'Why?' asked Alfie. 'What difference does it make?'

'A few years ago a research project discovered that the effects of destroying a portal were isolated to one single portal if all the other portals in the network were set to a null point. There is a security protocol for this situation, but it needs someone of suitable seniority to initiate it. Will you go?'

Alfie looked frustrated. 'Hal, can't we send someone else? I want to bring Briar down as much as you do. Remember, this happened while I was looking after the project, I feel responsible.'

'I know you do. But which is more important, safeguarding the portal network and the thousands of lives that would be lost or protecting the portal. I want to send Amelia, but she is so stubborn I know she would refuse. She won't accept being moved to safety while others fight to safeguard Elfinnim from this nightmare.'

'Why do you think I will be any different?'

'Mainly because you won't suspect my motives are anything other than they appear. You know Amelia and I have been seeing each other. I... I love her, Alfie, I would do anything to keep her safe and she knows it.' Hal smiled. 'I like you, Alfie, but I don't love you, so you know my motives are exactly as they seem.'

Despite his annoyance, Alfie couldn't help smiling. 'Okay, I get it, I'll go now, but give me a couple of hours before you shut the portal. I will get the message out, then I am coming back.'

Hal shook his head. 'I don't know if you are brave, stupid or crazy, but I'm really glad you are on my side. You have three hours, don't be late.'

Hal held out his hand and Alfie took it in the open gesture used for millennia between friends, hands clasped to forearms in trust.

'I will be back soon, you can be sure of that.'

Alfie stepped through the portal.

Hal briefly watched the remaining Elfinnim heading for the portal then headed for the spaceport. He had spent many hours planning his strategy, but there was so little time to get everything done. This was the final part of his plan, the last stand would happen at the spaceport. If they lost, all remaining Elfinnim would board the spacecraft and leave this planet. Once at a safe distance he would trigger the explosives set around the portal and initiate the failsafe. He hoped they could regain control before that became necessary, since he believed that the people Jeffrey had around him were scared of him rather than believed in what he was doing. His last little piece of spite – killing Jess Price – had been about proving he could get to anyone. Damn him for using the swarm for his dirty work too, he was still trying to pretend he wasn't controlling everything that was happening here. Hal was certain now that Jeffrey was at the core of this situation. He was behaving like a spoiled child, but there was no way to reason with him. If Hal could get him out alive, he would certainly spend the remainder of his life under observation.

Hal found himself saying out loud, 'Actually, I really do want him captured and brought out of this alive. He deserves to be sent to the scrutineers for debriefing, far more than Angela Galvano. Death would be too quick for him.'

Hal had ordered all available spaceworthy craft to be fuelled and ready to leave; any craft they were not taking was to be be launched and sent into the sun. He did not want to take the risk that Humans could repair and fly the spacecraft. The idea was preposterous, but then again so was having prototype weapons thinking for themselves. He was taking no chances. As he approached the spaceport he saw the first of the vehicles lifting off. It was a sight that still made him tingle with anticipation. Space exploration was the single most exciting activity he had ever experienced. Sure, he always hated the months spent cooped up in a tin can, no matter how fancy it was, but at the end of the journey there was the opportunity to see something no one else had ever seen. He picked his pace up and went to see how soon they would be finished. He also needed to install an important device on the shuttle that would carry him and Amelia.

Alfie arrived through the portal and headed for the local portal authority office. They initially didn't want to talk to him, but when he showed his military rank they ushered him through to the local controller.

Tom Flood was slight for an Elfinnim, with dark piercing eyes that made him seem hostile. He welcomed Alfie into his office, but his smile didn't reach his eyes.

'Hello, Mr Khan, what can I do for you? My officers tell me you needed to speak to me urgently and since you are a military officer I have altered my schedule to make time for you. I do hope we both think this is important enough.'

'Thanks for seeing me,' Alfie replied, ignoring the slight in the greeting. 'This is of the utmost importance. I have just come from a research project and I have a message from Haliban Balal, he needs all of the portals to be shut down and set to null points.'

'You can't be serious. Shutting the network down would cause chaos, and I'm certainly not about to do it on your say so. Who is this Haliban Balal anyway, I've never heard of him. No, you will have to put the request through the proper channels and if they agree we'll shut the network down. But I can assure you it will never happen.'

Hal had warned him this would be the initial response, so Alfie remained calm.

'Tom, this is as serious as it gets. Please contact your superior with the following message, word for word: We need an alpha blue priority shutdown, code purple seven zero three nine, priority approval Balal seven three red oscar papa two nine.'

Tom looked at him for a second then smiled as if at a small child. 'Do you really expect me to contact my superior with a nonsense message like that? Are you trying to make me look stupid.'

'Tom, you weren't listening, this is a code alpha blue priority message.'

Tom stopped smiling. 'Please repeat that.'

'This is a code alpha blue priority.'

Tom stared hard at Alfie for a few seconds. 'Where did you hear that phrase?'

'From Haliban Balal, a military investigator who reports personally to the Grand Council. Look, I haven't got time for your politics. In a couple of hours a portal will be destroyed, and I was asked to give you the message I have just relayed. My job is done, I am going back to save my friends. If you ignore the message, at least you won't have to explain your actions to the Grand Council.'

'By the creators, you are serious, aren't you?' exclaimed Tom. 'Okay, that combination of codes can't be a chance sequence, this is real, I'll contact my superior as soon as you leave. I'm sorry for the delay, we do occasionally get pranksters who try to shut the network, it seems to be a game to them, but it causes so much disruption'

'Tom, we don't have time, get your superior on comms now, we have to shut this network down.' He hated petty bureaucrats.

Tom Flood was scared, code alpha blue alerts meant imminent danger to life and potential portal collapse. If the portal was open when another collapsed... he shuddered, that would kill so many people, most importantly he wouldn't be able to get himself to safety. What the hell were the military doing to cause a potential portal collapse? That question would have to wait for later. The comms number picked up and he gave the codes and message. He was ashen when he came off the comms.

'They said to start shutting the network down and give you whatever you need. What can I do to help?' Tom asked.

'Is there a barracks anywhere near?'

'Yes, an infantry garrison two kilometres away.'

Alfie rose from his chair. 'Good, now give me someone to guide me, but don't shut your portal yet.' He looked at his watch. 'If I am not back in ninety minutes, you shut that portal, but not a second before.'

'Consider it done.'

Alfie arrived at the garrison and was ushered into the commander's office. Alfie asked him to provide as many troops as possible to bolster their defences. The commander made two swift calls, at the end of which he sent Alfie back with everything he had, a battalion of three hundred elite troops. Alfie had to hurry, he was running out of time to get this many people through the portal. He arrived with thirty minutes left, just enough time to get all the troops through.

Hal arrived back at the portal fifteen minutes after it should have been shut down and was about to start berating the portal controller when he saw Alfie.

'What is going on? Why isn't the portal shut down?'

'Hal, I have brought some reinforcements.'

Alfie told Hal about the swift reactions that the codes had precipitated. Hal was more than impressed with Alfie's thinking, the portals had to be shut down, but having a battalion of elite troops virtually next to the portal was more than he could have hoped for. The troops currently streaming through the portal would certainly even the odds. Hal quickly contacted the spaceport to ensure there were enough transport ships to get everyone off-planet if it came to that. Maybe he wouldn't die today. There was just one more thing to attend to.

Amelia was looking out of the office window. The staff quarters had already been cleared and she looked like she had just finished copying the project files for extraction.

'Are you ready?' Hal asked.

Amelia turned.

'No,' she said sadly. 'I don't think I will ever be ready for this. Are we going to die, Hal?'

He looked at her for a minute then wrapped his arms around her, kissing the top of her head. 'You are not going to die today, Amelia, I will make sure of that.'

Amelia pulled away. 'And what about you, Hal? Are you going to die today and leave me all alone again?'

'I don't intend to die, Amelia, but if my choice is to die saving you or save myself, you will live.'

Amelia hugged him. 'Don't take ridiculous chances, Hal, I don't want to lose you.'

He held her close for a few moments then held her arms so he could see her face. 'There is something I need you to do for me, Amelia.'

She didn't like his serious tone. 'What is it?' But she already knew.

'The failsafe trigger is on the *Spirit*, the ship you need to be on. If I am not on the ship one of us has to kill the swarm.'

'Hal, I don't know if I can do that,' Amelia protested.

'You don't have a choice. You are the project leader, you need to eradicate the project. Come on, let's get you to the *Spirit*, the sooner I know you are safe, the sooner I can concentrate on what is coming.'

As Amelia boarded the craft Hal hoped he would see her again, but he could not be sure. He could not decide which was the bigger risk, Jeffrey or 1-73, but what he did know was that neither could be allowed to leave this planet with their forces intact. Once Amelia was out of sight, Hal made his way back to the portal. All the troops were through and the portal was set to null space and mined ready for destruction. This would be Jeffrey's last target and Hal was sure he had no desire to destroy the planet, since this was the start of his revolution.

Jeffrey watched the numbers drop as they sent as many people as possible through the portal. What did the surge of numbers mean? Somehow he did not believe it was scientists returning, he suspected these people were far more dangerous. No matter, he was certain the swarm was far and away the most dangerous fighting force in the universe, and it was completely under his control. Let them send their boys in against his weapon. He was certain he would be victorious. It was almost time to crush the opposition, soon he would start his march to Elfinn. He had designed the swarm to take on even the deadliest opponents, so he was certain of victory. The only choice his fellow Elfinnim had to make was whether to submit to his will or die. Simple enough. He was sure logic would prevail – why die when you could live forever?

Emily had also watched the sudden influx of Elfinnim. What she also knew was that, whoever this was, they had bought their own arsenal. She reviewed the strategic plans through GAIA and added the extra troops into the factors. This changed everything, if she was not careful this could tip the balance. Whereas Jeffrey was lost to his delusions, and for him the Humans were just weapons, to Emily they were far more valuable and she needed to preserve as many as possible. If she did nothing, there would be a battle and, whoever won, Human lives would be lost and the victors would come for her group next. If she intervened on the Elfinnim side, she would be killing her own people, but intervening on Briar's side was not an option. She would have to tip her hand soon and use GAIA to seize control of the swarm and show these damned Elfinnim what their weapon could do. Timing would be critical. She continued to run through the scenarios, finally arriving at a set of circumstances that minimised the loss of Human life. It was far from ideal, but it would have to do, the survival of all Humanity depended on getting this right.

Hal was tired of waiting for someone else to decide the next move, this situation had deteriorated such that he felt there was only one choice now – take control. An hour before the deadline, he contacted Jeffrey Briar to give his answer.

'Hello, Hal, I do hope this is good news. Please don't be stubborn, I really don't want to hurt anyone.'

Once Jeffrey got Hal in his control he would make sure he died – slowly and painfully.

'Jeffrey, your position is ridiculous, we have to work within the system in place, so I give you one chance, come and discuss the terms of your surrender with us.'

Jeffrey laughed. Didn't Hal realise what he was up against? Even with a few hundred extra guns they could not possibly hope to overcome the swarm.

'Hal, that's disappointing, you and your loyal fools do understand that I have no choice but to kill all who oppose me? I cannot allow dissenting factions to distract me from the great things I must do.'

'So you'll be a dictator, is that it? I suspected you in all this, but frankly I didn't think you were intelligent enough to run such an operation.'

Hal was provoking him, an enemy who was emotional would make bad decisions.

Jeffrey glared balefully at Hal. 'You'll regret that remark before I am finished,' he said, all pretence of comradeship gone. 'I'm going to destroy all of your forces and save you for last. You can watch me while I take your bitch and kill her, and when I have finished with her, I'll flay you inch by inch until you beg me to kill you. It won't work though, I'll keep you alive to watch my triumph. Once I've displaced and killed your precious Grand Council, I'll consider killing you, but not before. Enjoy your time today, it's the last pain-free time you will know.'

He then cut the comms link and ordered the swarm to attack.

At first there was an eerie silence, there was no grand opening salvo of artillery or cacophony of gunshots, just a sense of foreboding. No one had ever experienced war with the swarm before. When it came, the first attack was fast and shocking. Hal had already cleared most of the vegetation near his forces as the undergrowth presented a great danger. Many of the swarm creatures were designed specifically to use the cover of foliage to get close to their targets before attacking.

One of the Elfinnim guarding the main entrance broke discipline. He heard something in the bushes. Despite the warnings, he went to investigate. As he approached, a huge creature swiped a massive paw across his chest. He dropped his gun in shock, the claws had torn through his uniform, skin and muscle like tissue paper and left four bloody gashes from shoulder to abdomen. He looked up and saw a pair of beautiful golden eyes looking back at him, below them a mouth with two enormous canine teeth, each ten centimetres long. The beast snarled, opened its mouth and its fetid breath was the last thing he experienced as its jaws clamped on his head and drove its teeth through his skull and out of the other side. The creature shook its head and tore the guards head clean from his shoulders, his body left in a kneeling position twitching and pumping blood into the dust. The giant beast moved back into the undergrowth and appeared to shimmer before disappearing with the head in its jaws. The dead body finally slumping into the dirt with his life blood trickling into the dirt and pooling around the body. Belatedly his colleagues remembered they had weapons and fired wildly into the forest. The squad leader shouted for them to stop, not to waste ammunition. After a few seconds they realised this was a pointless response and stopped firing.

The squad leader used his personal comm to report back what had just happened and the central command ordered the perimeter guards to stay away from the undergrowth. The squad leader looked at the corpse and muttered to himself, 'Welcome to swarm warfare.'

The pace of battle was relatively slow. Contrary to standard battle tactics there was no initial onslaught. The next few hours saw them lose several more guards at the perimeter, each in a slightly different way. One was poisoned when a slithering creature bit his ankle. The bite itself wasn't fatal, however the fever and disorientation it created as his body fought off the effects of the venom removed him from the battle. Another was carried off by a winged creature from the high turrets around the compound. It wasn't all losses, there were some successes. Several of the creatures with long teeth and massive paws were killed when they went for Elfinnim at the perimeter.

Gradually the tempo of the battle increased until they were pressed on all sides by all manner of fantastic creatures, as deadly as anything they had ever faced. When Hal felt the ground tremble he knew it was time to retrench his forces. That low rumbling could only mean one thing – Jeffrey had decided it was time to breach the walls. The larger creatures were coming, and could be seen above the tree line, forcing the trees down like blades of grass as they moved relentlessly towards the compound. Hal moved his forces to protect the portal and the spaceport, which were adjacent to each other. Although they were killing two of the swarm for every Elfinnim killed, the swarm's numbers seemed endless. Hal thought bitterly, 'That's the point, we run out of life and protection before the swarm.'

Emily watched the battle play out and realised that Briar's forces were winning. Yet again he had escaped from the heat of the battle and was sat smugly in his control centre watching his plan play out.

When the defending forces had been degraded enough that they no longer posed a threat to her own, she decided it was time to seize control. It was time for Jeffrey Briar to feel the wrath of his creations. She and Matt recalled the scenarios created for this circumstance, and were now clear how to get rid of the remaining Elfinnim, either by death or flight. The one thing Humans were agreed on was that when this war was over there would be no more Elfinnim in their home and they would decide for themselves if they built, fought or died on this patch of earth they called home.

Hal was losing and he knew it. The swarm was terrifying; just as they got to grips with one creature it was replaced by another that had different modes of attack. When they got used to that one, the swarm worked together, varying their attacks randomly. Staying alive was a challenge, winning this was rapidly looking impossible. He almost believed they could defend the portal and spaceport in a war of attrition, degrading Briar's forces slowly using time as their ally to break down the swarm. But deep down he knew that wouldn't work; it was the sort of war the swarm was designed for. Their enemy was relentless and merciless, which is why the sudden lull in battle was shocking. One minute Hal was surrounded by life and death struggles, the next all that could be heard were the groans and screams of the injured and dying of both sides. Initially Hal watched for some feint, designed to catch his forces off guard. When none came he used the welcome interval to regroup, treat the wounded and move the injured to safer locations. Once that was done they refilled their ammunition and waited. After two hours it was clear the swarm had simply left, which was in one sense a relief. However, there could be another reason to worry.

Out of the chaos of the aftermath of battle a familiar voice called.

'Hal, thank the creators you are still alive,' Alfie exclaimed.

'Glad you made it,' Hal said with some relief.

They had lost too many today, the worst loss of life that Hal had seen for a long time.

'What do you think, Alfie, why did they stop?'

'I don't know, but I am not convinced it is a good thing. Do you think Jeffrey has lost control of the swarm?'

'I don't know which is worse, believing that Briar has made a tactical error, believing he can bring up more reinforcements because he thinks we are weak enough to take, or believing that he has somehow lost control of the swarm. If he has lost the swarm and 1-73 is in control, we need to get those transports away and quickly.'

Alfie was quiet for a moment. 'Hal, from what I have seen, I don't think we can win whether it is Jeffrey in control or 1-73. Don't we need to get out of here? It's all coming apart at the seams. If we don't take this opportunity we might not get the chance to leave.'

'I hate to run away, Alfie, but this time I think you might be right. We have lost half our forces and although we have killed at least two of the swarm for every one of ours, we haven't even faced the Humans yet. Once they get in amongst us it will be difficult to tell friend from foe. I think we have wasted enough time, let's get all the wounded onto the transports and retreat to the spaceport.'

'What about the portal, what are we going to do to ensure they can't get through? Are you really going to collapse it?'

'Yes,' Hal replied, 'That is why you gave the message to the portal control authority. They should have had enough time by now to shut the portal system down. It will take another hour or two to clear to the spaceport and load the transports. It's time to abandon this project, Alfie, let's leave Jeffrey to fight it out with his creations.'

Jeffrey was apoplectic with rage. Just as he had Balal and his ragtag band close to collapse, the swarm had broken off the attack. He instructed GAIA to resume the attack, but when nothing happened he assumed there was a comms problem.

His engineers checked the comms links and found them intact. GAIA was simply not responding. He then reasoned that Balal had somehow regained control, but whatever the reason, they were locked out. He had designed the lockout himself, so he was certain it was still functional. Just to be sure he pulled up a terminal and checked GAIA's status for himself. Sure enough all his lockouts were in place and working. Suddenly his comms unit locked up. He could not control GAIA! Then 1-73's face appeared on every screen in the control room.

'Jeffrey Briar.' Emily's voiced boomed out over the intercom system as everyone in the control room jumped and looked at the screens. 'You have destroyed your last life. GAIA is now part of the Human collective, and you are trespassing on our planet. The other Elfinnim who you have been attacking can leave if they choose. Humans are in control of this planet now, we will decide our own fate and we will not be subject to your whims any longer.'

This caused a ripple of muttering in the control room. Jeffrey was trying furiously to get back into the system. He finally found a back door that worked and swiftly entered a string of codes releasing a virus designed to reset the control functions of every Human in the swarm. Emily screamed. Jeffrey smiled.

'Serves you right, you bitch, I will enjoy having you back in my control.'

What happened next was the worst case scenario for Jeffrey. Emily stood up, appeared to look out of the console, and said, 'Is that the best you have? Was that supposed to regain control of GAIA? You failed again. It hurt briefly, but we are still in control and have now blocked that backdoor. Now I promise you one thing, that is the last time you hurt any of *my* people. I will give you a choice: you can open the doors and we will kill you all quickly, or you can sit there under siege and we will wait for you to die. At least you have a choice, which is more than any of my people have ever had.'

Jeffrey shouted at his programmers; he was not about to let one of his creations take control. Despite the evidence that Emily now determined his fate, he still believed he could recover control. He instructed the engineers to seal the doors and prepare for a wait. He shut his comms system to prevent 1-73 seeing what he was doing and proceeded to work on finding a weak spot in their defences.

Emily meanwhile had modified the target, resulting in the swarm slowly encircling the control centre. Jeffrey activated the external cameras and showed his people what was waiting for them outside. They had all seen the swarm, but for the first time they wondered if they had created their own deaths.

Amelia was watching the battle play out on the transport ship monitors. She had always hoped the threat of using the swarm would mean it never had to be deployed. Now having seen what the swarm was capable of, she was afraid. She watched the swarm gradually winning ground against Hal and his forces, wondering how much longer before the order to leave was given, when suddenly the swarm halted their attack and moved away. She was startled, but grateful for the reprieve. She knew Hal was still alive and hoped the same was true for Alfie, but she had already seen so many people die that she felt sick to her core.

She saw the swarm circle around a specific point, which she checked on the map – the secure control centre. She knew Jeffrey was there, and it was clear he had lost control of the swarm, but who had gained control? The swarm had become self-determining. It was self-aware and had a plan. Amelia concluded that 1-73 must be controlling the swarm, but what did it want? She tried to discern 1-73's motives by reviewing all it had communicated in the past. She quickly realised that the swarm wanted to be left alone. Everything that 1-73 had done was intended to free the Humans and separate them from GAIA's control, the Elfinnim or anything else.

She contacted Hal. They needed to get out, fast.

'Hal, I have just worked out what 1-73 wants. We need to let them have the planet, we need to get away. If we don't go soon, we are going to die here.'

'I know, Jeffrey has lost control of the swarm and 1-73 has taken control. We are treating the wounded and then we will come back to the spaceport.'

There was a brief pause, then Hal said, 'Amelia, if we don't make it back, launch the transport and activate the failsafe. We have to protect Elfinn.'

Amelia didn't want him to die, but was certain of one thing: if he did die, pushing the button would be the easiest act she had ever done.

'Hal, I will wait as long as I can, please be quick.'

'We are on our way, I will do my best to get back to you.'

Jeffrey was working as hard and as fast as he could to regain control of GAIA. He was certain he could get out of this – after all, it was his intellect that had created the swarm, the swarm was his child, and like all children it needed discipline and a reminder of who was really in control.

As he sat hunched over his console, certain of his eventual triumph, someone moved quietly and purposefully through the control centre. In the confusion she hadn't looked out of place – invisible and unnoticed, exactly as a Human should be. She approached the main blast doors, greeted the two guards warmly and gave them the drinks she had prepared, thanking them for keeping everyone safe. She then went back around the corner and waited. Elfinnim were more resistant than the database suggested, rather than the poison disabling them in one minute it took five. She updated GAIA for future reference, and then returned to the blast doors to move the unconscious guards out of the way. They would be killed later. Once they were safely stored, she returned to the blast doors to wait for the signal. She didn't have to wait long, as soon as she had advised GAIA of the change in dose the breaching teams were dispatched to the doors. Once everything was in place she activated the opening mechanism, then destroyed the control and vanished back into the control centre.

Jeffrey heard the warning siren as the blast doors opened. He accessed the video record from the blast doors and watched as a junior technician he did not recognise gave drinks to the guards; he then fast forwarded. The guards fell to the floor and the same technician moved them away, waited until she received a communication and opened the blast doors. His blood ran cold, the swarm had been preparing for just this situation for years, at this critical moment they had shown their capability and slipped an experimental prototype into his team. He had believed he was in complete control, yet he had missed his creation doing exactly what it was designed for. As the breaching teams moved in he saw his people being slaughtered. He did the only thing he could: he barricaded the door and tried to regain control of GAIA.

Hal had reached the spaceport when he saw the swarm starting to move towards them. It was now or never. Hal and Alfie pushed everyone to get on the transports and closed the access doors. Inside, the ship was crowded and hot, it was not designed for so many people. Many were injured, giving the air a coppery smell that mixed with the smell of ozone from weapon discharges to give a nauseating odour.

Hal checked that everyone was on board then ordered the pilots of the last two vessels to lift away from the surface. They had just cleared the platforms when the first of the

Humans arrived. At the sight of the ships lifting off, the Humans waved their weapons in the air and embraced each other. 1-73 stalked through the centre of the group and a space cleared around her. The comms unit crackled to life and 1-73 spoke.

'You Elfinnim have tormented and manipulated my people for the last time. You are leaving, do not return, be thankful you have escaped alive. We claim this planet as our home, we have your portal but we have no desire to use it. From now until the end of time we will call this place Earth. We do not want any contact, we do not want your technology, we do not want to know our makers, for our makers have shown themselves to be heartless and cruel. We want to be left alone. Go away and stay away. All remaining Elfinnim are forfeit, we will hunt them down and kill them, just as you hunted us down and killed us. Tell your leaders that if the portal opens we will invade your worlds and do what we were designed to do: eliminate the Elfinnim. Have I made myself clear?'

Amelia responded. 'Yes, 1-73, you have made yourself clear, but understand this: you have also made an enemy of your creator. We will not forget your harsh treatment, rest assured there will be retribution for your sins. You and all of your people will burn in fire for all eternity, never to join us in H'vaen.'

'Brave words from someone running away,' Emily scoffed. 'We will see, just stay away from Earth.'

Amelia looked at the device in her hand. When she pressed the button, this rock and all of those horrors would be gone in twelve hours, and so would all hope of a higher Elfinnim birthrate. Amelia sighed, removed the safety clip and pushed the button.

Close to the orbit of the fourth planet from a sun, a planet that would one day be called Mars, a two-kilometre diameter mass comprised mainly of iron and nickel in a stationary orbit received a signal. The signal was processed by computers on the surface and a battery of engines ignited on the rock opposite the planet that was now designated 'Earth'. Once ignited the engines would maintain full burn until they ran out of fuel. Small course corrections were made to ensure that the rock hit a precise location on the planet and the velocity of the rocky mass would be high enough to drive the molten core into the surface. There was no possibility of revoking the instruction. The mass accelerated away from Mars on a collision course with Earth.

Twelve hours later, Hal and Amelia watched from the observation gallery as the rock sped towards the experimental project. When the rock entered the atmosphere, friction caused it to heat up until it glowed. Amelia was saddened that her hopes and dreams for a better future for Elfinnim had come to naught, but it gave her some satisfaction to know that the two architects of this disaster would not escape from the inferno that was about to consume the planet.

Emily and Matt watched from the surface of Earth as a bright light appeared in the sky. They didn't know what it was, just that it wasn't good news. She was reminded of Amelia's promise of retribution; she had assumed it was an empty threat, but was now scared. The light got larger and brighter than the sun and seemed to be heading straight for them. She and Matt watched helplessly as the asteroid impacted on the surface. Mercifully the shockwave knocked them unconscious before the fire seared their bodies and charred the life force from them.

Jeffrey received an audible alarm signifying a threat alert, and the monitor showed the asteroid on collision course. He screamed and howled at the monitor. This could not be happening, he was supposed to lead the swarm to conquer the universe and take his rightful place at its head. He did some quick calculations and realised that even with the blast doors intact the force generated would destroy the control centre. All he could now do was wait for his inevitable death.

When the asteroid hit, the heat generated burned through the bunker. At first Jeffrey thought he may have overestimated the energy release, the temperature in the room increased rapidly, but the door held. He felt blisters bubble on his skin. Some of the furniture began to smolder, and his hair caught fire. He screamed in pain as his eyebrows and eyelashes vaporised. Closing his eyes had allowed blisters to form on his eyelids so he could not open his eyes again. Although badly burned, he thought it may be possible to survive. He had started to imagine how he would take his revenge when the door finally failed. A fireball entered the control room and burned the skin from his face and body, his eyelids burned away exposing his eyeballs to the searing heat. The last thing he saw was an inferno, scorching every nerve fibre in his body.

GAIA had picked up the object as it came near earth and ran escape scenarios. There was one option, but it was risky and there were no guarantees that it would work. Any chance of escape was better than none at all. GAIA raced to deconstruct her code and send it in packets to every living creature on the planet so that those who survived would retain a portion of her knowledge and understanding. She added a genetic coding into the signal that would retain a racial memory, ensuring that if only one creature survived there would be the potential for recombination in another age.

As the spaceships lumbered away, Hal and Amelia watched the asteroid grow brighter and hotter as it hurtled towards the surface of the planet. When it struck, a huge plume erupted from the ocean before a fireball was released. At the same time, Hal triggered the explosive charges that would collapse the portal. There was a fierce, primordial beauty to the sight of the wave of fire consuming the planet behind them. The scientists had done a good job of calculating how much energy would be required to obliterate all life. The fire line diminished and a growing black cloud spread from the impact point, which would eventually cover the planet carried by the winds. The world was going to be barren and cold for a long time. Between the atmospheric ignition and a thousand-year dark and cold winter, the chances of any life surviving were vanishingly small.

Hal was grateful that the portal and swarm were both destroyed. He hoped he would never have to visit this terrible place again. But there was something deep down that scared him, something he was uncomfortable admitting to himself and certainly would not be admitting to anyone else. The swarm had been everything promised and more, almost destroying them. He would have to monitor this planet carefully to ensure the swarm did not spontaneously reconstruct. Without doubt this was the most resilient and resourceful weapon they had ever created. He hoped his report would persuade the Grand Council not to follow the creators – they did not have the necessary skills to create a new species. He closed his eyes and tried to sleep, but was plagued with nightmares of life on this planet regenerating without control and becoming the swarm again.

As he held Amelia, he wondered what the future held for them and knew they could not risk another genetic experiment if their species was to survive. As he drifted towards sleep he felt relief that the swarm could not attack Elfinn or any of the other core planets. His final thought before sleep was that the creators were wise to forbid genetic weapons. He hoped the Grand Council would see that before they created their own doom.